TWO GRAVES FOR THE BISHOP

Gerard Cappa

ISBN: 154290515X
ISBN 13: 9781542905152

Other Maknazpy titles by Gerard Cappa

<u>Blood from a Shadow</u>

<u>Black Boat Dancing</u>

Praise for the Maknazpy series:

"Writers from Chandler and Hammett through William Burroughs, Charles Willeford, James Elroy, Bret Easton Ellis and Don DeLillo have shown how the administration of cities is not corrupt, but inherently predatory. Speaking directly to supra-national, neo-liberal depredation, Jean-Patrick Manchette and Don DeLillo, are matched by Gerard Cappa, in Black Boat Dancing, and his earlier Blood from a Shadow. As with noir of the mid-20th century, protagonists are not destroyed but potentially redeemed by their own sin and suffering. They force their humanity to come to life. The ultimate 21st century heroism is to struggle for the control of one's own destiny. Con Maknazpy's struggle is a remarkable example - more complete, more blissfully anarchistic, than the nation-loving kind of hero" - Jay A Gertzman

"We are in the realm of tough guys doing tough guy things against other tough guys. There is something about author Gerard Cappa's style, as well as his hero Con Maknazpy, that carries echoes of Dashiell Hammett and the Continental Op. All the classic elements of the detective crime thriller are there: the smart-mouthed dame, nightclubs, les femmes fatale, and bodies scattered across the pages like raspberries on your morning cornflakes – A cracking good tale" Manhattan Book Review

"Mix of subtle allusion, rapidly paced violent set-pieces, and character reflection - I like the conversations his characters engage in about politics, capitalism, greed" – John L Murphy

"You come out of the novel knowing, like Maknazpy, that whatever the truth today, especially if it is truth as defined by the CIA, it will be different tomorrow. The action is non-stop and the sound of the jigsaw continual. This can lead to a dizzying experience for the reader. Take your time over each chapter, savor the dialog and enjoy the pieces coming together" - John J Gaynard

I gCuimhne
Stephen Cappa
(1956 – 2016)

Sláinte an bhradáin:
croí folláin, gob fliuch,
agus bás in Éirinn

REDBREAST

December 9th, Rio de Janeiro

It was his calling card on the kitchen table. The 40% currency of guilt-bonded absolution. Single Pot Still. Twelve Years Old. Two whiskey glasses prepped for the ritual, to be cupped and tongued, our reunion sealed with smacking lips and numb throats.

The drapes danced with the breeze from Leblon beach. His figure was dark against the bright sundeck.

'This is trouble,' I said. 'He'll bring his poison with him.'

Yasmin shrugged past me and flung the drapes back. He rose to meet her, then half-turned toward me when I appeared at her shoulder.

'Con Maknazpy! Thanks be to God, son!' He lurched forward and embraced me with a foaming kiss on my cheek. Yasmin offered her hand in welcome. He prised me away and flowed into a genteel half-bow before her, stroking her hand, oozing that old school charm that demanded Yasmin crack wide her bright smile like she was taken in by his gushing flattery and practiced twinkle.

'Yasmin, this is Monsignor Artie McCooey. The one I told you about, the priest that tried to kill me.'

Artie hitched back his sleeves, lost in his ritual, like his performance had some meaning, like he was back tricking his priest magic and I was his raw altar boy. The lip of the glass chimed against the mouth of the bottle. He set the glass on the table and slid the drink toward me. I didn't move.

'You like vatapá, Padre?' Yasmin asked.

'Yes, dear, as long as it is no trouble for you.'

Yasmin blew a kiss at the back of his head and flicked her tongue at me before turning to work the shrimp into a paste with the fish stock and coconut milk.

'I didn't think I'd be seeing you again, Artie,' I said.

'You know what they say, Con. You can't keep a good priest down.' Artie sipped and sighed into his storyteller routine. 'The Dear Lord above knows they tried, they knew I would take the rap for them that last time. I did my duty and took the knocks, the sacrificial lamb to slaughter.'

Poor Artie. The self-pity hung off him like the inflamed red jowls that quivered above his sharp priest collar. And he looked older, too. He must be about seventy, and still with the six foot frame that had carried the rough Irish swagger in his youth but now everything was just a little more tired, a little slower, a little bit closer to the end. I had the split second vision of me as Artie in thirty-whatever years but snapped out of it before the image could fester.

'That's crap, Artie. Your lunatic scheme would have had me shot down in the street by Homeland Security or stinking it out in Guantanamo for the rest of my natural.'

'Not at all, Con, not at all! That's what they wanted everyone to think. It was all just smoke and mirrors, smoke and mirrors.'

'Oh yeah? You remember the girl in Istanbul, don't you Artie? Sure you do. You were in that house when they carried her out. You going to tell me what happened to her was smoke and mirrors?'

'Ahh, you still carry that burden,' Artie tossed away the guilt with a shake of his head. 'Those sort of people, Con, that sort of girl – that's just what life is like for them, the unfortunate creatures. We can't be responsible for people like that.'

My chair scraped across the floor tiles, he lumbered backward but then scrambled forward to save the whiskey. All that anger and fear buried deep in my gut was boiling up through my throat now, the shame and helplessness about to explode in my hands around Artie's neck.

'Con! Stop this!' Yasmin grabbed my hair and shouted into my face. 'Never in my house. You promised me!' I backed off and held my hands up in surrender. She eased me back into my seat and fixed the table. 'Now, drink your whiskey and the meal will be ready in a few minutes, okay?'

Okay, I could screw the hurt back into my chest for now, somewhere dark and cold behind my heart, and so I let Artie sip his Redbreast, watched him hold the glass tight to his flared nostrils at each sip, slowly inhaling and exhaling the fumes as he wallowed the whiskey around his teeth. And I caught the slight tremor in his fingers.

'What are you doing here, Artie? You knew I would beat the shit out of you, maybe worse. I still might.' Yasmin flashed a warning scowl at me, only turned back to the vatapá when I shrugged obedience. 'So tell me, Artie, and no bullshit, what are you here for?'

Artie tilted forward with his fingers clasped as if ready to start a prayer session.

'I had to come, Con, I just had to.' His voice was low, and the tremor from his fingers had transferred to his throat. 'I need help and you are the only one left I can trust.'

A tear, or maybe an old man's mucus, blistered up in his right eye, on the red rim of his lower eyelid, like a milky scab pulsing over a rough scar.

'A heavy burden of duty has been placed on my shoulders. An honor, really, I suppose, but too much for one humble man like myself.'

I should have kicked his ass right there and then and dumped him out into the street. I knew it, that would have been the safe bet, but then my life was already scarred by the shrapnel from bad choices and squandered opportunities – Artie's poison just could be my next excuse.

'A good man is in trouble, Con, an innocent man. A good man betrayed and sacrificed, just as I was myself. All the rest of them have shunned him in his hour of need. I can't do that. I won't do that.'

Artie shuffled back in his chair when Yasmin curved around him to place a dish of cheesy puff-ball bread on the table. She lingered over him, hip against his shoulder, lifted my whiskey for a sniff and sip.

'Your friend is in trouble, Padre?' Yasmin squeezed his shoulder. 'What trouble? What did he do?'

'Well, he is accused of money laundering but he didn't do anything, he was framed, he is innocent!'

I tipped the bottle to Artie's glass and nudged the hot bread toward him.

'See, when you say he is innocent, Artie, does that mean there was no dirty money, or just that your friend didn't launder it?'

'It seems there was some money on the plane, yes, but I'm telling you he was set up!'

I was still considering kicking Artie's ass all the way down to Leblon beach but now he had tripped the curious switch.

'Okay, he was set-up, you and I sure know that shit happens, don't we? But before we go any further, Artie, I have three big questions. First, how much are we talking about here and who is this clean friend of yours?'

Artie sipped, cleared his throat, ran an index finger along the inside of his priest collar.

'It's very warm in here, isn't it?' he said.

'How much, Artie?'

'As far as I know they said there were five million Euros in his suitcases, but he didn't put it there.'

Yasmin worked both his shoulders now, teased the tension from his neck, her powerful thighs rocking against his shoulder blades, he could relax, amongst friends, but the more she worked him the hotter he became, the collar tightening like a noose, Pot Still sweat spangled on his forehead. Five million Euros, that's something like $7 million, enough to make my skin prickle also.

'So this guy was caught with five million but he didn't know he had it, right?' I said. 'Who is this five million Euro guy?'

'He is an old friend of mine!' Artie was getting a little aggressive now, didn't like my tone, but he let Yasmin keep on working his shoulders. 'It's Johannes Beikle, for God's sake! He was the Professor of Christian Philosophy at Wien University when I was there in the 80's! Smuggling my arse!'

Artie gulped his whiskey now, dumped the connoisseur act.

'Professors do bad stuff too sometimes,' I said.

'He's innocent! And he isn't a university Professor anymore, Monsignor Johannes Beikle has been in Rome at the IOR for the last twenty-five years.'

'IOR? What is this?' Yasmin said.

Artie wriggled away from her strong kneading fingers.

'Istituto per le Opere di Religione,' he said. 'The Vatican Bank!'

Yasmin looked at me and we burst out laughing in unison. Artie as a character witness for his Monsignor friend, five million dirty Euros and the Vatican Bank, what wasn't there to laugh about?

'I'm absolutely jubilant that you are so amused,' Artie was dry. 'It may delight you further to know that Johannes told me there was a fund of thirty million to start with, twenty five is still to be accounted for.'

Twenty-five million Euros? What's that, like $30 million?

'And thirdly?' Artie said. 'You said you had three big questions?'

Yeah, that's what I had said, right enough. I had been going to ask Artie why the actual fuck he had come to me with his good whiskey and bad karma, but a lead on a missing $30 million?

'Forget it, Artie,' I said. 'Let's enjoy Yasmin's fine vatapá and just forget that third question, I guess it wasn't such a big deal after all.'

CHAPTER ONE

Artie was still a player – high on the hubba bubba of power, fingering good and bad like beads on his rosary, slipping his mickey finn of wrong into right, wine into blood, truth into ashes.

'I can still eat like two men and a wee lad!' he clapped his hands against the straining clerical waistcoat, angled his seat back to drape his arms along the chrome railing that framed us into the balcony, and tilted his head toward the oppressive boom beat party a few blocks away below us on the beach.

'So that's what hell is like then?' he mused.

He rocked his weight further back, balanced on the two back legs of the chair, his black priest shoes swinging a counterweight. All I had to do was scoop up the two front legs and he would have flipped over the balcony and back into the darkness.

'Café, Padre?' Yasmin patted and squeezed his knee as she rose, and her eyes flashed an order to me to get down to business. Artie craned his neck to scope her ass as she headed for the kitchen. He savored the company of beautiful women, I remembered how he would flirt with their ingrained deference but played the victim if ever he was called out on one of his jokes. Yasmin would punch him in the mouth if he came on too fresh and the thought made me smile. But Artie didn't trust comedy when he wasn't included, made him uneasy because maybe he wasn't the center of attention, wasn't in control.

'This is a permanent arrangement?' Artie nodded a glance to Yasmin's empty seat.

'Sure,' I shrugged. 'As permanent as anything else.'

'And Rose and your son are still shacked up with our old friend Gallogly?'

He hitched his chair close to the table but I figured I could still boost him over the balcony before he could say "*Sanctifying Grace*" or "*Divine Institution*".

'Talk to me, Artie. People get killed for $30 million. What do you want me to do and what do I get out of it?'

He stroked his chin, now indecisive, hesitating, unsure if he should make the bargain, buying encouragement from me. I was wise to his phony tics and gestures, save it for the faithful.

'Find the man who set up Johannes Beikle. Persuade him to return to Rome and clear Beikle's name.'

Sure, for $30 million I could be *very* persuasive. But I knew Artie, this wouldn't be so simple, and if a fall guy was required I knew who would get the first and only nomination.

'What about the $30 million? How much of that comes my way?'

Artie rummaged a manicured nail around his ear as if a fist-sized flying insect had lodged itself in there.

'The money is merely a secondary issue.' He muttered the words like it created a foul taste in his mouth to consider Beikle's honor and the missing money in the same breath. 'Of course, Johannes raised it to fund a children's hospice in Rome but I'm sure we can compensate you for your trouble, if that's what you really want.'

Already with the guilt trip, Artie posed his mournful face, mugging disappointment at my self-interest.

'You are hiring a mercenary here, Artie, no free plays this time. Clear your friend and bring the money in? That's a 10% gig in normal circumstances.'

He was in his elbows-on-knees position now, the bloodshot eyes peeping up through the trimmed eyebrows.

'Of course, these aren't normal circumstances,' I was on a roll. 'We both know you are a lying bastard and will sell me out quicker than you can down that whiskey, so I guess $5 million should cover it.'

Artie screwed up his eyes and pursed his lips to forge the stern expression he probably perfected for the most shameless penitent.

'I include her in my prayers, you know, son. I offer my prayers for her and the souls of the faithful departed every day.'

'Rose? Don't worry about her, Artie, she is better off with Gallogly, I'm the first to admit it, it's no problem.'

'I'm talking about Didar,' he said. 'The poor girl in Istanbul. I pray for her every day, and her sorrowful mother.'

An Artie curve ball, the killshot to lodge in my throat and choke the impudence right out of me. He knew my place, even if I had forgotten.

'Five million, Artie,' I avoided his eyes. 'I need a million up front. No holding out on me this time, I get to know everything you know, right from the get-go, okay? I'll need guarantees, you pull your strings to get me access all areas. If it doesn't come off, I keep the million and we go our separate ways, right? But listen up good, Artie, any sign of you double-crossing me like you did last time and you will be delivering those prayers to the faithful departed in person, got it? You're not dealing with the dupe you thought I was last time, understand?'

Yasmin had heard enough, and pushed through the drapes with the tray. Artie switched on his fawning chivalry, stood to receive her and pull out her chair at the table – what a gentleman. Yasmin set the tray down and tipped me a wink before apologizing to Artie, she had to run to pick her son up from his Ju Jitsu class. Artie stayed on his feet, all the better to drink in the hip-sway rumba Yasmin vamped up for his benefit.

'Yeah, Artie, I know, jello on springs, now sit down and start from the beginning, no short cuts and no lies. Start with this guy we are looking for, what did Beikle tell you about him?'

Artie wrestled his priest collar loose and sipped a spoonful of coffee, trilled it around his tongue for a couple of seconds before sucking up the dregs of whiskey in his glass and tongueing the whiskey coffee mix around his gums.

'Poor Johannes wouldn't know anything,' he said. 'The bastard was using a false identity the whole time, that's how he was able to disappear, leaving Johannes to face the ignominy.'

'I know how that feels, believe me,' I said. 'Remember Istanbul? Before you conned me into that nightmare I was sitting at home, a regular guy leading a regular life. Maybe I should forget the five mill, and just beat the shit out of you and dump you over that balcony!'

Artie shook his head and croaked a hollow laugh.

'A regular guy? A regular life? Two years ago you were living the life of a zombie on your own in a dump in Hoboken! Your wife and child deserted up on Woodlawn! Wallowing in your own self-indulgent melancholy! That's how regular you were then, looks like you are doing okay now, though, doesn't it?' He made a theatrical sweep around the balcony. 'With your new girlfriend and your new life, what?'

'I *was* a zombie. That's what war does, you know? If you had seen what I saw in the Bushworld wars you would maybe understand, but hey, forget it! Let's exploit the PTSD guy and throw him to the wolves, right?'

Artie's hollow laugh rolled into a howl, he rubbed the back of his neck until he could control his breathing.

'Post Traumatic Stress my arse!' He started the guffaw again. 'You were like that as a child, I heard about you when I was in Fordham, your father came to see if I could help. You were just like him, exploding into a berserk rage over nothing, attacking everybody and everything around you. You must be the only soldier to get PTSD before you went to war, about twenty bucking years before!'

And Artie knew how to ignite my raw nerve, knew more about me than I liked people to know. That tangle of shared blood and familiar faces hinged me to him in a way I neither fully understood nor welcomed, but I couldn't escape it, Artie knew how to work my levers and I had to back off.

'Okay, forget it! I was just saying, that's all!' I retreated. 'Where do I start with this mystery man if Beikle can't help?'

'I know who he is,' Artie couldn't hide his swagger. 'You are going home, that's where the bastard is!'

Home? The United States? Maybe Artie didn't know as much as I thought. I was down here in Rio because of a very expensive buy-off that was good only so long as I stayed away from the US, and that's how it would be for the foreseeable future.

'There's a problem right there, Artie. I can't go home, that was the deal I made.'

'I know all about that, son,' Artie sighed, 'but I'm talking about *home* home - Ireland. That's where our man is, he thinks he is safe in Belfast.'

Belfast? Ireland? Was he screwing with me?

'Slow down, Artie, you've lost me here. Go back a couple of years. What about that cop? What about Inspector Swansea? They know we were there when he got wasted. I was covered in the old guy's blood and brains. I can't go back to Belfast! You can't go back there!'

'Don't worry I'm telling you! Our good friends in Washington resolved that issue. They know you weren't involved. Nobody over there is interested in you, and take my word for it, nobody wants to know about Swansea. God knows they can't afford to have anything to do with him looked at again, that's the least of our worries!'

This was all starting to slide away from me, the whole set-up was crazy. Everybody in Ireland had long memories for the old blood scores, I knew that to my cost, somebody would finger me.

'In fact, your de facto immunity for Swansea will be to our advantage. That's why you and I are the perfect team for this little task.'

Maybe Artie was crazy, maybe his enforced exile to Rome had sizzled a connection in his brain and this was all an Artie fantasy.

'I know who we are after, Con, false identity or not. He was part of Swansea's murder gang back in the old days, a Brit intelligence officer then, that's why he thinks he is safe back there now.'

$5 million is a lot of cash but I knew right there that I really should have tipped Artie over the balcony.

CHAPTER TWO

I told Artie I would meet him at noon at the Marina Palace hotel along the beach front. I was down there early to check it out and give myself some time on my own to think this through. The reception area was busy with guests arriving and leaving. A group of middle-aged Canadian men were already in the vacation swing and making sure the huddle of quiet Japanese women knew the Canucks were here to party. I slipped into the hotel bar, about twenty ordinary looking people doing ordinary things, nobody that I needed to look over twice. I took the side exit from the bar and crossed over the avenue to the beach. The little kiosk bar had a few tables and chairs arranged along the edge of the sidewalk. I called a beer and took a seat under a red parasol advertising 4G Nextel.

It was over 80 degrees again but the spirals of ocean breeze made it easier to breathe. Sometimes this city sucked the air right out of my lungs and clamped a gloved fist down my throat. Away from the beach, on the dry streets, it would hit me in the gut and punish me, like a snake bite had paralyzed my nervous system and

I would drown in my own juices. Especially if I had too much time to think, and to remember.

Artie would be here soon. I dragged the salty air into the deepest pockets of my chest, held it, teased the pressure, released it slowly, under control, safe. Artie was still bad news, priest collar or not, so why was I here? Don't think about it, just breathe, slow it down and take control, dull the dark energy. I didn't have a choice the times before, manipulated by their patriotic talk and my docile surrender to the big lie. Still time to walk away and leave Artie hanging. The breath control didn't work so good anymore. It was better when I could conjure the image of good times with the faces I loved but now I could only hold those pictures for a few seconds before they withered into shadows of the souls I had infected. A taxi pulled up at the Marina Palace. Artie emerged onto the sidewalk, sunglasses and a Brazil soccer shirt. Better to fight for the future than to regret the past. I left my beer behind and angled across the Avenue toward the hotel.

Artie moved through the lobby like he expected the throng to part before him. Yellow and green 'NEYMAR JR' soccer top, black priest pants, white socks and sandals. I tapped his shoulder and nodded toward the bar. A red and orange mural of Corcovado mountain and the Christ statue filled one wall. Artie parked himself on the soft seat right below the Christ statue as if the young couple already at the table didn't exist. I gestured to the remaining vacant seat and the bright young woman assured me they were leaving anyway. Artie clicked his fingers at the short stocky guy tending the bar and called for two cafezinhos. I hoped the guy would ignore Artie but he smiled a friendly wave and rattled a couple of tiny cups together.

Artie was in business mode.

'So, Con, what do you think? Will you volunteer to help me save a good man's name?'

It was that simple - help save a good man. The only problem was that I knew the shitstorms I had been dropped into before because of that simple good/bad choice, and the good never turned out to be all that good.

'I don't volunteer for anything anymore,' I said. 'Five million in clean cash might make it worth my trouble but I want to know what I'll be getting into.'

Artie pursed his lips and nodded his head like he was calculating the penance for a wayward altar boy.

'And, of course, I know from experience I can't trust anything you tell me to be the whole truth,' I said. 'A million dollars up front should keep you honest, and I walk the first hint you are holding out on me. I walk and sell you and your friend out to anybody who will pay. So, Artie, what do *you* think?'

He sighed his disappointment in me, perched the shades on top of his head and winced like he was wearing the martyr's crown. The waiter arrived with our coffee, two tiny cups whipped across the table, the menu flourished under our noses. Artie snapped the menu from the guy's nail-bitten fingers and dismissed him with a curt nod, no elaborate politeness show today. He pressed his nose close to the menu, Sushi served on a mini-surf board, Mango Sea Bass, Jumbo Shrimp Cocktail, his lunch deserved more of his attention, his respect, than I did. 'I'll have the chicken sandwich,' Artie said, like it was my job to place his order.

'Forget your stomach,' I said. 'You can eat after I leave, which is going to be in about 30 seconds if you don't start talking.'

Artie mumbled to himself under his breath, and I thought for a second his ego would win but even the biggest big-shot can fake humility when it suits.

'Johannes Beikle is a good man,' he said. 'He has been working for years to do something for the poor children suffering terminal illness. He has raised an incredible amount of cash over the years through his own hard work and perseverance but never enough to finance a purpose built hospice facility in Rome.' His sly glance hoped to catch me falling apart at his sob story. 'Anyway,' he said, 'Johannes has lobbied and begged for finance around half of Europe and beyond. Last year he was contacted by this character, calling himself Myler McGraw, said he was acting on behalf of a major philanthropic trust fund, and said he could put together a package to finance the children's hospice.'

Artie angled close to me now, close enough for me to taste his expensive cologne and the tang of breakfast whiskey on his breath.

'The deal was that the finances were available but the red tape in Italy was a problem,' he said. 'The only option was for Johannes to carry the cash from Vienna to Rome, lodge it in one of his IOR accounts, then release it to a health management company that the philanthropic trust would establish in Rome.'

That sounded like the typical half-assed scheme Artie's bluster would hit on, in hot water and out of his depth with the big boys who actually *do* make their own rules.

'Myler told Johannes the philanthropist would provide his private jet to transport the cash from Vienna to Rome, Myler would produce diplomatic immunity papers in the unlikely event that the customs authorities in Rome happened to show any interest, and this was the best way to save time and money. But when Johannes landed in Rome the Agenzia delle Dogane were waiting. They hauled him into an interrogation room and opened the cases with five million Euro bursting out. Myler and the other twenty-five million were nowhere to be seen. Johannes was fucked, as you might say.'

Artie sat back to sip his coffee, his diamond-tipped eyes challenging me to call him a liar. That was part of the package that was Monsignor Artie McCooey, all wrapped up in the incense-laced cloud of power and tradition that gave him first call on right and wrong. When he was right he was right, and when he was wrong his power franchise meant he was still right because those inconvenient wrongs could be ignored or ridiculed into limbo and forgotten.

'So what happened to this Myler guy?' I said. 'Is he the Brit spook?'

Artie's manicured fingers drummed a military beat on the table top.

'Johannes said he was American, with American diplomatic papers.' He slapped the table. 'But I know who that bastard is! As American as my arse!'

This would be the dangerous part, where I received the facts through Artie's truth filter.

'Johannes is more or less a prisoner in his apartment in the Vatican until his case goes before the courts again. Pity he didn't come to me before he let himself get roped into the whole sorry mess, I would have rumbled Myler straight away. That name would have been enough!'

Artie brushed imaginary crumbs off his pants. I was supposed to urge the rest of his tale out of him. I sat back with my hands behind my head.

'Myler McGraw?' he said. 'The smart arse is playing with Miler Magrath's name, one of our Bishops but the bastard went over to the other side. You know what it says on his gravestone? "*Here where I am placed I am not. I am not where I am not. Nor am I in both places, but I am in each.*" What's that tell you about him, eh? What's that tell you?'

It told me that Artie was still stuck half way up his own ass. And I didn't have time for another of Artie's Irish history lectures but if this Myler guy was so careless with a detail like that then maybe he shared Artie's big self-love flaw – that's the sort of weakness I want to know about in advance.

'If the name thing is so obvious to you then other people would catch it also,' I said. 'That's a big risk our Myler was taking, and not so smart. When was the real Bishop guy knocking about? During the Irish Troubles?'

Artie squeaked out his little smirk.

'During the "*Troubles*"? Well, he was born in 1522 and lived to 100, so, aye, Con son, I'd imagine he saw plenty of your Irish "*Troubles*", alright.'

'Oh really? I wondered why I didn't pick up news of his death on Twitter.'

'You may mock,' Artie said, 'but 400 years is no time in eternity!'

Yeah, I hear you, Artie, and ten minutes spent trying to make sense of his bullshit sure felt like an eternity, time to nail this down and get out of there.

'So what's Myler's real name? And how do you know so much about him?'

Artie got a big kick out of holding all the aces, it pumped his ego when he alone had inside info, and it pained him to share it too easily, too quickly.

'Johannes kept a record of all his fundraising activities,' Artie said. 'He has a pile of cuttings from newspapers and magazines, all the group photos with primped bankers and dolled-up business execs. We went through every single one – no sign of Myler anywhere even though he was at most of those events. Too smart, eh?' Artie nudged my knee and nodded a wink. 'He *thought* he was too smart! One of the young priests on Johannes' staff team is a great man for the selfie, have a look at this!'

Artie pulled his iPhone and tapped through a wall of photos until he found it, held it close to his nose to make sure, then slapped the iPhone into my hand. Five smiling men and a woman posed at the foot of a grand staircase, Johannes Beikle with his priest collar and what looked like a long black cape over his shoulders, the other men in tuxedos, the woman elegant in evening gown and jewels. 'Which one?' I asked. Artie needed me to drag it out of him, told me to look again, look at the big picture. They all looked the same, older men, tailored suits, over-groomed, burnished with wealth. She was younger, possibly a daughter but probably a trophy wife mistress. They all liked the camera. The stairway was framed by an ornate arch and heavy ornamental lights. A plaque on the arch read 'LOGEN AUFGANG'. Eight people in formal dress going up the stairs, their backs to the camera except for a young woman with her blonde hair piled high on her head and a fur collar draping her neck, stopped to rummage in her purse, her partner looking impatient on the step above her. Then I saw him - on the edge of the screen, partly hidden by the archway, turning back to check out the blonde girl, the lamplight behind blurring his features, spectacles with thick black frames, styled silver hair, and the look of a fox slinking away from a hen-house.

'Cameron Hamilton,' Artie said. 'He was a Military Liaison Officer in Belfast, back in the 80's and early 90's. He was the boy in the middle, the go-between for the Brits with the RUC Special Branch and MI5, and the Loyalist Death Squads, of course. I knew that bastard would surface one day and here he is.'

The fox in the photo was a man in his late 50's, of medium height and build, nothing extraordinary about him at all, except for the bleak sheen of death in his eyes that only signed up affiliates in our exclusive killers club would mark.

'You're talking, what, twenty-five years ago, Artie? You sure this is the same guy, from one lousy photo in bad light?'

Artie took the iPhone back and inspected the screen again like it was an old school photograph pitching him back to his happy childhood, then something snapped and he hammered his fist on the table.

'This bastard has the blood of fifty innocents on his hands! '*Paddy*' Hamilton, the Brits called him. He set up the ambushes for Inspector Swansea's killer cops and the SAS, and organized the arms shipments to their Loyalist proxy death squads! That's him alright, if I live to be 200 I won't forget this devil's face!'

The bar babble went dead, heads turned in our direction, and the waiter hovered nearby, unsure if this was going to be trouble, but Artie was in his own world of twenty-five years ago and the other people in the bar didn't exist. The old cynic was struggling now to hold it together, half turned away from me, shoulders quaking, heaving breaths and a muffled cry deep in his throat. It was a good time to push him a little further.

'Say it is him,' I said, 'how do you know he is back in Ireland? Isn't that the last place he would go to lie low?'

Artie slapped the back of his neck and puffed out his cheeks.

'When I realized who it was I asked people at home to see if anybody knew whatever happened to him,' he said. 'Somebody we know works at Belfast City Airport and recognized him, he's a regular flier to London, every couple of weeks.' Artie was making his comeback now, his voice stronger, looking me in the eye. 'Better than that, they noticed he was dropped and picked up at the airport by the same couple of cars every time, except one evening the car wasn't waiting on him so he jumped in a taxi.' Back on form, Artie teased me to ask or wait. I waited.

'The taxi took him to Loughside, about five minutes from the airport,' he said. 'That's Loughside, Con, HQ for British secret service.' He sat back now with his arms folded, triumphant.

'MI5? They're still there working against the IRA?'

'MI5, MI6, the crowd that listen to all our calls and read your emails, they're all in there but they're not interested in the IRA, that war's over. No, I'd imagine it's our friends in the East they're worried about.'

Artie was still a smooth talker but there was a whole big world out there, and I had seen some of it now and had been kicked in the balls too often to meekly accept his word as the only truth.

'Why do you need me?' I said. 'Why not get your friends in Ireland to turn Hamilton over?'

'Because that war is over and we want it to stay that way! There are plenty of people over there entitled to seek retribution from Paddy Hamilton but we don't want him executed! That wouldn't help the Peace Process and it wouldn't help Monsignor Johannes. You're a lone wolf, Con, that's what we need. Just get in and out with no fuss.'

I knew the routine, if anything goes wrong the lone wolf is suddenly the sacrificial lamb. It wasn't so long ago that I craved some of that lone wolf failure as the A1 route to numbed oblivion but I had started to feel alive again these last few months. Maybe Yasmin had something to do with that. And Rose and young Con were free of me also, and most days I could even forget that old guilt that used to crush the breath from my chest. All the good sense I had paid for dearly with pain and fear and shame told me to walk.

'You and I are really very alike, you know, Con son,' Artie said. 'I know you feel more comfortable taking refuge in that mantle of victimhood you construct for yourself, but we are very alike.'

Artie's resurrection from emotional wreck to smug bastard was surprisingly quick, maybe he was an even better actor than I had thought.

'Oh, I know you have had it rough,' he said, 'with the beatings and being held a prisoner and drugged and whatnot, I'm sure that must have been difficult. But this business of you being a broken soldier and a poor powerless puppet manipulated by the ruthless master class is really a lot of old bollocks, isn't it?'

His words hit me like a slap, first the numbness in my head, then the tingle as the old darkness started to pulse around my skull.

'Now take it easy,' he said, 'don't start any of your nonsense! What I'm saying is that men like us, the leaders, for want of a better word, have to make those sacrifices, we stand up and take it in the neck so that our people can plod through their nice safe comfortable lives. Are they ever grateful? No, of course not! But they only enjoy the luxury of being free to harangue and excoriate us because we are men enough to stand up and take the tough decisions. That's a compliment, by the way.'

Artie as the selfless saint, me as the knight in shining armor, that's how he could warp reality and sleep soundly at night, that's how they all did it.

'What?' he said, 'you think my ambition was to take responsibility for all this politicking and deal-making? Do you realize the compromises I have had to make?'

Artie settled back, his fingers linked across his fat belly, he was arranging a story.

'I'll tell you a story,' he said.

'When I was a young priest just starting out my only ambition was to serve Christ Our Lord and bring our people closer to Our Savior. I would have been happy working away in a quiet country parish, no dramas, no trappings of power, just a simple priest. At that time I was lucky enough to be offered a period of study at the Irish College in Rome. Those were the happiest days of my life, prayer, study, reflection, prayer. Prayer *was* my life! Anyhow, this time I was home in Armagh on a short break. News came through that a body had been found on the border. Word on the grapevine soon told us it was an unfortunate young lad who had been exposed as an informer. From a very highly respected Republican family, too, we knew them well, but an informer is an informer and the result is inevitable, God have mercy on his soul. His parents were on the scene as soon as they heard but the police and Brits wouldn't let them near the remains, said it was too dangerous and the body was probably booby-trapped, even threatened to arrest them.

'Word came back that the grieving parents had asked their own Parish Priest to intercede on their behalf, all he had to do was get confirmation from the IRA that there was no booby-trap and pass this on to the police. Now, I knew that PP myself, a spineless long drink of thin piss, if ever there was one! He refused to become involved, said he wasn't about to "*confer respectability on terrorists by engaging in communications*". Well, the gentlemen of the press got their teeth into that story and soon it was twisted into a choice between supporting the police and supporting the IRA. Our own PR people at Diocesan HQ in Armagh got nervous and stalled on any action. It was getting dark, and it looked like the remains would be left there overnight, so I got off my arse and went to the local IRA Officer in Command myself. No booby-traps. Next I phoned a crew from French TV News who were doing a program on the border and arranged to meet them at the police cordon. I linked the parents arm-in-arm and marched up to the police, with the French TV crew behind. I told them there were no booby-traps and then turned to the TV camera and declared that I intended to administer the Sacrament to the boy. Well, the cops nearly shit themselves and after a bit of huffing and puffing they cleared the way and I did my duty.'

Artie beckoned the waiter and asked for a low down on all the liquor they had on offer. He settled for a Sakerinha, ordered me a beer, and loosened his belt, ready to lecture me some more.

'Oh yes, the unfortunate lad was an informer alright,' he said. 'The IRA made audio recordings of last statements and confessions and passed them on to the families, at least when they were Republican families. When I approached the IRA O/C he gave me the tape to pass on to the parents. It was a very sad case, Con, I can tell you. It turns out the poor boy was actually a homosexual, you know, and the Brits somehow knew about it. They set him up and caught him in a gay honey-trap, then blackmailed him into working for them, passing on information on his comrades. I listened to the tape myself, and it would have drawn a tear from a stone.'

'So the kid was executed because he was gay?' I said.

'He was executed because he was an informer,' Artie said. 'What a waste, eh? And you know what one of the cops said to me when I was praying over his remains? He said, "*I wouldn't waste your breath on him, Priest McCooey, he's only a scum IRA poofter!*" And do you know who that policeman was? It was our old friend the late Detective Inspector Swansea, just starting out on his long and ignoble career!'

The drinks arrived, I held the chilled bottle against my cheek, Artie sipped his smooth Sake cocktail. I was supposed to chisel some extra sense from his story, like the words were only a shadow of the real meaning hidden in his nod and wink tic-tac. Artie rearranged himself on his seat and a little grunt escaped from both ends of his body.

'I'm saying we all have to make sacrifices, that's all. I could easily have spent my life with my head down saying my prayers. But I stepped up to make the difficult decisions that other clergy were afraid of. Plenty of those gutless wimps are delighted to snipe away at me behind my back with their snide remarks and character assassination, but they are only free to get on with their nice holy lives because I'm the one who stands up and takes the flak.'

'I can't say I ever decided to stand up for anything, Artie, it all sort of just happened, just bad luck and bad timing. I never got to make the choice like you did.'

Artie flashed his I-know-more-than-you-do smirk. He knew some of it, I had told him myself once when I was drunk and couldn't deal with the blood guilt on my own anymore. But even I didn't know exactly how much savagery I had unleashed, and I had even less of a clue how it was possible I could have turned into that wild beast. The top military forensic psychiatrists and neuroscientists in the United States didn't really know either, their best guess was that some screwed up wiring in my "*amygdala sparked a hyper fight or flight response and then permitted the function of a normal human being afterwards by rewriting the implicit emotional memory*".

'They used to say a hero is born, not made,' Artie said, 'but it seems now that everybody in a uniform with a gun is made a hero. But you are a different sort of animal, Con, you are the real thing.'

He knew too much, and probably had read the witness accounts that filled in the blanks my own brain couldn't accept.

'I have changed, Artie. I have control now, I won't be in those situations again.'

'I'll offer my prayers for that, son, and trust in God the torment of your Ríastrad is over for good.'

'My what?'

'Your Ríastrad, the demon battle frenzy that afflicts you. Didn't your fancy neuroscientists ever hear of the Ríastrad?'

'Drop it, Artie, it doesn't need a label anymore because it won't be happening again,' I said, 'but get back to your own story. How come you could get in contact with an IRA Commander so easily? I thought all that stuff was top secret, isn't it odd that you knew who he was?'

Artie laughed out loud. 'For feck's sake why wouldn't I know him? Wasn't he was my own cousin?!'

Artie jock-slapped me on the shoulder, tried to cajole me into laughter as if there really was something funny about all this, something I just hadn't noticed yet but that, when I did, would suck me into Artie's world of forced humor and false optimism.

'A million dollars up front, Artie, then we are in business.'

Artie's laughter stalled into a throat clearing cough and he studied me from behind the rim of his Sakerinha. We were in business, I had made it easy for him and he was already calculating his next move. I guessed he was figuring out an extra choke-hold to keep me docile, something else to blackmail me with if I wavered or pulled too tight on his leash.

'Remember now, Con, this will be in and out quietly, no big fuss, you hear me? I will make arrangements. I'll have trusted people there to support you. You won't even need to speak to anyone else, only the few people we can trust, understand?'

I understood, Artie couldn't help but suffer a slight unease, anxious that I might ruin his meticulous planning with my carelessness, or my Ríastrad, as he called it. He shouldn't have worried. I had no intention of putting myself at the mercy of his 'trusted' supporters. I would make my own plans, turn the screw on Paddy Hamilton and find his rainbow with a $30 million pot of gold. I might even rescue Monsignor Johannes Beikle and restore him to the pedestal Artie had reserved for him.

But I didn't try to fool myself that I was leaving the pleasures of Yasmin's bed and the Rio sunshine to save Beikle, or even for the dirty money. No, but I could already sense that dormant thrill tingle at the base of my skull, maybe it was my warped amygdala or some other primitive slice of my brain that even the neuros hadn't discovered, but it was stirring now and pulsing through my veins like a flood tide. I wasn't in it for the money or the false glory of righting a wrong. I was in because I missed the delicious kick of fear and menace, the demon bang that was the only sure way to banish the old ghosts, even at the risk of creating new ones.

I was going home, okay, but bringing the Ríastrad with me.

CHAPTER THREE

February 1st, Ireland

There is no border in Ireland, no border patrols, no checkpoints, no uniforms, and I only realized the coach had crossed when the African guy beside me swivelled his head to gape at the ragged British flags that suddenly appeared on the light poles and lampposts. The elusive Irish border has been the recycled fuse paper at the core of their fighting for ninety years, or nine hundred, and somebody should have noticed it had gone, but then I figured saying there was no border in Ireland was like saying there was no slavery in the United States.

The sugar dusted hills above Belfast were coming closer now, alive in the early morning sunshine, waiting for me. I fingered my new passport - Conor McAnespie, Éireannach/Irish. I thought it would be green but Artie said all European passports were purple. I had half expected to be rumbled at the first passport control in Rio airport but Artie had somehow managed to fix me up with the real thing. I passed through Amsterdam with no problem, then the guy in Dublin hardly looked at it. So, either Artie could pull strings at a higher level than I had thought or there were other players in this game, maybe at the level where they get to decide who is expendable - I already knew where I sat in that hierarchy.

Rio was heaving in the high 80's when I ran out on her, slinking away like a dog with my tail between my legs whilst Yasmin and her kids were down at the beach, but this freezing Belfast bus station was still deep in Sunday morning slumber, and the gray chill licked my face before wrapping itself around me like a piss-soaked shroud. Artie's guy was waiting, a skinny kid with bad skin and a worse suit. 'Mr McAnespie?' He offered a cold greasy hand for a pretend shake and pressed a small envelope in my fist before jumping into the tiny car that was waiting on him. It looked like it was his mother driving, and they almost got totalled by another bus as they lurched out of the station. Welcome to Belfast, I thought to myself.

The envelope had a door key inside and a phone number and address scribbled on the back – "*18 Sandymount Street, blue door*". I tore off the phone number and shredded it into an unreadable pulp, then poked the pieces into a half empty beer bottle that some drunk had left under a bench in the station, a sniff of my fingers confirmed it wasn't beer the bastard had left in the bottle. A small mall led out to the street, I stopped to let the other bus passengers pass and checked out a bookstore window, nobody following but I stopped again in the exit to the wide street. I had been here before, this was where it had all started, when I had still been dumb enough to think I was immune from the power-addicted predators who were born in the right, before Swansea's execution had kick started my crazy learning curve.

I shunned the taxis outside and turned left toward the city center. Still only a few people on the streets, it was a couple of minutes before I found someone to ask directions to Sandymount Street. They were a couple of Dutch tourists meandering around the streets looking for something to do, the next person was a Spanish student, and the next group were English business types at a conference. I was thinking of risking a taxi when a little round guy motored around the corner, the exaggerated shoulder roll anchored to the fat gut ballast. 'You're going the wrong way, mate! Up there, past Lavery's, on up to the left, past The Elms, go left after Queen's and on up to the Birdcage. That street is up there somewhere, about twenty minutes.'

Sandymount is a narrow street of modest red brick houses outnumbered by the cars sardined along both sides. Artie's friend was a landlord with a portfolio of rented properties in this student area, and number 18 was vacant at present. The blue door was about half way down, on the left, the only ground floor window boarded up and a broken table lay in the tiny garden which was no more than an excuse to separate the house from the street by a wall only three-bricks high. The key struggled to open the door, looked like a new lock had recently been fitted. It was dark and cold inside, a narrow hallway, the door to the room with the broken window was locked. The hallway opened into a tight living area, shabby armchairs piled up in one corner, the worn carpet covered in dark stains, broken glass and cigarette burns, a lamp with no base wedged at an angle in the other corner. The adjoining kitchen was so cramped I could touch the walls on each side without stretching. Pots and pans were stacked in the sink, the work area was sprinkled with rodent droppings and a stale odor to match. A small yard ran parallel with the kitchen, enclosed by an eight foot high red brick wall.

The first floor was two locked rooms plus a bathroom with a stained purple bath and peach colored sink and toilet. The second floor had two doors, the unlocked room overlooked the street below. It was even colder in here, ice glistened inside the windows and my breath steamed out in cloud bubbles. An old bed frame, a small lamp on a cheap bedside table and faded curtains were the only furnishings but someone had left me a present - a new mattress, a duck down fifteen tog duvet, an electric underblanket, sheets and two goose down pillows, all still in their shop packaging. A large envelope was tucked into the electric blanket package, £5,000 in used notes. Maybe this Irish hospitality wasn't so bad after all.

Back down to the kitchen, I found a knife sharp enough to open the packaging and quickly put the bed together. By the time I returned from dumping the packaging in the back yard the electric blanket was starting to pump some heat into that ice-box. I needed food but, after twenty hours on the road, I needed sleep more.

I woke up in a daze, a couple of seconds of panic before I could unscramble my brain, somebody was down there banging on the door. I jumped out of bed and pulled the curtain aside just enough to see into the street. There was a blue taxi stopped outside, with two other taxis and a white van stacked behind, unable to pass in the narrow street. The taxi man screamed in through the letter-box, 'Taxi for McAnespie!' I pulled on my pants and ran down to the door.

'Come back tomorrow,' I said.

'Tomorrow? Are you fucking wise?! Do you want this taxi or not?'

'Come back tomorrow, same time,' I said, and closed the door on his astonished purple face. Artie would freak out when word got back that I had gone off radar but he had better get used to it quickly if he wanted to keep up with me because I had already started my play six weeks ago, and Artie's pals weren't high on my priority list.

The gate in the yard opened to an alleyway that ran along the back of Sandymount Street. I turned right and emerged at the end of the street, dodged down low behind the parked cars and crossed into the next street. I made my way back toward the city center, down Stranmillis and past the grand red brick pile of Queen's University of Belfast. A black London-style taxi came toward me with his '*For Hire*' sign lit up.

The driver talked too much, had some sort of blue badge permit for exploiting tourists, wanted to take me to the Titanic Belfast exhibition. I told him I was a Canadian, here to research family roots. That was a mistake – he was also an expert on the pedigree of all the families in Belfast. I told him to drop me at the Merchant Hotel. He said he could stick around and take me to the Public Records Office if I wanted to search their genealogy records. That was beside the Titanic exhibition anyway, he could show me around both. I told him the hotel would be fine for now.

The Merchant Hotel is a real knock-out, sweeping steps leading up to the grand doorway, four pairs of classical columns framing the entrance, and some Roman gods up top. This looked just like the top of the range indulgence he was accustomed to, and the interior is even more spectacular than the grand exterior, all plush red velvet and a diamond sparkling chandelier under a jaw-dropping glass dome. I didn't expect this in Belfast.

'Can I help you, sir?'

'Yeah, thanks, a friend of mine is staying here – a Russian guest. He is expecting me.'

The guy craned his head sideways for a moment.

'I believe the gentleman is in the bar at the moment, sir. May I show you the way?'

The bar is a heartbreaker as well, not at all like the Irish bars around McLean Avenue and Hell's Kitchen, but a bar is a bar, and my man was waiting. He was at the end of the long counter and stood to greet me with exaggerated warmth, his arms reaching out like I was a baby taking his first steps.

'Well, my friend,' he whispered in my ear, 'what brings a CIA Assassin to this lovely place?'

'Let's judge how lovely the place is when we get our hands on $30 million,' I pressed my mouth close to Yakov's face. 'Right now I'm going to have a drink with a KGB gangster.'

CHAPTER FOUR

Yakov was a killer. His killer scent spiked the air around him. I buried my ghosts with shame, Yakov flashed his kills as a badge of honor, like scalps hanging around his neck and each one making him stronger, feeding his power. His round tanned face was at home in the high class hotel, and his fellow guests maybe assumed his easy confidence was spawned from the wealth that gave him status, made him a good guy, one of them, to share in the mutual respect and deference of their club - but he was still a killer.

'Michael Leeks said I was a fool to let you walk away from Lisbon,' he said.

'Michael Leeks? Who the fuck's Michael Leeks?'

'My colleagues! You dumb American fuck! I said my colleagues! Don't you speak English?! My colleagues said I was a fool!'

'Yeah, well I guess your colleagues don't know how much you made out of our Lisbon arrangement, do they? Anyway, that's ancient history, we have a new project to discuss.'

Yakov wedged his broad back into the elegant chair, cranked his thick neck to glance over to the barman and, without a word, the guy set about the rattle and roll of his business.

'I am here on business, Maknazpy,' Yakov drawled, 'important business for my enterprises. I can spare a few minutes to listen but I will not be caught up in your dirty deals, understand? Anything goes wrong and you are on your own, and something always does go wrong where you are involved, doesn't it?'

The pressure on Yakov to assert his alpha male swagger would have exhausted lesser men yet this Silverback showed no sign of being dethroned anytime soon, but it didn't cost me anything to let that ride, he wasn't here because he wasn't interested, and he hadn't sent his nephew all the way out to meet me in Rio because he didn't want in on my act.

'Okay, I won't hold you back from your big shot business,' I said, 'your nephew Pyotr passed on my message, so what do you think? What did you find out about my missing money in Rome?'

I didn't expect a straight answer.

'When you are at home in your little apartment in New York do you notice when your neighbor buys himself a new little car?' he said. 'No, maybe not in your sick America but in civilized societies people notice what their neighbors do, then they can respect their property, give them space to do their thing, understand? The same in my business, when a neighbor, another business person moves that much money, that *sort* of money, we know about it. Then we can respect their space, they don't interfere with our business and we don't interfere with theirs, everyone is happy.'

'So you do know about it, then?' I said.

'I was not involved personally,' he said, 'but something about this operation was not honest and that makes me a little nervous.'

The bar guy performed a discreet cough as he approached and Yakov flipped back to his genial tourist face.

'Here is a treat for you, my friend! The famous Moscow Mule created by an artist!'

The artist placed the drinks on the table and acknowledged Yakov's bullshit with just the right balance of grace and deference before leaving us alone in the corner. The drinks were in copper mugs, with a kicking mule and the words '*Moscow Mule*' etched on the front, vodka and mixers fizzing and sparking over the brim, lime and cucumber slices topped with a sprig of spearmint. Yakov made a big play of drawing in the aroma, circling the drink under his nose, holding his breath, touching his tongue to the tip of the mug without drinking any.

'I am opening a hotel in Leningrad, St Petersburg as the revisionists call it,' he said. 'That is why I am here, doing research. They have won the awards here, '*World's Best Hotel Bar*' and '*World's Best Cocktail Menu*', but they know I'm coming after them and will take it to the next level. So remember, when things go bad for you, my friend, that's my story – here as a genuine businessman and owner of a 6 star hotel. Don't even waste your time mentioning my name.'

'Sure, maybe I'll leave you to it,' I said. 'Thirty million dollars on the line and I have a lead on the main man. I'm pretty sure I can find any help I need in this town and you can sit here sipping cocktails until they rename Petersburg again.'

Yakov's indulgent smile said he couldn't care less, his eyes said he might tear my head off my neck. He snatched my Moscow Mule mug and two thick fingers scooped out the lime and cucumber, tore the cucumber into two strips and bit into the lime wedge before ripping it apart. He arranged the fruit and my drink across the table; cucumber, lime, mug, lime, cucumber. The barman looked the other way. This was Yakov pushing the boundaries, flaunting his power, making it easier to insult and control me in future. The burn started its coil around my throat but I would keep my cool this time, no matter how far he pushed.

'Virtual banking,' he said, 'on the dark market.'

I loosened my collar, suddenly too hot in here.

'Say you want to move cash without moving cash, say you value your privacy,' he said. 'This cucumber is a bank, okay, just a normal bank like normal people put their little money in.' He fingered the sliver of cucumber closest to him and performed a tight circle on the table like he was driving a Ouija board.

'I walk into this bank, say it is in New York, and direct the nice people in there to wire my money to this particular place, okay?' The particular place was now the wedge of lime on his side of the table. 'It's your money, they wire it anywhere you say, yes? So, they wire it here to this money exchanger, real money in the normal system.' The lime oozed its pungent juice under the fat fingers. 'Let's say this exchanger is sitting somewhere beautiful, like Cayman Islands, okay?' Now he tapped his oversized gold sovereign ring against the copper mug. 'Pay attention! This is where it becomes interesting. Now say you have the virtual bank, the dark bank that serves its customer market without the attention of Big Brother and the government tax robbers.'

He swilled a long swallow from the mug and slapped it down on the table. 'This dark bank is maybe sitting in Nauru or Niue or some other fucking rock in the ocean that no-one has ever heard of. The exchanger in Cayman, our lime friend here, is instructed to wire virtual currency to the virtual bank in Nauru, understand? That is one half of the deal. Then the virtual bank in Nauru wires virtual cash to a different exchanger,' he bent forward to squeeze the second lime wedge, on my side of the table. 'This exchanger is maybe somewhere like Switzerland or Austria, say maybe Vienna, you see? Then the exchanger in Vienna receives the virtual currency and converts it into real hard currency and then wires the real hard currency to an account in a real, normal bank in Vienna, get it?'

He scooped the second strip of cucumber up and dunked it into my drink before throwing it back on to his dirty yellow tongue.

I didn't get it. Didn't the real currency stick at the first exchanger in the Cayman Islands? How did the virtual bank in Nauru wire anything at all to the second exchanger in Vienna?

'Fuck!' Yakov exploded. 'The first exchanger takes a cut from the hard currency, right? They all take a cut, maybe 10%, maybe more depending on how dark the deal has to be. The first exchanger keeps *all* the hard cash, okay, but these guys do business together all the time. The next time the transfer could be coming in the other direction, maybe the second exchanger is the one wiring virtual cash to the first one, it all evens out over time, it is a two way street!'

'Okay, okay,' I said, 'I get you now, but when you say *maybe* Vienna, you're telling me the second exchanger *was* in Vienna, aren't you?'

'Let's just say some people are very interested to know what happened to a certain Viennese finance operation that was doing good business close to the Prater in Leopoldstadt. It started small about five years ago and then suddenly became a big time dealer, and taking only a little cut compared to the others.'

Yakov plucked the Viennese exchanger lime into his bear paw and squeezed it to pulp, squirting the juice into my face and all over the table top.

'All of a sudden it disappeared,' he said, 'about the time your priest turned up in Rome with bags of dirty cash.'

'He turned up with some of it,' I said, 'another $30 million is still out there somewhere, and I'm talking about real folding money, not that virtual crap.'

'I know, I know,' Yakov said, 'and thirty million must sound like a lot of money to you, Maknazpy my friend, but believe me, there is a lot more at risk here than your $30 million. My colleagues who are interested to find your Viennese lime sent the dogs after him, top people, ex-special forces and police insiders, no money spared. No ordinary person could stay free for long but two Polish man-hunters were found floating in the Danube, a German ex-detective choked in a British police cell, and two others have disappeared. The trail stopped in London. I say your Viennese lime has friends, ass licking hypocrites rewarded with immunity and entitlement. There is much more than your $30 million to worry about.'

He didn't say how much more and I figured that was good and bad - good for the obvious greedy reason, bad because I wasn't the only one on Hamilton's tail and maybe Yakov's colleagues would be more persuasive this time when they told him I was a risk.

'I know what you are thinking, Maknazpy,' he said it in a low, laughing growl. 'You think I came here to fuck you over and take all the cash for myself, isn't that so?'

Yeah, that was exactly so.

'Don't worry about it!' he said. 'Some things are more important than money, like trust and like confidence in the economic system. Our businesses can't function efficiently if the system is broken, if it isn't honest.' We both grinned. 'These government desperados and bank robber barons aren't honest but their system works for them because that's the only way it can work – the more dishonest they are the better they are rewarded – but it doesn't work like that in our world, my friend. A bad apple will turn the whole barrel bad. Bankers on the dark market must be honest, they must be kept honest, or else the whole financial model breaks down.'

'I sure hope you can work with me on this one, Yakov,' I said, 'but if you and your people are planning on double-crossing me you are going to have a big problem, starting from right now.'

'Calm down, calm down, crazy Irish Yank!' he said. 'You will be well rewarded, very well, but sometimes money is not the most important thing.'

I heard it, but I didn't believe it.

'No, the most important thing this time is that this Viennese lime,' he pulped the fruit between his fingers some more, 'this bad apple, dies a very slow, very painful, very humiliating and very public death. You will get your dirty money, we will get this thief's heart on a stick, and his masters will find out they have more to lose than we do!'

Yakov wouldn't let me leave until he bear hugged me, smearing lime and cucumber juice over the back of my neck and all down my jacket. I knew he had only told me as much as he wanted me to know, and I could work around that just fine. Artie also knew more than he had told but that was just another piece of fruit to be juggled. I paused at the top of the sweeping entrance steps and let the damp Belfast air rinse over me. The game had started for real now, and the buzz was a good enough reason to be alive. A London-style black taxi choked into life and limped off in a cloud of fumes, turning down the lane of cobblestones before I could see the driver. That's the way it was going to be, and I was ready.

CHAPTER FIVE

The purple faced driver edged his blue taxi past the removal van doing its best to block Sandymount Street.

'So you decided today is more convenient for you than yesterday then, boss? That's very nice of you,' he laid it on heavy, lord of all he surveyed within his blue taxi kingdom. 'It makes no odds to me anyway, you know, I get paid so I do, but there's a wee girl I lift down Balmoral, she's regular, had to cancel her yesterday, know what I mean, but I get paid, no odds to me.'

'Where are we going?'

'I was told to go west. The depot will give directions when I get over there. I just drive, as long as I get paid it's no odds to me, sure it's not?'

He didn't turn his purple face toward me but I caught his quick glances in the rear-view mirror.

'It's cold,' I said, 'can you get some heat in here?'

He started to twist toward me but thought better of it, sighed a deep breath, and hit the air-con. Hot air blasted around my ankles, and purple face sank deeper into his seat, muttering to himself.

We were leaving student land now, houses with price tags nosing up as we climbed a tree-lined hill, then down to a wider road, hard-grafted high hedges and trees shielding comfort zones from the commuter transients, turned down again into a broad avenue, the Belfast hills straight ahead, still frozen in their time. Purple face played a running commentary to himself on the piss poor driving he met along the way. Traffic gorged to a crawl as the motorway drew closer, purple face blustered his way ahead, laughed in victory when he got the jump on an old lady, and then we were speeding toward the city center.

'This is us here, boss, The Balls on the Falls!'

It was a huge see through skeleton of a metal globe floating high above the motorway, with a smaller ball, about half-size, somehow suspended inside the bigger one - a seductive illusion that there was an alternative universe, a better one, almost within touch.

'That's supposed to be art!' he whined. 'I'm fucking taxiing over pot-holes and *that's* what they spend my fucking taxes on?!'

He tapped a tablet on his lap as we left the motorway and linked on to the vehicles backed up at traffic lights. I heard the reply beep on his screen, he bumped two wheels up on the pavement to crawl past a school bus and took a left into a small side street of red brick row houses, then a right and accelerated too fast up the narrow ravine of tarmac between the parked cars.

'This is you, boss.' He thumb pointed to a solid red brick building. 'The Cultúrlann. Welcome to West Belfast!'

I had expected the meet-up with Artie's contact to be in some quiet country lane or in a deserted back street but this was an unusually public place, a buzzing spine of shops and offices with the city traffic funnelled almost to a standstill at the nearby junction. There must have been a hundred pairs of eyes that could have recalled me being dropped by the blue taxi and going into the Cultúrlann building.

I tailed along behind a gaggle of kids in school uniform going through the gate and up the steps. They stalled at the small lobby inside, laughing and goofing around, and it was only then I realized they weren't speaking English. They parted to let me pass, a door led to an open plan main hall - a trendy looking bistro café to the right, a bookshop on the left. I could see about ten or twelve people in the café, a group of young women taking up two tables, a couple of old men, some guys working over tablets, and two middle-aged men, suits and ties, sitting near the door, waiting for me. They looked up as I approached the table, then looked behind me as she tugged my elbow.

'Over here, I have a table,' she said, and nudged me toward the corner. She was a dark haired woman in her 40's or 50's, tall and very slim with black, black eyes, well dressed in a dark business suit, and I guessed she used really expensive hair and skin products.

'You were supposed to be here yesterday,' she said, 'you are lucky I was able to alter my diary.'

Her navy blue woollen overcoat with silver buttons was carefully draped over a seat, the matching leather bag sat on the table with her open MacBook.

'I'm Brigid,' she said.

No handshake, no greeting hug or cheek kissing, but she was close enough for her premium perfume to do its job.

'You know who I am, Brigid.' I didn't feel like trivial chit-chat. 'How much has Artie told you?'

The fragile lines around her black eyes puckered into deeper cracks. 'You know our Monsignor McCooey,' she rolled her black eyes, 'he either tells you what you want to hear or what he thinks you should know.'

'Yeah, I've got that T-Shirt also,' I said. 'So what did Artie think *you* should know?'

'Just that a friend of his was in trouble and an old friend of ours was behind it.'

'You have a history with this Hamilton guy?'

Brigid arched her back and stroked the curve of her neck with both hands, tossed her head back to shake her hair over her wide shoulders, and held me steady with her eyes, not in an alluring, beguiling way, more like a snake hypnotizing its prey, or a cat toying with a mouse.

'What's that saying? Those who know history are condemned to repeat it?' She shrugged the coat over her shoulders. 'I've moved on, Mr America. What exactly does Monsignor McCooey want to do about Hamilton? How are you supposed to do it on your own?'

That stumped me for a second, I knew what I would do when we boosted him out of his spook penthouse, and Yakov was laying down the backroom support right now, but I needed Brigid's people to get to Hamilton in the first place.

'Well, let's meet with your people and see what we've got,' I said. 'Then we'll take it from there.'

'My people? What do you mean? What "*people*"?'

'The IRA,' I said, 'your fucking IRA people!'

She laughed out loud now, and her shoulders still quaked even after she clamped her hand over her mouth.

'The IRA?' she said, 'they've gone away, you know, been gone away a long time now. Is that what that mad bastard McCooey told you? The 'Ra would come to the rescue? I think you'd better go home now, son, before you embarrass yourself.'

So, Artie's nod and wink scheme was already full of holes, that was no big surprise.

'Anyway,' Brigid said, 'Aren't you the one being well paid? Why should I stick my neck out so you can walk off with a hundred grand in your mercenary back pocket?'

Artie's big mouth. The million up front didn't happen, he cried off at the last minute, said he had no access to any cash but would look after me when the big money came in. Artie's bullshit, but the game was buzzing through my skull by then and I needed the hunt more than I needed the money – and I had my own ideas about the cash anyway.

'I'm here because McCooey needs my help,' I said. 'I thought that's why you were here also. If you have some beef with Artie over money that's your business, not mine, but if you aren't here to work with me on this thing then I don't know why you are wasting my time.'

'You're a cheeky bastard!' She jabbed a finger in my chest and thrust her neck forward so that she was right in my face. 'Don't be fucking coming over here acting the big hero! You're nothing but a fucking mercenary scumbag, a killer for hire, so don't give me that shit about fucking helping people, right?'

There was something fierce deep inside her, and it was straining hard to escape through her mouth and eyes and into my face. I caught the two guys behind moving closer.

'How many innocent women and children did you kill in Iraq anyway?' She poked her venom into my chest, I shifted away and angled myself to keep the two men in view.

'I was a soldier,' I shrugged. 'It was war, it was shit, war shit happens.'

'What? Like you can just sit there and shrug your fucking shoulders and say "*shit happens*" and that's okay?' Brigid slammed me. 'You were a murderer in uniform, you were scum!'

'You were an IRA terrorist, Brigid, so don't lay your rose-tinted morality on me, okay?'

She recoiled like I'd unloaded a taser up her ass but quickly bounced back to attack mode.

'I was no terrorist!' She gripped my wrist and dug her sharp talons into my flesh. 'The only terrorists I saw around here were trigger-happy fuckers like you in uniform. They brought their war here to us, to our streets, I didn't go half way around the world looking for them.'

'A terrorist is a terrorist, Brigid, no matter what self-deluding excuses you make for yourself.'

'You're in the wrong place to be mouthing off about who was or wasn't a terrorist, soldier boy, but I suppose it isn't your fault – must be hard to escape all that Neo-Con brainwash that put you in Iraq in the first place.' She smiled without releasing her grip. 'But you look like you are in control of yourself. Monsignor McCooey warned me you were volatile, on a knife edge, that's not good for this sort of work.'

'You're testing me, Brigid? If you want to bust my balls you gotta know I'm going to react.'

She pulled my wrist forward with one hand and pushed my sweatshirt sleeve up my arm.

'What's that about then?' she smirked.

She knew what it was. It was the green, white and orange 'IRA' tattoo branded into my skin.

'That doesn't mean shit,' I said. 'Friends of mine paid a guy one time when I was too drunk to stand. They could have tattooed Bin Laden's butt on there for all I knew about it.'

She released her grip and eased back to stretch her legs and link her fingers across her stomach. Now she looked like a battle-weary teacher still wrangling for submission from an unruly student. I sensed the two guys relaxing into stand down.

'Your friends?' she smiled. 'You mean Golden Boy Ferdia McErlane, don't you? Monsignor McCooey warned me not to mention his name in case it set you off to throw a psycho.'

Artie hadn't even mentioned his name to me, but how much and what else had the big-mouthed fuck told her about Iraq and everything else?

'It's in the past,' I played it down. 'What's done is done, don't worry, I don't freak out about it anymore.'

'I knew him, you know,' her tone was softer now, 'or at least I knew his family, his uncles.'

Yes, Ferdy's adored McCooey uncles, Artie's cousins, ambushed by Swansea and Hamilton, I saw the black granite totem to their memory the last time I was here.

'You *were* in the IRA then?' I said.

She shrugged.

'A different life,' she sighed, 'what's done is done. And that's the problem, I really don't have any *"people"*, so we are on our own on this one.'

I turned my eyes to the two guys.

'What about these two?' I said. 'They sure look like they are your people.'

'Aye, they work for me, okay, but unless you need them for a bit of extreme action office management and accounting I reckon they'll be about as much use to you as rosary beads at an Orangeman's funeral.'

Two wiry guys, neither over 170 pounds, both with bald heads shaved, one with a purple sheen arcing from chin to ear, the other with a neglected gray goatee and white eyebrows. The waitress arrived to ladle their table with burgers, fries and salad, laughed on cue when graybeard said something funny. Brigid rolled her eyes.

'That's Tomás,' she said. 'His cousin runs a taxi firm in south Belfast, Wee Joe has his ear to the ground.'

Tomás was at least fifty, maybe fifty-five, and his round head bobbed and weaved like it was attached to the thin neck with a rogue spring.

'Taxi-men in this town don't miss much,' she said, 'the word is that there is a big house in the country outside Lisburn, about ten miles from here, that becomes a big boy's fun palace at the weekend. A couple of Wee Joe's drivers disappear with two seven-seater cabs for a couple of hours every now and again. He heard they were driving the entertainment to the party house, working girls, girls from Eastern Europe and China.'

'So what about Hamilton?' I said. 'Somebody has seen him there?'

'The party boys arrive later, and have their own transport,' she said, 'but one night the fella bringing the girls didn't show up so the girls phoned the depot and got Wee Joe. By the time he got out there he ran slap into the Hooray Henrys arriving. They were already high and couldn't wait to haul the girls out of the taxi. Hamilton was there, not fussed about the girls, and standing in the background, but he was there alright.'

'Sure it was Hamilton?'

Brigid puffed out her cheeks and did the eye-roll thing, twisted in her seat and called something to Tomás, something in Irish but I knew it meant 'get your ass over here'. Tomás screwed up his face and muttered something to purple head but then shoved a fistful of fries into his mouth before making a big deal of getting up and coming over. Brigid issued another order and pointed to his belt. He wasn't keen but she insisted, he said something else with a 'Fuck's Sake!' tagged on to the Irish and then he looked up at the ceiling as he pulled the belt apart and worked his pants open. It's not easy to make me uncomfortable but Tomás was getting there. The girls at the tables half way up the room giggled and elbowed. Tomás dropped his pants to his knees, the girls cheered and whistled, Brigid nodded to his pink hairy thighs. Tomás turned sideways. The right thigh wasn't pink and hairy at all. It just wasn't there. The flesh and muscle had been scoured out to leave a mess like gray plastic, melted to bubbled lava then warped to a hideous marble.

'Wee Joe's brother wasn't so lucky,' Brigid said. 'They took him down then put one in the back of his head. Tomás went over the bridge and washed up down the river.'

'Left half my leg on that fucking bridge, must go back down there for it some time,' Tomás joked, and shook his ass at the sniggering girls before pulling his pants up.

'If Wee Joe says he saw Paddy Hamilton, he saw Paddy Hamilton,' Brigid said.

'Well, I suppose that's a start,' I said. 'What else? Can you pull together whatever you've got on Hamilton? I'll work something out.'

'That's it,' she shook her head, rolled her eyes. 'If you had been here twenty-five years ago I could have told you what that bastard had for his breakfast but it's like I said, that was a different world.'

Brigid started to collect her things, swathed a purple and red scarf around her neck, standing over me to twist the silver buttons with crisp efficiency.

'PJ was the best Intelligence Officer we ever had,' she nodded to the sheen of purple stubble and red skin grazing at the other table. 'He'll give you a lift over to Stranmillis, maybe he can fill in some of the blanks.'

One of the girls saw Brigid was about to leave and they all swivelled in their seats to wave goodbye, Brigid smiled sweetly and curved a little wave back.

'Monsignor McCooey says you don't believe in phones?' she said. 'No e-mails, no nothing? You think you are under surveillance, mercenary man?'

'Aren't we all, Brigid?' I rolled my eyes at her. 'Aren't we all?'

Maybe PJ had been a terrific Intelligence Officer in a past life but he was a shit driver in the present one. His purple face scowled over the wheel at the road ahead to death-stare each vehicle and pedestrian for a few moments, then he would slump back in his seat and turn his eyes to me, as if he could pre-pay his road attention and his snaps of furious intensity could build some safety credit to be milked until a near miss sparked the next fierce staring bout.

He wanted to know if I ever thought about the people I had killed. Did I see their faces in my dreams? Hear their screams in the dark? The crying mothers? The children? He peered at me with the same cold eyes as all the shrinks and head doctors that had ever pinned me to a couch. I knew all the answers, too, all the right words to disarm them, make them think they alone had managed to break my case, let them self-validate their craft and science. There would be no payback for indulging PJ, though, so I wasn't playing ball.

'So what business is Brigid in?' I asked, 'what do you do for her?'

'She's a busy woman, done very well for herself, so she has. The office is there beside the Cultúrlann, she has property interests and a couple of other things, catering and commercial cleaning, courier work, couple of other wee things, you know,' he squinted a quick glance at the road and then back to me. 'I suppose you got all sorts of psychological counselling, that sort of stuff? Did it work or was it a load of old ballicks?'

The back of his hands and the loose skin on his neck said PJ was late fifties, maybe sixty, but he had the tight frame that said he still worked out, kept himself in shape, just in case.

'What did you try?' He wasn't letting go. 'Cognitive therapy? Psychodynamic Story-telling?'

Maybe PJ was still the ace Intelligence Officer, or maybe he was interested to find out about treatments he never had access to.

'What about you, PJ?' I said. 'You ever get the flashbacks? Ever pray you could go back in time and change just one thing?'

'I never killed anybody,' PJ said, 'my hands are clean that way, so they are.'

He was backing off now, but I kept pushing.

'You were the top Intelligence Officer. The calls you made decided who lived, who died.'

He pushed his face forward to glare at the bus turning too slowly for him.

'Most guys I know that brought a problem home from Iraq with them can trace it straight back to somebody like you,' I leaned closer to cramp his space. 'Yeah, most guys can deal with the enemy contact, mano a mano is no problem. It's when they get pumped with bad Intell or some officer prick pushes too hard and some non-com gets hurt, like a kid or an old woman or some other innocent bystander, that's when the regular human inside the uniform rebels. That ever happen to you, PJ, like did you ever make the bad call and some innocent civilian got whacked? Guys like you and Hamilton weren't so different, fingering people you thought you knew about but the Intell got mixed up on the street, or you just plain got it wrong?'

The vein above his temple popped and pulsed like an eel trapped under his skin and I thought he was about to blow but then he turned his face away from me, only I don't think he noticed me catching his sly smile. Either way, he cut the probing and started to give me the low down on Hamilton.

I needed a photograph, more detail about Hamilton's routine, who he was in contact with and where I could find him. PJ shook his head, didn't have any material like that anymore, all his records were dumped years ago and that sort of stuff becomes obsolete very quickly anyway. He didn't even have much on Hamilton back then in the day when he was a Military Liaison Officer. They knew a little, from whispers and gossip they harvested, say, from big mouthed cops when they thought they were safe amongst their own, in a bar or rugby club or somewhere like that. Other frames of the big picture, usually better quality, they picked up in police interrogation rooms. Some interrogators were better than others but they mostly all used the same tactic of trying to extract info from the prisoner by conning the guy that the police already knew all the details and that the prisoner's only hope of saving themselves was to come clean. Sometimes the cop might let a casual word slip, maybe trivial and insignificant in that context, but later on that slip would find its way back to PJ or somebody like him. All those random fragments, of careless words, of who was where and who knew what, all of it would be stripped down and analysed, then put back together, first this way, then that way, then as many ways as necessary until something clicked and PJ could magic the casual word into a silver bullet.

'I always had the feeling that Hamilton was right there in front of me,' PJ said, 'but I could just never nail him. I never gave up, knew I would expose him in the end if I just had time. Then it was all over. The Ceasefire was declared in '94 but I kept working on my files, just in case. In the end, they told me it *was* the end, move on, and that was it. Now I count Brigid's money and take abuse from the tenants like that cheeky wee student bastard the other day, him and his mates had a house party and somebody shoved a towel down the toilet, now he's on to me slabbering about flood repairs.'

I recognized this melancholy oozing out of PJ. Part of him still lived on the nostalgia of his glory days, the adrenaline, the fear, the sense of belonging to something big, of doing something big, of being part of history. Another part of him was still paying the debt, a toxic cocktail of guilt and hurt, grief and loss, and the demon that haunted all our dreams, that poisonous voice in your own head screaming that it was all a waste of their time and your life.

'Anyway,' he said, 'it was only later on that I finally worked out who Hamilton was, and the info came from your part of the world, from Washington, to be exact.'

PJ smiled at the memory. Some retired Brit, a Colonel or General, was gifted a place as a director on some big-time bank or insurance company. It was the sort of big deal finance gig that gets you invited to those corporate fundraisers, paying maybe ten grand to get in the door. PJ figured this was about fifteen years ago, and the General rolled up to this fundraiser in Washington. This guy had a taste for fine brandy, especially when he wasn't paying, and after a few his tongue was looser than his wallet. He started to regale the other guests with tales of his adventures, and this guy had been all over, like Iraq the first time around, Bosnia, Kosovo, the Malvinas. A lot of the company had seen service themselves, and he felt at home and free to boast and exaggerate. He started to spoof about here, about how they taught the Paddies a lesson. It never occurred to him that Presidents of big American corporations could be cousins of the people he was laughing at.

'We had Hamilton's name the next day,' PJ said, 'and enough details to fill in a lot of those blanks in my records - setting up ambushes with Swansea's trigger men, feeding information to Loyalist Paramilitaries, arranging arms supplies to their proxy death squads.'

Other pieces started to come together. Like, where a violent death is involved, a Coroner's Inquest is held and the Coroner, a sort of Judge, hears all the evidence about how the person was killed. For most of those guys ambushed by Swansea and Hamilton there have never been Inquests because the Brits say there are still sensitive security issues involved that can't be aired in open court. Some of those deaths go back 25 or 30 years or more and the Inquests haven't been completed yet. Sometimes, though, police or army personnel do give evidence in secret, like say this is Soldier 'A', and that is Police Officer 'B'. PJ had been stood down a long time but he kept his interest in those Inquests that did get started. He soon mapped a pattern, and there was always evidence concerning a mysterious Brit officer who was involved in organizing these operations. PJ worked out Hamilton was involved in most of the high profile shootings.

'Then there was the drugs,' he said. '2005, he was stopped in a convoy at the Turkish border with Syria, a truck full of heroin from Afghanistan on its way to the west. He was looking at 30 years behind bars but somehow he walked away. A different American friend of ours told me it was a US operation, buying the loyalty of Afghan warlords by taking their drugs off them at above market value.'

'Sounds like you have good sources in the US, PJ.'

He pushed the car radio, Blondie was still waiting on the telephone, PJ croaked the chorus, hammered the rhythm on the wheel.

'Last I heard of him he turned up in Libya, about 2012 or 13,' he said. 'Same old trick, divide and rule. Paying a bounty to one set of militia to fight another set. Sounds familiar, eh?'

'You heard that from your American friends, right?'

'Some of it,' he smiled, 'but we used to have friends in Libya too, in the old days. Spent a bit of time there myself, so I did, many moons ago.'

'You were in Libya with Gadaffi?'

'Well, not him personally, fuck's sake!' PJ said. 'In fact, I spent most of my time with some excellent Cuban instructors, so I did.'

He left that hanging in the air like I was supposed to be impressed or pump him for more.

'These good American friends of yours,' I said, 'they ever have anything to say about me?'

PJ laughed and drummed the wheel.

'I'll drop you here,' he said, 'that's Stranmillis Road there. See how narrow it is? There's an old graveyard behind that wall. They can't widen the road because there's a mass grave from the Great Hunger time on the other side, a big outbreak of typhoid. They're afraid if they disturb the bodies the old poison will be released. You can't be too careful with that sort of thing, sure you can't? Never know what harm you might do by fucking about with things you don't understand, know what I mean?'

'Your American friends told you that about me?' I said.

PJ laughed. 'I'll arrange a meeting with Wee Joe. How do we contact you if you have no phone?'

'I'll be in touch,' I said, 'I know where you are.'

I could see PJ still eyeballing me in the rear view mirror as he coasted off. I knew he was a smart guy, and he probably thought he was smart enough to work me out, taking the background stuff he had been told and marrying it to his first hand impression to create his idea of who or what I was. He wasn't the first to take a crack at that one, and he was nowhere near the smartest. And someday I might even open up about the guilt thing but it wouldn't be to PJ or anybody like him but in the meantime it was just enough for me to function as I always had, with a big black hole in my memory and the hazy promise that there would be a next time, and that this next time would be my chance to make things right, to wipe that slate clean.

I was at the end of the typhoid wall when I saw them, the blue lights pulsing their orbit around the roof tops. I kept walking just like a regular citizen. Two police Land Rovers blocked Sandymount Street, and a dozen cops were fanning out along Stranmillis Road, redirecting traffic, evacuating shops and offices. I stepped into a fast food joint and watched from the doorway. Some workers from the shop up the street came out for a look and then drifted back inside as the cops tried to corral them away. Customers in the food outlets strung along Stranmillis ignored the cop commands until they got served their meals and then walked off slowly, looking over their shoulders to see if anything would happen before their food got cold. A woman stuck her head into this doorway and shouted something in Chinese to the guy behind the counter. He muttered to himself after she raced off to spread the word, and told me the police had found a suspicious device in Sandymount Street. I asked him if that sort of thing still happened around here much.

'No, never around this area, never' he said, 'sometimes there might be a small bomb under someone's car in other places maybe but never here. What is there in Sandymount Street? Only students! Why would there be a bomb there?'

The two Land Rovers blocking Sandymount parted ways to create space for the two large saloon cars with blacked-out windows to turn into the street. The first saloon passed by, the second stopped. A tall man in a formal business suit, middle-aged with close cropped silver hair, stepped from a rear passenger door. The senior uniformed cop, also middle-aged but thicker in the middle, lurched forward to greet him. A double-handed shake, no salutes or formal protocol, these two were old friends or comrades but weren't in regular work contact. Smiles and laughter, then the silver fox slapped the uniform on the shoulder and hopped back into the saloon, carrying on the banter through the opened window as the car disappeared into Sandymount Street. The two Land Rovers bumped back off the kerb to block the street.

I left the doorway and turned right, heading back to the city centre. Half way down Stranmillis the key to 18 Sandymount Street arced high over the wall. I pictured it nesting there on PJ's poisonous typhoid pit where nobody would ever disturb it.

CHAPTER SIX

Yakov wasn't in the Merchant. He had hired the hotel's Roller, chauffeur and all, to take in the sights along the coast. I told the receptionist Mr Yakovich had a business appointment with me, and that I would wait in a nearby bar. This guy was too attentive for comfort, like he would recall every detail about me if anyone happened to ask. Okay, some risks I would have to suck up but other alarm bells couldn't be ignored, like the London black taxi idling at the corner of the cobblestone street.

It was the same black cab that had dropped me here the first time, the same number on the yellow plate and the same '*Titanic Belfast*' sticker on the rear window. I passed slowly, casually glancing around, the driver had his nose stuck against a tablet like he should be wearing reading glasses. I took it easy, turned as if I had forgotten something in the hotel, stole a better look, could see it wasn't the driver from the first time but, unless my imagination was in freefall, it *was* the squat little swagger guy that I had run into at random when I needed directions after I got off the coach from Dublin. Even in a small town like this, some coincidences aren't a coincidence. I turned right into the cobblestone street and jogged along to a doorway. The taxi edged forward, the driver looked down the street. I walked on, turned left down an alleyway and entered the bar.

The space between the doorway and the empty seating area was filled with the chat and laughter of a troop of about ten or twelve cheery drinkers; three eager young attorneys or accountants in sharp suits fringing a couple of sister queen bees heavy with glamor and promise, some weather scoured men in spattered work shirts, a couple of student types and an old guy, always an old guy in these places. A big round workman acknowledged my presence with a nod and stepped aside, inviting me to pass. The rest shuffled closer to create a path for me and quietened down so the barman could hear my call for a beer then kicked back into their fun as I took a seat.

The crowd simmered down again and I saw another figure enter and slip up to the bar, a wiry guy, medium height, nothing extraordinary, younger at second look, and with that unmistakable defiant poise that said this was a street guy, a hustler, a pimp, a petty crook – or an undercover cop. He kept his head down, working his cellphone, oblivious to the company. I kept watching him not watching me long enough to dispel any doubt.

I was starting to enjoy my beer too much by the time Yakov appeared. The men shifted nervously, sipping their beers, avoiding eye contact with him and each other. Yakov planted his feet wide apart and made a big deal about rubbing some heat into his hands. The confident women eyed him up, scented his cold risk reward musk and exchanged their secret code with a wrinkled brow. The wiry guy didn't move, but I saw Yakov register him before he turned and strutted over to me.

'I don't think it is such a good idea you coming to my hotel,' he clapped me on the shoulder, 'I don't need the sort of attention you bring, understand?'

Sure, he knew I was being watched.

'So, any problem my friend?' he said.

I shrugged, no problems, at least not any that he didn't already know about.

'I've got a good lead on Hamilton,' I said. 'He leaves that MI5 compound to indulge his private passions. That's when he is vulnerable. That's when we put the drop on him.'

Yakov beamed and rubbed his red hands some more.

'I like it!' he said. 'I like it when these champions of your western moral superiority drop the pants! We had a wise old instructor when I was young, a Hero of the Soviet Union, he used to tell us this thing, "*Drop the pants, drop the guard!*" That's good, huh? Drop the pants, drop the guard!' Yakov rocked back in his chair to laugh but I could see he was sneaking a look at the wiry man.

'So no problems your side?' I said.

'What problem?' He spread his hands wide. 'You bring Hamilton to me, problem over!'

'That's the bit I need to know about, right there,' I said, 'between the "*I bring him to you*" and the "*Problem over*". Considering you are going to waste this guy, how do I get my money? How do we clear Artie's friend Beikle in Rome?'

'Beikle? The priest?' Yakov shrugged. 'What do you care about a priest, Maknazpy?'

'I gave my word I would help him,' I said. 'You understand that, don't you, Yakov? Giving your word about something?'

He sniggered into his massive red paw.

'He is a priest,' he said, 'he should like being locked up, plenty of time to say his prayers to the big make-believe God in the sky.'

'I gave my word,' I said.

Yakov peered into my face, like he was expecting me to be joking. 'Okay, okay, we will see what we can do, don't worry about your priest.'

No, I wasn't joking. Whatever way this turned out, I guessed I would need somebody or something to take the heat off me if things got dirty. A couple of Monsignors, maybe the Pope in Rome, could cover a lot of dirty ass if they needed to.

'And how exactly do I get my share of the cash?' I said.

'Yes! Now that is important!' He dropped a hammer fist above my knee that hurt like a kick from a mule, though I swear his hand moved less than 6 inches. 'How you get paid, that is what you need to think about, Maknazpy! Forget all the other shit!'

Yakov squinted close up into my face searching for my pain but I didn't flinch.

'Hamilton has the encryption package for the money exchange that was in Vienna. He gives us the package, it is like having keys to a bank. Simple.'

'He *gives* it?' I said. 'Simple as that?'

'He gives, we take. What matters?' Yakov dismissed my question with a sweep of his palm across his jaw. 'Look, Maknazpy, I can tell you how it works but what for? With respect, it is too complicated for a man like you to understand.'

Yakov managed to say it so his deep disrespect slapped my face.

'Try me,' I said. 'Maybe I'm not as dumb as you think.'

Yakov sighed and pulled a twisted grin like he was an exasperated parent dredging up the last crumbs of indulgent patience for a lost cause child.

'This business is done over the Web, yes? It has to be secure so it is encrypted, yes?' He mouthed the words and his hot breath slowly into my face. 'Two types of encryption key, public and private. The message is sent from A to B using the public encryption but still only A and B can read it, yes? But A also has his own private encryption key, and B must receive this also so that he confirms the message is really from A.'

'Okay, so Hamilton is A,' I said. 'What about B? He's still in Vienna? Why don't your people just pay *him* a visit? What's the big deal about Hamilton?'

'Because Hamilton has locked the door with his code! He has fixed it so the B code is useless without his A code. And the people working the B code isn't one person,' Yakov gritted his teeth. 'This B is a band of disgraced Swiss and Austrian bankers, merely banking apparatchiks, happy to operate outside the rules, they do what they are told. Either way, these bankers with dirty hands will be useful to us in future so they are permitted to continue.'

He meant they were permitted to continue living.

'So where is Artie's missing $30 million?' I said. 'Back in Vienna?'

Yakov did his couldn't-care-less shrug.

'Who knows? It could be in the Vatican Bank, it could be anywhere. But this is no problem, trust me. You will be well rewarded. There is plenty more where that came from. Just bring me Hamilton and I will take care of the rest, no problem.'

'So what does this encryption key look like? I said. 'Is it like a password or something?'

'Fuck!' Yakov's patience was blown. 'It is a piece of software! He will keep it close, so just get him and we get the key.'

'And how do I get my share?'

Yakov tried the hammer to my thigh again but I snatched his wrist and pinned it to the table.

'After you bring me Hamilton and we conclude our business with him, I will personally transfer $5 million to any account you want, anywhere in the world,' he said. 'You can stand beside me and watch me do it, if you don't trust me.'

'That's before you whack him, right?'

'What does that matter to you?' he said. 'You get your money, we work something out for your priest, what more do you want?'

'And Michael Leeks won't think it's a problem?' I said.

Yakov blinked like I was speaking backwards.

'Your colleagues,' I said. 'As long as they don't think I'll be a problem and decide to take the risk free route.'

'Don't worry about them,' he said. 'I take care of them. I take care of you. No problem.'

'That's what I like about you, Yakov. You're such a Good News guy, so full of positive energy and goodwill to all men.'

'Of course, goodwill to all men. All men except your Hamilton.' He caught me with a hammer fist again. 'Hamilton I will crush. All his bosses will know. That will be good news.'

CHAPTER SEVEN

It was after 6 p.m. when I got back to the Cultúrlann. The homeward traffic pumped tired workers through the cold and dark, on their nightly parole from daily grind back to the bright warmth of family and freedom. Yasmin might be on Leblon beach right now, keeping cool and maybe wondering where I was and if I was coming back. Rose would be fixing lunch for Gallogly and young Con, a million things on her mind. I would contact both of them soon, when the time was right, when I had the words fixed in my head, when things were better, not right now but sometime soon.

The lady in the Cultúrlann directed me to Brigid's office, it was on the road, she said, just keep going and I couldn't miss it. After a couple of minutes I guessed I had missed it. It started to rain, that angry vindictive rain they have here that they accept as a penance. I stopped to look around. A plaque above a doorway said '*Alameda Terrace*'. The tripwire in my brain snapped me back to that house on the clifftop in Portugal, '*Almeida Terrace*', and the line between real and unreal started to melt in the rain. The only thing I could believe was before my eyes; steam rising from the shapeless carcass on the ground, the old man's fish dead eyes, the little girl's severed hand picked from the sewer. The demon had one hand on my throat, choking me, the ghosts screamed revenge inside my skull. My knees were weak and my head spinning, I grabbed a lamp-post to steady myself.

'You alright there, mate?' the voice appeared from the dark. I turned toward him, almost stumbled into his arms, he caught me and eased me into the car. The voice was Tomás, and the driver was PJ.

Brigid's voice was harsh in the bare room. She cut her conversation and slipped the cellphone into her pocket as PJ opened the door to usher me in.

'Your eyes look weird, Con,' Brigid said, 'are you okay?'

The small room was crowded with the three of us standing there, and the naked bulb doused her features with a stark light.

'You heard I was trying to find you?' I said.

Brigid and PJ exchanged shrugs and mystified looks.

'No, I didn't hear nothing,' PJ said. 'Me and Tomás were just driving down the road and we saw you standing there.'

Maybe it was another coincidence, good fortune that they should come along to deliver me into this labyrinth of no-escape streets.

'Why?' Brigid said. 'Has something happened?'

'No, no, nothing at all,' I said. 'That's the point, though, nothing is happening. Artie told me preparations would be made before I got here. He said he had all the right connections and I would have plenty back up.'

'Look, I don't know what Monsignor McCooey told you!' Brigid screamed at me like I was one of her house decorators that had screwed up. 'If I had a magic wand I would wave it for you. I said we would do our best but if that's not good enough then you can just fuck off back to America, alright?!'

PJ stayed very still and silent behind me. Tomás was out on the street, his back against the small window, blowing smoke into the cold black air.

'Take it easy, Brigid, take it easy,' I said. 'I'm grateful for your help and I'm not putting you down here.'

Brigid twisted the silver buttons of her coat, looked like she was about to throw me out into the street. I sensed PJ was gesturing behind my back, telling her to cool it, hear what I had to say.

'I just think Artie McCooey owes it to all of us to step up here,' I said. 'He's the reason we are doing this thing, and he does his usual trick, gets people to do his dirty work and sits back to keep his own hands clean.'

Brigid glanced at PJ and worked hard to control her breathing, calming herself, slowing it down.

'I know Artie too well,' I said, 'there's no way he isn't somewhere close at hand, keeping an eye on what's happening. I think he's here in Belfast somewhere, and I think you know where that is.'

Brigid laughed in my face, 'I don't fucking know where the bastard is!'

PJ did his usual shoulder shrug. I stepped around PJ into the street, gripped Tomás' wrist before snatching the cellphone from his hand and dragging him into the room. I twisted Tomás' elbow up his back with one hand and tapped the last dialled number on his phone. Brigid pulled out her own cellphone and started to make a call, PJ quietly shuffled around to the door. I swept Tomás' ankles and he crumpled to the floor with my knee pinning his head against the wall.

'Fucking get off!!' he shouted. I bumped his head off the wall, just a little, and nodded PJ to stay put.

The voice said 'Yes?'

'Yes yourself, McCooey, you dirty bastard!' I said, before the phone went dead.

'Where is he, PJ? You know I'll find him anyway, so unless you want to see Tomás' head cracked open you'll save me the trouble of looking.'

PJ and Brigid thought about it, Tomás cursed and screamed.

'I know there's a big house up the Antrim Road,' Brigid said. 'Some sort of residential accommodation for visiting clergy, maybe he is up there.'

'Maybe he is,' I said. 'Like, there are so many coincidences in this city that I guess there's a very good chance that maybe he is.'

PJ cruised through the thin streets as if he was my tour guide giving me a running commentary on the notable sights. 'And that's Cumann Chluain Árd, very famous Irish language institution, getting some building work done.'

Brigid simmered beside me in the back, Tomás muttered to himself in front.

'That's the Royal, surgeons in there developed the expertise in gunshot wounds that later became useful to your medics in Iraq,' PJ said, then added, 'and everywhere else you invaded.'

I rested my hands on the back of Tomás' seat, close enough to his neck to keep him tame.

'That's the famous International Mural Wall, tourists come from all over the world to see it, pity it's dark now.'

Brigid stared out her window but I could feel the rage trembling through her body.

Traffic lights stopped us at a wide no-man's land intersection.

'This is Millfield, what's left of it. This is where Brigid's perfume got its name from, *Midnight in Millfield,* isn't that right, Brigid, love?'

Brigid kicked the back of his seat, Tomás laughed and PJ pulled his '*What'd I do*?' face. He eyed me up in his rear view mirror, must have thought his blarney gimmick had cooled the anger in the car, and we edged through the traffic in silence. Before long we were in a different part of town and PJ turned off the main road into a deluxe residential area, fine double-fronted houses reserved behind high hedges and mature gardens.

'Down here somewhere, I think,' PJ said. 'That there's the Bishop's place, I think our one is on down here, so it is.'

PJ knew exactly which house it was, I let him pretend to be unsure. We stopped outside high black gates, with only the roof of the house visible. I made to get out but the door was locked. 'Child lock,' PJ chuckled, and Tomás didn't hide his irritation at having to get out to open my door from the outside. Brigid was still insisting I didn't exist, and stared out the opposite window.

'Thanks for the ride,' I said. 'Pick me up here tomorrow morning at 10 a.m. and we'll go see your Wee Joe, okay?'

They took off without a word, except for the '*Dickhead!*' that Tomás shouted back at me.

The security gate was a heavy piece of hardware, for sure, but the hedging and shrubs that would thicken into a robust boundary in the summer were still in their winter clothes, and I squeezed through a gap easily. The house was a sturdy red-brick with four very large bay windows. A river of gravel driveway, about 75 yards, flowed through a carefully landscaped garden of lawn and ornamental trees before opening its sandy mouth to form a parking area for three high end cars, two Bimmers and a Merc coupé. The house itself was in darkness at the front, except for a dim light in the arched entrance porch.

I jogged up to the porch, then followed the path around the side. There were more extensive gardens rolling into the darkness at the back, and a light shining from a side room. I kept low, the side room was a small kitchen with a wooden-framed glass door.

They couldn't see me out here in the dark, but four elderly priests were cramped around a narrow kitchen table, playing cards and smoking their lungs out.

I tried the door handle, it opened and I stepped into the smoke zone. The priests were locked into their cardplay and only one, yellow-skinned and with a head of oiled black hair, much too black for his age, raised his head to inspect me through the spectacles hanging off the end of his nose.

'Monsignor McCooey is expecting me,' I said.

They all turned to check me out, and yellow-skin nodded, 'Top of the stairs.' I started to move but he stopped me with a raised hand and a gruff bark. 'Hey boy! Shut that bloody door behind you! Some of us around here have to pay the heating bill you know!' I did as I was told and moved quietly past them, out into an empty dining area. 'Big Dick McCooey at his work again!' Yellow face made sure I heard him and the rest didn't care if I heard the malicious laughter that ruptured into a chorus of hacking coughs behind me.

The dining area led to a hallway and grand stairs with an ornately carved mahogany handrail guided me upwards into the darkness, then a corridor and another stairway, narrow this time, and light from an open bedroom door at the top. The low voices in the room stopped as I reached the top yet I could sense their delicate anticipation, like a mob of friends were in there ready to spring a surprise birthday party.

I pushed the door further open, saw the low table at the end of the bed. There was a luggage bag on the table. Even in this gloomy light I knew it was my luggage bag. I stepped into the room, two old-fashioned armchairs on either side of the empty fireplace, two men drinking brandy, Artie McCooey and the Silver Fox policeman from Sandymount Street.

'Like a bad penny, you always show up!' Artie struggled out of the armchair and stumbled toward me with his hand outstretched.

I recalled the temptation to tip him over that balcony back in Rio. He pumped my hand like I was bringing him life support and he dragged me toward the Fox.

'I'm glad you are here, Con, it's time you met my dear friend, Superintendent Colin McIntyre, Police Service of Northern Ireland, and one of the good guys.'

McIntyre was a big guy, well over six feet tall and easily 250 pounds. He had that look like a starved monk, with no flesh padding his face, only the tanned skin stretched tight across the sharp cheekbones and eye sockets. The green eyes were more cunning than smiling, and the crushing handshake wasn't enough to buy my trust.

'Nice to meet you at last, Mr Maknazpy,' McIntyre said, 'Monsignor McCooey has very kindly explained your mission. It's a sensitive situation, no doubt, but I'm sure we can work together for the greater good.'

Artie rattled another brandy glass out of a cupboard and dragged a low stool out from behind the bed. He poured too much into my glass before topping up his own.

'So, what are your plans for Hamilton?' Artie said. 'Have you made contact yet?'

I looked at McIntyre and sipped my brandy.

'Hamilton? Never heard of him,' I said.

McIntyre laughed and swirled the brandy under his nose.

'Oh come on now, Con!' Artie sounded in pain. 'You're amongst friends here, no need for that sullen attitude of yours!'

If the 250 pound McIntyre hadn't been there I would have smashed Artie's teeth down his throat. And if he didn't wipe that stupid look off his face I might do it anyway.

'My name is McAnespie. I'm in town to search for my Irish roots. I'm going back to the United States this week. I've never heard of anybody called Hamilton and I'm not on any sort of a mission, for the greater good or otherwise.'

'Don't try to act the smart arse, Con, it doesn't become you. If it wasn't for Colin you would be lying in the morgue right now. That's if they had been able to scrape you back together.'

'Suspect device in Sandymount Street, right? Funny thing about that,' I said, 'I just heard on the car radio the suspicious device wasn't so suspicious after all, allegedly just some trash a student had dumped in the street. Very convenient to raise a scare like that and evacuate the street if you want to break into somebody's house, isn't it?'

'My guys risked their lives disarming half a kilo of Semtex,' McIntyre said. 'You were a dead man if you had opened that door.'

'Oh really? Semtex? Wasn't that the IRA's explosive of choice, and didn't I hear it was all decommissioned years ago?'

'Come on, Con!' Artie groaned. 'You're making a tit of yourself and embarrassing me! Colin disarmed that bomb himself! He didn't call the army disposal men in, he did it himself so he could keep a lid on it, and he put the news people off the scent as well!'

McIntyre didn't get excited, just sat there sipping his brandy and looking cool, like we were exchanging opinions on the weather or sport or how bad the traffic was. He didn't fool me, though. Those fox green eyes were sizing me up like I was a chicken who hadn't yet heard of slaughter.

'Police officers here are trained in bomb disposal?' I said.

'Not really much need for it here anymore, I'm very pleased to tell you,' McIntyre said. 'Mind you, I was seconded to Baghdad some years ago, training the Iraqi police. I learned more than I taught, if truth be told. In fact, I would nearly think whoever rigged that welcome present for you had attended the same training course on anti-personnel devices as I did myself. That couldn't be possible, of course.'

'Somebody like Hamilton, you mean?' I said.

'That would be the Hamilton you have never heard of? No, surely he wouldn't be involved in that sort of reckless illegality, surely not.'

'Your people have been tailing me around this town since I got here, right?'

McIntyre clicked into another zone.

'No, not really enough manpower at my disposal for that,' he said. 'I posted a couple of boys to keep an eye on Sandymount Street, that's all. You are being followed?'

My gut said he was for real but I had already said too much.

'Nah, just a little jumpy, I guess,' I lied. 'You know what it's like when the pressure starts to get to you.'

McIntyre's instinct took over, honed by all the grim years of making thumbs up or down calls for hustlers and liars, deciding the future of cold eyed killers and power hungry empire builders. I knew he had my number but I slurped the brandy like I didn't give a fuck. McIntyre didn't buy it.

'I can offer you protection only so far as I know that what you are doing isn't unlawful,' he said. 'I understand from Monsignor McCooey you intend to expose serious financial crimes that have some relevance to this jurisdiction. I am keen to assist but a certain degree of trust is a precondition, and an absolute acceptance of the primacy of the law of this land.'

He sipped his brandy and left his homily hanging like I was supposed to hop on the soapbox and pledge my honor to his greater good.

'Sure, trust is fine,' I said. 'Isn't that so, Artie?' Artie managed to keep his head held high and squirm an encouraging nod. 'Only problem is, from my experience I've found the people that preach most about trust and the greater good and being lawful and all that shit are the ones who scrabble up to the high moral ground and then pull the ladder up after them. I usually find myself left to fight it out down below in all the crap somebody else has dropped on me. Isn't that so, Artie?'

Artie avoided McIntyre's eyes but glared at me. 'Mouth open and ears closed, that's your problem,' he scolded. 'If you listened to what I told you in the first place you wouldn't get yourself into trouble. I said Colin is one of the good guys, didn't I? If you were capable of even rudimentary abductive reasoning you would have grasped I was warning you that there aren't only good guys involved.'

The image of how Artie's teeth would crack under my fist made me grin.

'There is the Dark Side, as Colin calls it,' Artie looked serious, 'men and women devoid of Colin's integrity and moral principle.'

The Saint Colin of the Holy Bullshit sat there with a smug look on his tight skinned face, waiting for his prompt. I tossed back the brandy and dropped the glass to the floor. Artie fidgeted in his armchair and gestured for him to continue their tag team routine.

'The Dark Side,' McIntyre tried for gravity but sounded like a voiceover in a darkened cinema. 'It pains me greatly but my duty and conscience won't allow me to deny their existence. Don't get me wrong, I am proud of the men and women of the Police Service. But I stand in front of new recruits every year, young men and young women, and I solemnly pledge to make Northern Ireland a safer place for all our people, Protestant, Roman Catholic and Dissenter, from every community and ethnic background. I can safely say the vast, vast majority of our officers are 100% committed to that ideal. All are equal before the law, and our young officers are making this wee country of ours safe, confident and peaceful.'

McIntyre paused to make sure I was seduced by his vision of noble sacrifice and service but I had heard such stirring rhetoric too many times, and had bagged the charred remains of too many sacrificial lambs.

'There are, unfortunately, a very small number of the old guard who can't let go of the past,' he said, 'They see progression as surrender, reform as betrayal. We call them the Dark Side because they are a cabal of few numbers but they're untouchable, at least as far as conventional policing and justice is concerned. Your friend Paddy Hamilton is bullet-proof and he knows it.'

That time PJ asked how I coped with guilt I didn't tell him my defense was to blame someone else. And it was true, there was always somebody or something creating the situations I had found myself in, dotting me in as an afterthought squiggle in their big picture painting. What I didn't much talk about, though, was that other truth, that I had made a choice each time before their games started. It was like that couple of seconds you have before surrendering yourself to a crazy water slide, stepping in there knowing you can't go back and tossing and spinning out of control to the bottom.

'Say I *was* interested in Hamilton,' I said, 'what back-up can you deliver?'

'I can't task my officers overtly,' McIntyre said, 'but I can pass on certain surveillance – like activity around that house I know you have an interest in.'

McIntyre carried his charisma easily, and it was hard to tell if it came with his position or if guys like him naturally rose to the top. His eyes and voice said he was with me on that last step of the crazy ride, with Artie complicit at our backs, urging us on, the two of them and the brandy crafting this blood brother bond to make my choice this time so easy that there was no choice. And it wasn't only the brandy fumed camaraderie they promised, but an invite into that inner sanctum where worthy men are protected by their own and by the prism that shaped all consequence and collateral to match their good intentions. Their only problem was that I had been on this ride before also, and I knew that for their caste, when the water cut up too rough, there would be an escape hatch leading to the calm forgiving shallows while I would be propelled into white water rapids with no lifeline.

'I need some guarantees here, Colin,' I said, 'if things turn sour I won't be an easy fall guy, you know, I'll make life pretty tough for all of you.'

'I'll do what I can within the law,' he said, 'but isn't your best guarantee the fact that I am sitting here now discussing this with you? No offense intended, but meeting you like this puts me in a compromising position too.'

'You're compromised by meeting me? What about Artie? With all his old IRA friends and all?'

Artie's red face turned gray, McIntyre grinned.

'Ah now, Monsignor McCooey and I have an excellent working relationship,' he smiled. 'We are both working for the possibilities of the future. That's what we call progress around here and, after all, what choice do we have, boys? What choice do we really have?'

CHAPTER EIGHT

Artie's black shape twitched and grunted in the miserable morning gloom. He hadn't exactly been a generous host last night, wasn't really into that Good Samaritan thing, no, the selfish prick had tried to throw me out into the street and only quit his red-eyed bluster when I heaved my naked hairy butt into the bed, leaving him to huff and shuffle in the armchair until the brandy tugged him into a doped silence. The bed had been a luxury after the icebox in Sandymount Street, even if the yellow brown stains on the sheets pushed me to the edge of the soft mattress, but Artie's discomfort alone was satisfaction enough.

I didn't sleep too good, though, the old chronic visions had been viciously relentless, canting my doomed penance that was never geared to purge the guilt.

The clammy bedsheets had been glued to me when I jolted awake in my sweaty panic and I knew I wouldn't, daren't, sleep again that night, so dressed and sat quietly on the bed until now when I heard movement down below. Artie's head was tilted unnaturally over the edge of the armchair and, just for a second, I feared that I might have snapped his neck during the night. No, he was alive, his throat rasping through the caustic fallout from cigar and brandy. His delicate priest jacket lay at his feet, and keys and loose change jangled as I patted the pockets. I felt the weight on the inside pocket, behind the *'Gammarelli Roma'* label, and slipped his iPhone out before draping the jacket over his knees.

The stairway was cold and dark, the iPhone led me down the threadbare carpet, and then further down to the spot where the chilly dampness creeped me out as if a priest ghost was spitting his malediction in my ear. There was a presence there, not one of the spirits I carried as my burden, but something ingrained in that dank space, something evil and hostile – maybe my own black heart raised its hackles - and I quickly skipped down the last few steps before twisting back to see nothing in the darkness. A light was on in the kitchen and my nerves pushed me through the door with more force than I had intended.

My entrance startled me more than the four card players, still dealing their tricks and trumps around the small mountain of cigarette butts that had sprouted overnight. The kitchen door was wide open but the envelope of stale smoke hung in the air like it was suspended in an invisible cage.

'Are you ready for your breakfast now, love?' It was a little gray haired lady, with kindly eyes and a soft smile.

'Thank you, ma'am,' I said, 'if it is no trouble for you.'

'Aye, no trouble, no trouble at all!' the yellow faced priest scoffed into his cards. 'Who's bucking paying for it, that's what I'd like to know! Who's paying? His Lordship Prince of the Church up the stairs?'

The little lady ruffled my hair as I passed into the frosty garden. 'Don't listen to him, son, that one says more than his prayers.' Yellow face raised his voice, making sure I heard him, 'Wait and I'll take a run up the Antrim Road and see if there are any more waifs and strays looking for their free breakfast! Maybe I'll find a crowd of starving Tinkers, or maybe some hungry Protestants, how about that?'

His rant trailed off behind me as I hunkered down against a tree in the corner of the long garden to google the Merchant's number. Almost 8 a.m., Yakov was sure to be awake. The receptionist answered almost immediately but she stalled when I asked for Yakov, came back to lie he wasn't available and offered to pass on my message. I didn't have time for this bullshit, told her I was Yakov's nephew, Pyotr, and I needed to speak to him urgently about an illness in the family.

'Pyotr! You better have good reason for disturbing my business schedule!' This was Yakov's real voice, full-on menace and threat. 'Have you heard from my cousin yet? When will he come?'

'Very soon,' I said. 'Have you made arrangements for his treatment? You will need to have nurses ready when I call again, maybe this week, I think.'

'Don't worry, the treatment is ready, this will be no problem. But don't call me again until my cousin is with you, yes? I am a busy man. I am here on business, understand?'

I understood, and so would the surveillance techs but the transcript had enough ambiguity to suit Yakov and a call from Artie's phone wouldn't be my problem. One of the poker priests came out to stretch and yawn but wasn't close enough to hear me. I scrolled through Artie's log, two calls received from 'T' yesterday evening, hit the number, four rings before Tomás answered.

'Yes?' Then something in Irish, a question, only a couple of words, maybe a 'How are you' greeting.

'Hi, Dickhead here,' I said. 'How's your head? I'm ready for that taxi, say 45 minutes, okay?'

Tomás grunted and cut the phone.

Wee Joe didn't speak much. He kept his mouth shut and his eyes on the road like this was a regular taxi job, with Tomás in front and PJ back here with me. We trundled along quietly in the morning traffic until we met a funeral procession coming down the road toward us. PJ told Wee Joe to pull in and wait for the funeral to pass. The empty hearse inched along, "*Grandad*" honored in a floral tribute, six young men shouldered the coffin, and a cluster of middle-aged men shuffled through the rain, with faces strained from crying or the strain of not crying.

'God rest his soul,' PJ said.

'You know him?' I asked.

'Don't know his name, no,' PJ said, 'but he was one of our own, wasn't he? Our own kind, a human being. His passing deserves an acknowledgement, doesn't it?'

I couldn't believe the balls on this guy, like he was making out he was somehow my moral superior, like life was cheap in my world and he was a saint?

'Yeah, whatever,' I said, 'how long before we get to this place?'

PJ shook his head and turned away, pretending to say a short prayer for the dead man.

'You know tears are different depending what causes them?' Tomás said. 'I seen a thing, they looked at the structures under a microscope, different tears for different emotions - grief, joy, guilt, onions. They're all different.'

'Where'd you see that?' Wee Joe said.

'Facebook,' Tomás said.

Wee Joe thought about it and nodded. His wispy thin hair was tangled into a kind of ponytail and the outsized navigator style spectacles rooted him back in the 80's. Wee Joe was coming alive now. 'This is Wolfhill,' he told me, 'where the last wolf in Ireland was killed. One of the last places!'

Tomás laughed with him, PJ scrolled through his iPhone, and I sat apart in my bubble with the echo of Yakov's menace in my head. We were on a narrow country road now, Belfast was behind, on the other side of the wolf mountain. The flat country rolled out far below and into the distance, and the horizon was framed by the miraged silver of the great lake that looks like the heart of the northern lands.

'Brigid said this place was in Lisburn,' I said. 'That's south-west of Belfast according to any map I've seen. How come we are headed north-west?'

'*Near* Lisburn, she told you, *near* Lisburn,' PJ said. 'Her geography is crap anyway, it's closer to Aldergrove, close to the airport.'

'The International Airport?'

'Yeah, close to the International Airport,' PJ said, 'and to the Brit base next door, RAF Aldergrove.'

'There's a Royal Air Force base here?' I said, 'how close?

'Close,' PJ shrugged. 'How far can you throw a stone?'

So this was great! I was in a car full of known IRA operatives heading to recon a target sitting next to a British military base. That's the first detail anyone with brains would have told me, except these sly bastards had the brains not to tell me, to string me along until it was too late to back out.

'You Yanks had an airbase out here as well, you know, during the Second World War,' Wee Joe said. 'I can take you on a tour if you want, the runways and all are still there. I do guided tours, you know, locations from Game of Thrones, the Titanic, the Troubles. Just if you're interested, like. I'll do you a special deal.'

His little piggy eyes squinted back at me. He looked and sounded as if he was serious, as if there was really a chance I would take some vacation time out so he could milk a few bucks out of me. Wee Joe reminded me of Yakov, and I thought maybe I should introduce them but, then again, they would all be introduced to Yakov and his people soon enough, just not in the way they would like.

'No thanks, Wee Joe. This tour to the RAF base will do fine,' I said.

'Who the fuck are you calling "*Wee*" Joe!? My name's Joseph! Who'd you hear calling me "*Wee*"!? Nobody fucking calls me "*Wee*", understand!?' Cheeky bastard!'

Wee Joe glared furiously at Tomás for a moment and then retreated into silent mode, his foot a little heavier on the gas, and we bumped along the rest of the country road in silence. That suited me, all that "good buddy" shit was a distraction and these guys would be better kept at arm's length. They hadn't yet realized just how different our agendas would be but, when they did, it could very easily become a big problem, so, for now, I was fine with letting them think they were stringing me along, and fine with dropping the small talk and false laughter.

I knew we were close when the military chopper buzzed over our heads. It was a small utility model, weaving maneuvers too close to the black trees and dead fields. We kept driving, and the chopper pulled a tight 360 to latch on tight behind us, just off to the right. 'Fuck!' Wee Joe broke his silence, 'here's his mate!' A second chopper popped up from behind us, and steadied itself in parallel with the first one, hanging back just to our left. 'Keep driving, Joseph,' PJ said, 'they're only training, not interested in us.' The choppers sat on our tail, like they were noisy kites roped to the car.

'We're coming up to the turn off here,' Wee Joe said.

'Forget it. Keep going to fuck until these wasps find somewhere else to play,' PJ said, 'we'll come back when they're gone.'

The first chopper pulled into a steep climb and veered off over the fields, the second chopper reacted almost immediately and chased after it, the two of them twisting and ducking like kids playing tag.

'Dickheads!' Tomás said. 'Pissing about like that, they'll give some old farmer a heart attack.'

'Fucking nearly give me a heart attack!' Wee Joe said.

'You sure they didn't make us?' I gripped PJ's wrist.

'Don't worry about it,' he said, 'they're always like that out here, training exercises and generally fucking about. The poor bastards will probably find themselves in Syria or Iraq next week, or some other place they have no business being. Turn back now, Joseph, the coast is clear.'

Wee Joe made the turn and paused at the junction of the target road.

'See that wee lane?' It was a rough track between a gap in the hedge. 'A cop car sits in there on party nights.'

'What about coming from the other direction?' I said, 'where does this road lead to?'

'Nowhere,' PJ said. 'A dead end.'

'Well, it leads to the Brit base, actually, about three quarters of a mile away,' Wee Joe said.

'Like I said, a dead end, nowhere.' PJ said. 'The only way you're getting near that house is down this road, cop car or not.'

Wee Joe slowed as we approached the house. It was about 100 yards back, accessed from this road by a main entrance and gravel driveway that looped around the front of the house and then doubled back to a small gate that must once have been the tradesmen's entrance. The house itself was big, three gray floors, with eight large windows spread across the upper two levels, six different chimney stacks, and a wing extending back from each gable-end. There looked to be work in progress, a lattice of scaffolding masked the gable-end to the right and various building material was stacked close-by.

'Is it occupied?' I said. 'Looks kind of neglected to me.'

'Dunno,' Wee Joe said, 'I've only been here at night with the girls and there is plenty of life about it then.'

An untended orchard sprouted from the left side, and a thicket of ornamental trees and shrubs promised some cover from the right. One of the entrance pillars was collapsed, or maybe demolished to make way for wider vehicles, and the heavy wrought-iron gates were propped against a silver-barked tree. No sign of cameras or security systems from here. We reversed into the main entrance and Joe cut the engine. I snapped some photos to Artie's phone. The choppers droned and whined in the distance but were out of sight.

'What's behind the main building?' I asked, 'any sort of space for security?'

'Dunno that either.' Wee Joe said. 'I drop the girls here at this gate and then piss off. They are collected the same place later on, any of them that are going home, anyway. I looked it up on Google maps but no good. Pixelated. This whole area is out of bounds, even for Google.'

'And how long back to Belfast?' I said. 'Twenty minutes? Any other routes we can take?'

'Plenty of back roads around here,' Tomás said, 'once you get past the cop car on guard. That's your problem right there. How are you going to manage that?'

The three of them waited for an answer, like I was a rookie being set an initiation challenge before being accepted in to their man club.

'Search me!' I said. 'I'm the stranger here, I'd hoped you smart guys would have all the answers. Maybe Brigid will know. Let's go see what she says about it.'

Tomás and Wee Joe looked to PJ, waiting on his words of wisdom. He sat tight, like he was testing how long he could hold his breath, and I could almost see all the possible scenarios running through his head, running and re-running until he was satisfied he had all angles covered.

Two young guys in orange day-glo track-suits appeared on the road, running toward us with heads down and ear-pieces wired up to their sleeves. Maybe local athletes, maybe servicemen from the base, but they had no reason to take any notice of us, either way. Not right then, but later, after Hamilton's big surprise reunion, random witnesses like these were exactly the sort of prize gift an investigator would sell his wife for.

'They're fucking two Brits!' PJ said, 'let's go!'

CHAPTER NINE

Aldergrove, February 20th

Friday night was party night at the big house. I burned the images from Artie's phone into my head and dumped the phone on his bed, he had made sure to be offside when PJ picked me up in the dirty white workman's van. Three athletic young men hunkered down in the back. I didn't know who they were or what they were, didn't want to know and didn't want them to know anything about me. Tomás was waiting in an identical van on the other side of the wolf mountain, just like we practised on the test run last Friday. The country roads were deserted before us and we drove in silence, no bravado, no jokes, none of their *craic,* just the frantic tic-tac of adrenaline and testosterone sparking the air between us.

'So you're sure the cop car won't be on guard?' PJ said.

'No problem,' I said.

Superintendent McIntyre had sent the word through Artie. The party was on tonight, and the usual discreet baby-sitters had been discreetly tasked to other duties miles away which meant they had to leave their post at 11 p.m. It was 11.45 when we pulled in behind the Alfa Spider sitting pretty above the web of dark roads between the International Airport and the great lake. Wee Joe had dropped the girls, noted the cop car on its usual spot, then returned to Belfast to ditch the taxi and get back here in time to see the squad car take off. Tomás' van rolled in tight behind us.

'Cops left an hour ago,' Wee Joe said, 'nobody in or out since then and no other traffic passing down any of these roads.'

My guts told me to cut Wee Joe out of this but Brigid insisted on another pair of eyes. She said the Brits and police Special Branch had a favorite dirty trick in the old days, said they would remove security checkpoints to give their Loyalist proxy hit squads a free run at a target but then grab the gunmen *after* the hit. When it worked out good it was always a real win/win – RUC Special Branch came out with a hit against Republicans and also deflected claims of collusion by catching the killers red handed. Brigid didn't ask how I knew the usual cop guard wouldn't be a problem but she wasn't about to trust my contact would guarantee safe passage in *and* out of there. Anyway, she reckoned, nobody knew the twisting country roads around there like Wee Joe, so he was in, and would stay back here to watch our backs.

PJ took the van past the house, slow and easy, Tomás tagging behind. Most of the house was dark except for the wing on the left side, closest to the orchard. Music, laughter, loud voices, all amplified in the dark. A woman screamed, didn't sound like she was in trouble. PJ swung the van around in the entrance to a field and killed the lights before sliding up close to the gate pillar of the main entrance. We pulled on ski masks and silently stepped out of the van, no talk, no slamming doors, everything slowed down, reduced to the next quiet movement, no panic, no rush. Tomás and two big guys joined us behind the gate pillar, a driver left behind the wheel of each van, four younger men crouching low behind PJ and Tomás as I scanned the ground before us.

Some voices were definitely outside the house, but high on some cocktail of alcohol and drugs so we should be able to get real close before anybody noticed. The lights back there outlined a high wall between the house and that end of the orchard, enough to give good cover. I tapped PJ's shoulder and motioned them to follow. Half way there, somebody stood on a fallen branch and the crack of dead wood splintered the night air like a gunshot. We lay flat against the hard cold earth. I strained to hear a reaction, waiting for the boots to crunch across the gravel path with spotlights and guns. Nothing happened, the party boomed on, but I stayed flat and waited. Thirty seconds feels like forever when the adrenaline is pumping. PJ's guys started to shuffle. I kept them still for another minute, then another. An old guy up there with the larynx of a spoiled choirboy chanted along with Skynyrd's *Free Bird.* I pushed them low and slow until we made the wall. A backing group of young females flattered his *Alabama* now, maybe five or six voices that I could make out.

If Hamilton was one of these party jokers outside the house this was going to be easy. If he wasn't, we had a problem. There had to be a lot of places he could be hidden away in there, old real estate like this was built to be a maze of corridors and stairs and secret rooms. This Skynyrd tribute group outside would react badly if we had to storm through, and the commotion would give the other orgy heads inside a warning we couldn't afford. The girls wouldn't be a problem. They would freak out at first but they weren't being paid to be heroes, and would slink into the background when they realized we were no threat to them. Hamilton's VIP comrades, on the other hand, wouldn't be VIP's in the first place unless they were branded with the smug arrogance to fool themselves into believing they *were* heroes, and the drink and drugs would only inject them with more hero juice. A cracked head here and there would quickly tame their warrior hearts but my problem was time. Time wasted getting my hands on Hamilton was time for an alarm call to go out. That RAF base was on the doorstep and McIntyre's conveniently absent squad car could soon draw down reinforcements to cover our escape routes like a blanket.

'PJ, have a look and see if Hamilton is in that group outside.'

PJ felt his way past me, and one of his young guys moved with him but bumped into me in the darkness. The prick had a pistol in a double-handed grip and nearly dropped it as he stumbled over me. I pushed him off me and grabbed PJ by the back of his collar.

'I told you no guns!' I hissed into his ear, 'what the fuck he is doing here with that thing?!'

'It's okay, it's okay,' PJ twisted out of my grip. 'The wee lad's just a bit nervous, the wee gun helps with his self confidence.'

That was supposed to reassure me?

'Look,' PJ whispered close to my face, 'it's not like he's fucking going to shoot anybody, is it? But were you never young yourself? Did you not feel safer with a piece in your hand?'

Was he serious? Or busting my balls again? He shrugged away from me and I heard his knees creak to my left as he bent down to scout around the wall. The rest of them were to my right, pressed tight against the wall, but I could see now the young guys were all carrying. This was starting to look more like an assassination run than a kidnap.

'No, that's not him,' PJ said. 'There's three men out there and four girls. One of the men is underneath one of the girls. The other two look like they're off their heads, wouldn't know if they're Bertie or Gertie. But no Hamilton.'

'Look PJ,' I said, 'there is a lot of cash riding on Hamilton, on getting him out of here in one piece. A real lot of money. He is worthless dead, understand?'

PJ sniggered. 'We know. Brigid is waiting to talk real money when we get a hold of Hamilton. We knew there was more at stake than Monsignor McCooey deigned to tell us. Once we have

Hamilton by the neck, we will have you and McCooey by the balls. Don't worry, Brigid will square it up with both of you, being fair to everybody, know what I mean?'

If he meant Brigid would demand a bigger piece of the pie, that would be okay, and strictly Artie's problem. I had my own plans, so Artie and Brigid could fight over the empty pot when me and the cash were long gone. As long as he didn't mean Hamilton's name was down for an old time IRA revenge killing, I could keep them sweet just long enough to get out of there.

'There's a hedge over there,' Tomás said, 'looks like we could follow it to get around the back of the house.'

We groped our way through the dark, somebody had doused too much aftershave, and another wore a watch with a too luminous face. The karaoke crooners were behind us now, murdering '*Bad Moon Rising*', and other lights and sounds were coming from straight ahead. Tomás nudged me forward to a gate that opened to the rear of the house. There was another building here, long and low-roofed, looked like it had originally been some kind of storeroom or work space. It was about twenty-five yards from the main house, and we were some thirty yards back again. Loud music and dim lights leaked out from three of the four windows and vague shapes hovered like ghosts behind the white drapes. The fourth window had black curtains but a high powered spotlight cut a razor blade of light across the rough concrete, stretching toward us like an accusing bony finger.

'Bingo!' Tomás slapped my back. 'Hamilton is in there. I can smell him.'

PJ pulled on the gate, the rusty hinges screeched. We squeezed through. Tomás signalled two of the young guys to make for the corner of the outbuilding, they pitched into the darkness fast and low, like a pair of trained dogs, like they had practised this a hundred times. A door opened at the back of the main house. We all spread flat on the ground. Shapes filtered out from the door, two tall men carrying a small figure between them, the figure's feet dragging behind on the ground. The men were in a hurry, marching the slight limp figure toward the outbuilding without a word between them. A security light mounted above the door of the outbuilding tripped alive as they approached. I could see two middle-aged men wearing tuxedos and open-necked white shirts, and a young boy, maybe thirteen or fourteen years old, his head rocking loose against his chest and his bare feet scraping along the ground. The men had that savage look of hunters about to take their kill. The kid couldn't have walked even if he had been conscious, his pants hog-tied his ankles, and a stream of blood smeared down the back of his legs. The men pushed the boy in through the door and the hungry pack inside erupted into howls and roars of delight.

'Fuck this, Tómas!' One of the young muscle jumped to his feet and PJ had to haul him down again.

'I know!' PJ said, 'I know, son, but keep your head! We have a job to do here, keep your discipline, keep to the plan!'

PJ was right, I knew it, but I couldn't help thinking of my own son, and Yasmin's kids, and all the brutalized children I hadn't defended, sometimes scarred by the enemy, sometimes by my own comrades, and my stomach twisted into a violent knot.

'You okay there, Con?' PJ said, holding my face in his hands, then snapping me back to business with three short slaps. 'You need to keep yourself under control,' he said, 'or else we'll have a problem, hear me?'

'I'm fine, PJ, under control. Let's do this fucking thing and get out of here!'

The security light made the dark shadows of the yard even darker, and we scuttled across to join the first two at the corner of the house.

'Right! You two in first,' Tomás poked their chests, 'let me and PJ pick out Hamilton, then you two grab him, you two come in behind and cover, right?'

Right, they knew what they were doing, they already had it all worked out. The security light cut out and we hit the door like a thunderclap. There was a small hallway, to the left was a tight corridor with three doors to the dim rooms, and to the right was a single door to the blazing light where all the screams came from. The two guys went in first, ready to take down any opposition. We pushed in behind them but then froze before the numbing ferocity of the scene. A squirming mass of plump and pink bodies devoured the kid with his pants round his ankles, lifeless under them, being torn and ripped by their pure flesh greed but unable even to whimper. Eight men were on him, or fighting to get on him, like red-eyed piranhas in frenzy, all naked except for the two still in tuxedos. One of our young guys moved to intervene but Tomás smacked the back of his head and yanked him by the collar. PJ walked past the scrum on the middle of the floor as if it was nothing more than a couple of kittens play fighting over a ball of wool, and slowly raised his hand to point at the quiet man sitting alone in the corner. The man looked up at PJ the way you might when you see someone you think you should recognize but don't.

'Alright Paddy?' PJ smiled.

Now Hamilton realized who this was, what this was. He twisted a rueful, resigned smile back.

'Alright, PJ? Long time, no see.'

The convulsing swarm on the floor continued but one or two on the fringes started to notice their world begin to burn. Tomás nodded, two of his guys grabbed Hamilton's arms and wrangled him into a standing half crouch, Tomás skipped forward and pile-drived all his weight behind a punch into Hamilton's gut that buckled his legs and only the two guys kept him upright. Confusion and fear rippled through the heaving parasites on the floor. Tomás took a step back then rammed the hard heel of his hand up into Hamilton's face. Hamilton's blood fanned out like water from a fire sprinkler and splashed across the faces of the animals on their knees closest to him. PJ thumbed toward the door and the two guys hauled Hamilton forward. Reality was hitting home hard now, and the wolf pack moved to its feet, like it was a single organism with one head and many limbs. A couple of them moved to pull Hamilton back and block the exit. One of the tuxedo men pushed his hand into Tomas's chest and Tomás' guy stepped forward and smacked the handgun hard into the tuxedo balls. Tuxedo folded, but Tomás' guy smacked him again only this time he squeezed the trigger and the tuxedo groin exploded out the back of his trousers.

'Get out to fuck!' PJ shouted, and shoved Hamilton toward the door.

The gun guy fired into the ceiling and the pack quivered back like a glass high rise hit with aftershock, and then instinct creased them back into a corner, leaving one lone wolf still feeding on the comatose young boy. He was a man in his fifties, with eyes dilated so much that he didn't look human anymore. He had taken a bite out of his own tongue in his manic rage and his lathered blood and saliva glooped on the boy's snowy white back as he gorged without mercy. We had Hamilton at the door now and our exit was clear. The gun guy said 'Fuck it!', took two steps forward before cranking the gun tightly into the base of the vampire's skull. The back of the head burst like a kid's balloon, a skull balloon full of blood and brains, and splattered a pink arc that radiated a semi-circle across the floor and sprayed a gray film over the hot spotlight. The rest of his face didn't realize the back of his skull had vaporized, and his eyes and mouth still worked their animal fever until finally the body stalled and crumbled.

'Holy fuck!' Tomás winced. 'Now what?'

The gun guy pulled the boy away from the dead man and his big comrade helped him lift the boy to his feet. PJ pushed the other two to get Hamilton outside, but kept his face blank while Tomás and the others waited for his decision.

'We can't take that wee lad with us,' PJ said. 'I'm sorry, boys, we can't do it. We can't take care of him.'

'We're not leaving him here!' the gun guy said. 'I'll fucking nut all the dirty bastards first!'

I tapped PJ's shoulder and nodded over to the corner where Hamilton had been sitting. Two more naked kids were lying there behind a couch, unconscious, with their knees folded up to their chests and their wrists tied to their ankles. The smaller boy, about twelve years old, skinny and with curly blond hair, looked like he had been whipped with a thick leather belt and blood oozed from the red and purple weals criss-crossing his back. The other kid was about fifteen, with black hair shaved close to his skull, and his dark skin was patterned with red bite marks all across his shoulders and arms.

'Fucking no way we're taking the three of them!' PJ said. 'Fucking no way! We can't do anything for them, we can't take them to hospital!'

PJ called it right, we needed to slip away into the darkness, but I lifted the black haired kid, with his wrists tied to his ankles he cradled in my arms like young Con did when he was a baby. The big comrade lifted the blond kid, and we followed the gun guy out.

'You're right about the risk, PJ,' I said, 'but we'll all regret it for the rest of our lives if we walk away. Believe me, I'm speaking from experience here.'

PJ pushed past me and ran out to catch up with Tomás and the two guys hauling Hamilton across the yard. He grabbed Hamilton by the collar and pressed his mouth close to his ear, then pulled his cell phone and made a call. I was close behind now and could see the phone's light display as it pulsed the call. PJ killed the call without speaking. We were at the corner of the house now, coming up to the orchard wall. The music still pumped from inside the main house and the croaking karaoke kids of generation-x were too high to even see us until we were knocking them out of our way but the girls knew danger when they saw it coming and were already half way down the path to the gate. We caught up with the slowest girl, carrying her heels in one hand and what looked like somebody's wallet and watch clamped between her skinny elbow and ribs. The girls ahead scattered, the white van raced up the path toward us before pulling a drifting 360 on the loose gravel. PJ was in the van first, helped drag Hamilton in the back, Tomás and the other two jumped in and the van took off before they could slam the door closed.

The rear lights bounced and weaved away from us like a red-eyed devil in the night. The boy was a dead-weight in my arms, maybe he was already dead, and the cold air stung my nostrils. The other two were younger than me, and fitter, and overtook me now, sprinting down the path to the other van. The girl with the heels latched on to me, pretending to help carry the boy but using me to help drag her down the path. The van waited with the doors open, revving and straining to take off. I dumped the kid in the back and clambered in behind him.

'Get her out!'

The heels girl wedged herself in the back of the van before I could pull the door closed.

'Get that hoor out to fuck!'

She was hanging on to me like a limpet, it wasn't worth the trouble, I thumped the driver on the shoulder and he hit the gas. The acceleration tipped us off balance and we sprawled across the van, me, the girl, the two young guys and the three doped boys. PJ and Tomás were out of sight.

'Where you from?' one of the guys asked her.

'Belfast!' she snapped in a thick Russian accent, 'I live Ormeau Road, Belfast. Where you fuckers from?'

The two guys looked at each other, shrugged, and tore the ski masks off their faces. We started to pull at the plastic ties on the boys but they were too tight. There was nothing in the van to cut them off. The girl pushed me out of the way, collapsed a heel on her shoe and drew out the hidden short sharp blade. She sliced the ties on the boys and started rubbing hard on the closest boy's legs.

'They are cold! Rub! Rub hard!' she ordered, and the two guys started rubbing, trying to rub some spark of life back into the clay limbs. We layered them in our jackets and jumpers and sweatshirts, and kept rubbing their hands and feet and faces. One of them looked too far gone, the other two close behind.

Two sets of tail-lights were getting further away, I shouted to the driver to catch up with PJ and Wee Joe. The road forked, PJ and Wee Joe went right, we went left.

'There's a doctor lives this way,' the driver shouted over his shoulder. 'Tomás says I'm to drop these kids at his house first.'

'Where's the safe house?' I said. 'Isn't it Belfast? Looks like PJ is headed the other direction.'

The driver shook his head, didn't look back at me.

'You wouldn't know where it was even if I told you,' he said, 'and I'm not telling you.'

The adrenaline high was starting to seep away. I climbed into the front to sit beside the driver and left the others to work the three boys as best they could. The girl seemed to have some experience, maybe dealing with a drug overdose was part of her on the job training, maybe she used to be a nurse, maybe a doctor. Yasmin's voice and perfume were in my head but I couldn't conjure a picture of her, other images flashed and scrambled before my eyes.

'You guys seemed to have that all pretty well worked out,' I said, 'like you had rehearsed it plenty, like you didn't need me at all, and now Hamilton is going one way and I'm going another.'

The driver didn't flinch, kept on driving as if I hadn't said a word.

'Kind of makes me wonder what I'm doing here,' I pressed a little more. 'Like, somebody's making a major mistake if they take me for a fall guy.'

'I don't know, mate,' he said, 'I thought you were the big boss. I just keep my mouth shut and do what I'm told.'

That used to be my own formula for survival and guilt-free sleep but, somehow, that husk of cheap and easy denial had curdled and died long ago, leaving me at the mercy of the shame and stigma churning me up inside like corpse maggots.

'Two cars coming up fast behind us!'

'Where did they come from?' I said.

'Out of nowhere!' the young guy said, 'out of fucking nowhere!'

The driver was spooked, took the corner too fast, almost lost control, somehow wrangled the van straight again, then slammed the brakes and skidded to a stop. Two vehicles were blocking the road ahead, sitting side by side facing us, waiting. The spotlights ignited in our faces, blinding us and obscuring the figures on the road. The cars behind screamed up close. We sat in silence then for a few stretched moments, only the choked sobs of one of the boys and the cracks from the engine cooling in the winter night.

'We have you surrounded!' A deep voice boomed. 'Anybody moves and we'll riddle that pile of shit!'

The young guys crouched at the sliding door of the van, handguns clenched, eager for the Butch and Sundance climax to validate their hero halos and etch their celebrity in stone. A long freeze-frame, no movement, no contact, but I could sense the shadows maneuvering into the perfect kill spots all around us. A MP5 tapped the driver-side window, a black shape, two more behind him, silhouetted by the spotlights, on the opposite side of the van from the sliding door where the young guys waited for their kamikaze chance.

'Everybody out! Lie on the ground! Hands behind your head!'

I opened my door slowly, spread my hands open and high.

'Forget it, boys,' I said, 'way too much firepower out there.'

I stepped out of the van and a strong pair of hands grabbed my neck and forced me to the tarmac. The driver followed, then the girl, the two desperados had to be dragged out but at least they didn't insist on the ultimate sacrifice.

'Keep your faces to the ground and don't move!' The same deep voice. 'Don't move and you won't get hurt!'

Two of them knelt to shine a light in front of my face, then forced a rough hood over my eyes. The Russian girl cursed and bit at the hands hooding her, and the other three struggled until they were stomped and kicked into submission. My hands were behind my head, I peeled the hood back just enough to see out of one eye. Two figures shone torches into the rear of the van. They just looked, no reaction to the three boys lying before them. They hopped out and one came running to the figure standing close to me. 'He's not here.' The figure turned and walked off behind the cars with their lights blinding me. A door opened in another car behind and the interior light shimmered on the damp road. I couldn't see or hear much, but I figured there were three or four shapes standing back there. Then that car door closed and the whole episode happened in reverse, the cars in front killed their lights, black shapes disappeared, the cars behind spun away into the darkness.

'Christ the night!' the driver puffed, 'I thought they were going to nut the lot of us! Who even were those dickheads?!'

'You wouldn't know even if I told you,' I said, 'and I'm not telling you, but get this pile of shit moving before they have second thoughts.'

We piled into the van, only this time the Russian girl squeezed into the front, half sitting on my lap. She hadn't been wearing much to start with, and had wrapped her thin silky top around one of the boys, so now she felt practically naked on my lap. Close up like this she was a good looking girl, very alive and very full of attitude. She turned her back on the driver and sat sideways across my thighs, with her arms around my neck and nuzzling her nose into my throat.

'I am cold,' she said, 'I need your heat.'

It wasn't the worst sensation I had felt that night but I had been down this road before and it never worked out good for the job in hand and certainly never worked out good for the girl.

'Don't worry about it,' I said, 'you're getting out soon. We will drop you at the doctor's house.'

She snaked a little tighter around my neck, working her ass in a gentle rhythm. 'I don't want out,' her wet mouth was hot on my ear, 'I want stay with you.'

'No, you don't,' I said. 'You want to get out as soon as you can. Then walk away and don't look back.'

Her right hand was stroking my face, I didn't stop her.

'The authorities will come,' she said, 'my papers are not good. The authorities will make trouble for me, make me tell everything I see at that house.'

'You didn't see anything,' I said, 'you met some guys on the way out and hitched a ride. You didn't see anything.'

'I see what the authorities tell me I see.' She nipped my ear. 'My name is Yana. I stay. No trouble for me, no trouble for you.'

Yana was always going to be trouble. Right then that was the only thing in the world I could be sure of. I knew that trouble was rocking right here on my lap. I knew it but I just didn't care.

CHAPTER TEN

From the outside it looked like a typical deserted barn behind a deserted house at the end of a deserted lane. A shipping container nested inside to hide the secret army. The main section had six camp beds, a gas stove, and an electric heater and lights rigged to a silent generator. Tomás held the door to the small cell at the back and nodded me forward. Hamilton stood facing into the corner, hands tied, blue boiler-suit, bare feet. PJ putting the squeeze from one side, Brigid in his face from the other.

She wasn't asking where the money was or how he was going to clear Beikle. She wasn't asking anything, just purging her venom into his ear, telling him he was a worthless piece of shit, had pissed on his father's grave, would be branded forever as a two-faced murdering scumbag and it would have been kinder to his mother if he had sucked on a .45 years ago. Brigid was good. She would have reduced me to a blubbering wreck in about ten minutes. Hamilton stared onto the corner as if he was in the room on his own.

'Any trouble with the doctor?' Tomás whispered.

'The doctor was fine. The kids will be in hospital by now,' I said. 'Bring Brigid and PJ outside. We need to talk.'

I waited beside the stove. Yana wrapped a sleeping bag around her shoulders and greedily soaked up the glow from the electric heater. The young guys watched her from their creaking camp beds, forcing cool disinterest but still buzzing from the action and craving more kicks.

Brigid stormed out of the interrogation cell with a face like poison. The young guys shifted uneasily. Yana casually glanced over her shoulder and gave Brigid a routine once over, taking her measure head to toe, then toe to head.

'Who the fuck is this whore?!' Brigid yelled.

'Calm down, calm down,' I said. 'Your guys took their masks off, she saw their faces. It was either leave her to the police or bring her along.'

Brigid stood over Yana like she might yank the hair from her head. Yana shrugged off the sleeping bag and stretched to her full height. Brigid was tall but Yana was a little taller, even in her bare feet. Brigid's black eyes and black hair looked a little dull in that light, a little tired. Yana's blonde hair and baby blue eyes pulsed with vitality and promised excitement. Brigid didn't like Yana already. I tapped her shoulder and motioned her outside.

The two white vans were squeezed into the corner of the barn with a tarpaulin over them.

'How did you get here, Brigid?' I said.

'Fuck off, Yank!'

'Where's Wee Joe's car?' I said.

'He scouted in front of us, then went on home,' PJ said.

'Yeah, real lucky you didn't take the same road as us, isn't it?' I said. 'They were waiting on us, in front and behind.'

'Very fucking nice of them to let you go!' Tomás said. 'Friends of yours, were they?'

I tightened his collar with my left hand, gave an extra twist to raise him to his toes.

'Don't ever try that shit with me, Tomás,' I said, 'we were the decoy to make sure you had a free run out here. The three of you set me up and, listen good, getting me pissed off wasn't a good idea!'

'You're talking balloon bollocks now, Mercenary Man,' Brigid said, 'why would we hand up our own men, and risk us all being fingered? Anyway, how come they *did* let you go?'

'They only wanted Hamilton,' I said. 'They knew we were coming for him and they sat back and let us do the dirty work and then pounced.'

'Who's *they?'* PJ said.

'You're the big intelligence man, PJ,' I said, 'why don't you give it a shot? Only a handful of people knew our plans, that shouldn't be so hard to figure for a smart guy like you.'

PJ brushed past me and swaggered off to check the barn doors were secure. The looks between Brigid and Tomás told me they weren't sure what PJ was thinking either. That was good as far as I was concerned, maybe a split in the camp, maybe some long standing rivalry that I didn't know about but could exploit.

'I'll speak to Hamilton now, on my own,' I said.

'Not a good idea,' Tomás said. 'The prick is still acting the big man with his "*fuck you all*" attitude. Wait until the morning. My boys will keep him without sleep in that ice-box, no food, no water. He'll be easier to talk to tomorrow.'

'Now,' I said. 'You can sit up all night reading him bedtime stories if you like but I'm seeing him right now, on my own.'

Tomás started to muster up his own *fuck you* attitude until Brigid put a hand on his chest and eased him back.

'Five minutes, that's it!' she said. 'Then keep out of the way and let us work on him overnight. But here, big golden bollocks, work out what you're going to do with your Russian prostitute before it's time to go, alright?'

Tomás smirked behind her back like a schoolboy.

'So you are the famous Maknazpy!' Hamilton said. 'You're not what I expected. Trigger men usually have dead eyes.'

The immaculate grooming from Artie's photo was gone, the white hair hung over his red eyes and his face was purple like a wino's. Blood seeped from his nose and his lips were rough and swollen. I knew he would try to play me.

'Let's keep this simple,' I said. 'These people want to kill you. You give me the encryption key and the rest of Beikle's cash and I will get you out of here.'

Hamilton laughed at me like I was a dumb bonehead. He was wasting his time, I was never going to be suckered into any of his manipulation games.

'Beikle? You really think this is about Beikle, the pirate priest?'

'Okay. You can forget Beikle,' I said, 'I'm here for the cash. Deliver the cash and you can walk out of here, otherwise you disappear with a bullet in your skull.'

There were two small stools at the door for the interrogators to use, I told Hamilton to take one and pulled the other one for myself. He took his time settling down, adjusting the stool so we were face to face, manspreading his legs to overlap mine. I wanted him to think this was a break for him, knew he would figure it would give him more scope to play his mind games and assert his superiority. Operators like Hamilton always think they are so smart they can twist every situation to their advantage. He could have his small victories, I wanted the money.

'The money exchange set-up in Vienna,' I said. 'Give me the encryption key.'

'That's not why I'm here,' he said.

He was here because I was here and I was here because I wanted the money but I wasn't getting into a debate about it.

'Where is the encryption key?' I said.

'That's not why you are here, either. They fed you that dope as bait to get you here but it's a smokescreen. They need a sucker to take the blame and they picked you. Who was it brought you into it? That other pirate priest McCooey? You trusted McCooey again?'

The flicker in his eyes said he had picked up the doubt in my mind but he was mistaken if he thought he had created it. I was wary of Artie and the whole package right from the start and I had no intention of being cannon-fodder this time.

'You have problems of your own right now so don't be worried on my behalf,' I said. 'Where is the encryption key?'

Hamilton thought he was getting on top now. He cracked a fake grin and his lip started to bleed again.

'Okay, fine,' he said, 'We can go get you the bloody thing but what use will it be to you? It's obsolete! Blown! That key won't work anymore because the Russian Mafia have blocked the other end. If they get it *they* can unlock the cash but no-one else can touch it. Unless ...'

I whipped an open handed slap against his left ear, he crumbled off the stool but I grabbed him by the throat before he hit the ground and threw him back into the corner, pressing his face into the rough metal.

'You don't get to negotiate with me, Hamilton! Where is the key?!'

He was dazed, maybe I hit his ear too hard and he couldn't hear properly. I slapped him again and pulled his head back by his hair.

'Okay! Okay! For fuck's sake! What're you trying to prove? You're the big action hero and you can treat me like dirt if you feel like it?'

'Where's the encryption key?'

'You were fucking sitting on it, you dickhead! I hid it in the house I was using before your friends put the screws on me - 18 Sandymount Street! It was under your arse the whole time!'

I shoved his face into the corner again so he couldn't see my confusion. He was too smart, scrambling truth and lies on the hoof, Judas kissing his way to survival.

'That's right, Maknazpy! Sandymount Street! Who sent you there? Why? So it looks good when they pin my murder on you?'

He had that stupid grin on his face again, and blood running from his nose and lips so that his teeth were vampire red.

'Okay! Let's go get it then, Hamilton, just you and me – and if it's not there I *will* execute you on the spot! How you like that for a plan?'

He wiped his nose with the back of his hand and a sticky plug of black blood smeared across his cheek.

'You think those three are ever letting me out of here alive?' he said. 'You're more naive than I thought!'

'Deliver the cash and you'll see their thirst for revenge melt away,' I said. 'Or are you really such a big shot that they'll throw it all away to get even?'

'It's not about me,' he said. 'Those three have been under suspicion from their own people for the last twenty years. The word on the street back then was MI5 had an informer in that unit. It suited the IRA and MI5 to let that one slide at the time, don't jeopardize the ceasefire, primacy of the Peace Process and all that.'

I knew they weren't only here to do Artie a favor but was the crock of gold really enough without something else, something deep in their twisted history, something I wouldn't understand?

'So? Who is it?' I said. 'Who's the informer?'

Hamilton did that hollow laugh that chugged his shoulders and frothed the blood on his tongue.

'You're not in Abu Ghraib now, my Yankee friend!' he said. 'And it isn't that simple. It wouldn't stop at one name, this sort of thing never does. There would be another name, and another, stretching all the way back to the 1970's.' He sniffed a trickle of blood back up a nostril. 'They will whack me anyway, name or not. Or one of them will whack me before the others beat the name out of me.'

'Say I get you out of here,' I said, 'say I take care of it and get you out, I get the encryption key and you walk. You disappear back to Vienna or Libya or wherever people like you run to. But double-cross me and *I'll* whack you. You really know I'll whack you, right?'

He twisted his neck to eye me, calculating his next move, fitting me into his plan, another stepping stone, a neck to stand on.

'I'm the only option you have right now, Hamilton.'

'What about the Russians?' he said.

'Let me worry about the Russians.'

'Is that girl here?' he asked.

'What girl?'

'The Russian girl. She wasn't right. Tall blonde. Tonight was her first night. I saw her and knew straight away she wasn't right. Is she here?'

'No,' I said. 'No Russian girls here.'

CHAPTER ELEVEN

Yana claimed the camp bed closest to the heater and wrapped the sleeping bag into a tight cocoon so only a stray tussle of silky blonde hair was visible. Brigid hunkered down in front of the heater. The homely glow rippled a soft honey mask across her face but her black eyes were more coldly intense than ever. It was freezing in here, the cold metal sucked the goodness from the heater's miserable warmth, and the young guys distracted themselves from the boredom and cold by sneaking a glance at Yana's shape curved into the bag when they thought Brigid wasn't watching.

'What did he say?' Brigid tapped me on the ankle as I bent to rub some warmth into my hands.

'Nothing. I'll try again in the morning.'

She fixed those black eyes on me and I didn't have to be a mind reader to work out there was something major going on behind them, like a maelstrom of fury, maybe, or a severe and irresistible depression.

'Took him a long time to say nothing,' she said.

'So what did he say to you?' I challenged. 'Or what answer did you want to hear?'

'Nothing. PJ and Tomás are in there now. We'll keep working him. He'll talk.'

'You're cool about that, then?' I said. 'You're out here and PJ and Tomás are in there without you, asking questions, maybe getting the answer they want?'

'*Cool*? I'm fucking freezing!' Brigid hopped up like a sprightly teen and skipped past me like I wasn't there, then swung back to jab two fingers into my chest. 'And what about *her*? Is your prostitute *cool*?' She jabbed me again then spun away, taking the next bed to Yana and forcing the young guy who had been stretched out on it to move.

Brigid *could* be an informer. She wouldn't be first choice if you were a gambling man yet it could easily be her. I'd been twisted and turned and shafted often enough not to rely on instinct, and just because she pumped up that hostile hard-ass shell didn't mean she was clean. She sat upright on the bed now, with that uptight ballerina pose, her spine and neck stretched straight and chin held high. It could easily be her, even if those hard black eyes would never surrender the secret.

I slid in close behind Yana on the narrow camp bed. She kept her firm grip on the sleeping bag but didn't exactly squirm away from me. I burrowed in as tight as I could to the gap between the mattress and her. There was some warmth there, or at least it wasn't as cold. Her hair was very fine and delicate, and I breathed deeply to draw in the fresh clean aroma. She started to move in the bag, slowly, working herself against me, working me. I could feel Brigid's eyes burning into the back of my head, and sensed the young guys agitated in their beds with envy. Yana kept moving, then slipped the zipper of the bag down and turned to face me. She snuggled close, and drew the bag behind her as she rolled on top. Her mouth was hot on my neck and her ass was warm to my hands. I was going to wait until it was Brigid's turn to go work Hamilton over but Yana's slow teasing dance was killing me. I pushed the bag down and pulled Yana behind me. The young guys sat up like meerkats. 'What a dickhead!' Brigid called after me.

She had one hand around my waist and the other played in my pocket. It was almost totally dark out here but I felt my way and led her over to the corner of the barn and backed her up against the van hidden under the tarpaulin.

'It is cold!' she said. 'Too cold for me.'

'You're Russian, aren't you? This isn't cold for you.'

She was wearing a heavy woollen jumper one of the young guys had handed over when he thought it might buy him the chance to strip it off her later. She shivered and pulled the collar up to her chin.

'Not here,' she used her soft persuasive voice, 'I will make it nice when you take me away with you, later, it will be fantastic for you, I promise.'

I took her by the hips and lifted her ass up on the hood of the van.

'But I'll make it fantastic for you here, Yana baby, right now, I promise I will.'

The tarpaulin slipped and I held her steady with one hand and reached down the back of her long sleek legs and tipped one high heel off, then the other.

'No! Not now! Later! I just want you hold me now and make me warm!'

'Okay, okay, Yana, I'll make you plenty warm.'

I pulled her ass off the hood and twisted her around so she was pressed tight against it, face down with my weight pinning her from behind. I fumbled in the darkness until I found the long tarpaulin strap and whipped it around her neck. She reacted like a pro, striking down hard at my knees and shins. I worked my thighs to trap her kicking legs against the van and pulled the strap tighter around her throat. She clawed backwards, going for my eyes, but I dodged down and twisted the strap. She tried to lever herself sideways to escape the pressure on her windpipe but I countered and shifted my weight to pin her shoulders square on the hood. She was going, choking on her death rattle, the fight in her body slipping away. I loosened the strap just enough to let her gasp some air.

'Yakov knew what would happen if he double-crossed me,' I said. 'So this isn't my fault. I haven't any choice. Blame your boss, he knew what would happen.'

She tried to cry out but I tightened it again before she could reclaim her breathing. I held it steady, not enough yet to finish her but enough for her to think it was the end. I counted to eight before loosening it again.

'Nyet! Nyet! I not know this Yakov. He not my boss!'

'Oh yes!' I laughed in her ear, 'you *do* know this Yakov! He fucking sent you here to double-cross me! Where is the bastard!? You have some sort of tracker, haven't you? I swear I'll squeeze this fucking strap until your eyes pop out! So listen good! One chance! How are you signalling to him!? When is he comimg!?'

I held it for a couple of seconds before slacking off. She panted for air and gouged her fingers into her throat to pull the strap away.

'I'm CIA, you fucking asshole!' Yana croaked. 'I'm CIA!'

Even with the choked voice, she didn't sound much like a Muscovite anymore. I let her pull the strap away and she went down on her hands and knees, still choking and coughing, trying to suck air down her crushed throat.

'Go get me a drink, you fucker!!'

I bumped my way in the darkness back to the container and scrabbled about to find the door. Brigid was in the cell room with Hamilton and PJ was back out here.

'You shouldn't be out there,' he warned. 'In here is insulated, if the Brits have a chopper up with a thermal camera they'll never see us in here but out in the barn is too risky. Come on back on in.'

I grabbed a bottle of water from beside the stove and felt my way back over to Yana, her groans and wheezes made it easier when I got close. I held the bottle to her lips but she smacked me away and took the bottle herself, glugging and choking, mucus down her nose and tears in her eyes.

'Maybe you are with CIA and maybe you're not. Don't much matter to me either way, Yana – or whatever your name is.'

She spluttered and spit the water and phlegm into the darkness, still panting, pulling in quick gulps of air.

'There's a very angry Irish lady in there and she already doesn't like you much. If she suspects you are anything different than a working girl she'll have you buried out here.'

'No she won't!' Yana was getting her voice back. 'She'll shit herself! Her own people will bury *her* if I break a fingernail out here.'

This new Yana had that elevated sense of self worth common to Operators, but I knew plenty of whores like that also.

'You have fucked up big time, Maknazpy!' She was taking control now. 'If this Op gets blown because of your amateur bungling you'll pay for it.'

Her voice was still weak and she pushed close to my face, spitting saliva in my mouth as she balled me out. Her aggro face was hitting the wrong buttons and I felt the red pressure rising from my neck. I forced myself to chill out, couldn't afford to lose it now.

'So what are you doing here, *Yana*?'

'That doesn't concern you, Maknazpy! You need to back off right now and do exactly like I tell you, understand?'

I wasn't sold yet, an American accent didn't mean she wasn't working for Yakov.

'We need to get Hamilton out of here,' she croaked, 'you back me up and you get to keep that big pay off from the last Op you fucked up. Fuck this one up and all your bank accounts will be cleaned out. That includes the nest eggs you set up for your wife in Hampton Bays and your girlfriend in Rio. Are we clear?'

That didn't mean shit, Yakov knew about those deals, he was part of them.

'And I know all about your psychotic episode rages,' she patted my cheek, 'I read your file. You need to keep that bad boy under control, okay?'

She was making their mistake of assuming I could be compressed and distilled into the ink on their pages. Maybe she *was* genuine. People like that, brainwashed by the anointed elite and the righteous snake charmers, they needed the world to be created in that neat predictable format and needed people like me, their sheeple, to conform to their filing system.

This Yana had honed the double sharp edge of indulged arrogance and cruel indifference, like many of the sociopathic power drones. Didn't look like she was Yakov's girl, though, and at least that was something because if he *had* double-crossed me it would mean I was on my own and ear deep in shit.

'Have you a cell phone?' I asked.

'Inside,' she nodded toward the container unit, 'in the wallet I snatched from that sleazeball creep. That Brigid bitch took it off me.'

The door to the container unit opened and PJ was framed in the doorway. He wanted us back inside but was shy of intruding on my imagined reckless rutting. I took Yana's wrist and told her to pull the jumper over her throat before we went back in. She twisted her arm, grabbed my wrist, skipped forward to knee me in the balls.

'The Mick lady is right!' she crowed in my ear, 'you really are a premium dickhead!'

CHAPTER TWELVE

The plan was to keep the squeeze on Hamilton all through the night. Brigid, PJ and Tomás taking turns to rattle him, a couple of the young guys to add muscle, or sometimes all of them if PJ wanted to rack up the menace. Tomás could scream and bluster for an hour or so before his voice would crack. Brigid's malice unsettled the rest of us, except maybe for Yana. PJ milled his questions through his head like killer chess openings while he waited his shift then unloaded his moves to draw Hamilton to the endgame. The plan was for the crew to rest up whilst Hamilton's resistance was being whittled down, layer by layer. That was the plan, but the air was too cold and too heavy with their frantic aggression so none of us got any sleep, except for Yana, and I figured she was faking it.

By six in the morning Brigid's fury was spent through the black pinholes of her red-rimmed eyes. PJ looked ten years older and the tremor in his fingers sloshed coffee over his boots. Now it was time for Tomás to rock Hamilton's world again but he could hardly rock himself up off the camp bed. I told him to take it easy, I would work on Hamilton until he was ready.

'Still here, Maknazpy?' Hamilton said. 'I thought you had more sense. You should have hooked it while you had the chance.'

Hamilton was fresh and cheerful, like a man looking forward to the day ahead, a man with appetite, ambition, like his destiny was to finish each day better than he had started.

'The only thing going to get *hooked* around here is your neck, Hamilton, that's unless I save you. And you know I won't put myself to any trouble unless you deliver the encryption key.'

'Yeah, I know,' Hamilton chuckled, 'life's full of golden apples for me right now, isn't it? Stay here and toy with the Three Stooges or volunteer to let you gift wrap me for Yakov's Russians? Very magnanimous of you sir! Much obliged!'

He knew I was in contact with Yakov?

'Yakov played you good in Lisbon, didn't he? Maybe he had you drafted in to this? Let you think it was all your own idea, like you're calling the shots? And yet perhaps I do you a grave disfavor, sir, perhaps you really *are* so important they decided you were a necessary prerequisite, a Superman, with your big *ríastrad* and all that.'

Artie! That ríastrad shit could only have come from that slippery bastard McCooey! The smirking contempt in Hamilton's face begged to be smashed and pulped out of existence but there was a panic swelling my gut and rising thick in my throat, the brutal panic when the bubble of self deception fractures and can't smother the shame of being who I am, who I was allowed to be, would ever be. It was all slipping away.

'That Russian girl is here,' I said. 'Brigid agrees with you, something not right about her.'

Hamilton didn't blink, didn't flinch a muscle.

'They have her outside with a hood over her head. Tomás and his boys are going to take her across a field to a manure pit to bury her, don't think they will risk the sound of a gunshot.'

Hamilton posed the blank expression of a man determined not to react – but he *should* have reacted, even just a little, a pulse in the eye, a tightening of the jaw, even an almost imperceptible shrug, but there should have been something.

'Did she say anything?' Hamilton asked.

'Didn't get much of a chance to say anything before Tomás knocked her out cold. Just said her name was Yana, that ring any bells with you?'

'She might know something, might be useful to us,' he said, 'go and stop them, bring her back, she might help us to get out of here.'

'Why? You were right first time,' I said. 'If she's Russian maybe she's working for Yakov and then she will only be trouble. Let Tomás take care of it.'

Hamilton strained to hold my stare but I could see him weakening, knew there was turmoil behind the eyes.

'She's not Russian,' he said, his voice cracked, as if my panic had infected him, as if the shame had jumped from me to him. I sat back, spread my palms out wide, inviting him to continue.

'She's one of ours!' he said, 'Get out there for fuck's sake and stop them! She's one of ours!'

'One of *yours* you mean?' I said, 'you telling me she is a Brit spy?'

He stood up and turned his back to me, bowed his head and linked his fingers like he might start to pray, wedged his elbows against the corner and spat on the floor.

'We're not working for the Brits!' he said. 'We're reporting back to Maryland, that's all you need to know, now get the fuck out there and stop wasting time!'

Maryland and not Virginia? Not Langley?

'Yeah? Well, Hamilton, you might think I'm a worthless piece of shit and you are far too intelligent to need to tell me anything but right now I decide if you live or die, right? I have just dragged your ass from a house where young kids are being drugged, raped, beaten and fuck knows what. Unless you prove different, it looks to me that you were there to satisfy your own perverted desires, and you deserve to be exterminated like the other two rats we left lying on the floor. So we'll try that one again, okay? Who exactly are you working for and why are you here?'

Hamilton's shoulders heaved, he buried his face in his hands, he looked like he was about to cry.

'It's my job,' he said, quietly, like this was his real voice emerging from the years of trained bullshit. 'I hide bugs where nobody will discover them. I wiretap people and places that are supposed to be untouchable. I set up black finance networks to trap terrorists and drug lords. And I catch child abusers on film and break up their networks.'

'You and the woman are both CIA?'

He shook his head. 'I think she probably is. I'm only contracting for the National Security Agency. This is a Special Collection Service job, Maknazpy, joint agency operation. You're wasting time. Get out there and stop them. I'll tell you anything you want to know afterwards.'

Hamilton was docile now, like nothing mattered except to save Yana. That figured, I guessed - he was an old guy, maybe twenty-five or thirty years older than her, but that figured.

Tomás hammered three blows against the door before he came in, Brigid and PJ right behind him.

'We'll take over now,' he said, 'get some rest and we'll keep Paddy the Brit company for another while.'

I pulled Hamilton's head back by the hair so his ear was against my mouth. 'Be ready,' I whispered, 'when I come in we'll be moving fast, so keep alert and pay attention.' I slapped him hard for Tomas' benefit and pushed him back down into the corner.

'He's all yours, Tomás,' I said, 'You enjoy Hamilton's cheery company, Yana's waiting for me in her warm bed.'

Hamilton had snapped into his "*fuck you*" mode when I looked back over my shoulder but he had, as Artie McCooey might say, a face like a slapped arse.

Yana's bed was cold but not as cold as the icy stare she fixed me when I snuggled up tight against her.

'Is that cell phone still in Brigid's bag?'

She nodded, and pointed her chin toward the small stove. I got up and stretched in front of the heater as if I was sucking in as much warmth as would let me sleep. The young guys snored or shivered with their heads buried deep in their sleeping bags. I shifted sideways and hunkered down to the bag and quietly drew the zipper. Toiletries, a change of underwear, new and expensive, a lavender cashmere sweater, an iPad and a pair of sneakers. I patted it down, something in a side pocket, the guy's wallet and an incredibly thin iPhone. Some sort of identity card, Florian Timmermans, Belgique. I slipped the phone into my sock and stood up to stretch and rub my arms in front of the heater. Nobody moved, only Yana following me with her wide awake blue eyes. I headed for the door, going into the barn for a piss, if anyone asked. The door of the container unit squealed like a pig when I pushed it open, still no reaction. Black dark out here, I felt my way over to the vehicles and squatted down before turning on the phone. The screen display was too bright and stupid jingle too shrill, lucky Brigid and PJ were otherwise engaged, and lucky the iPhone didn't need an access code. Googled the Merchant's number, same efficient receptionist, same story, Yakov's nephew, imminent family bereavement. Hurry the fuck up. The polite voice came back - Mr Yakovich not available, would I like to leave a message? No I fucking wouldn't! Yakov was *supposed* to be waiting on my call. 'Thank you,' I mumbled, 'I'll call back in a few minutes.' Only I might not have a few minutes. The door to the unit rasped open.

'You out here?' Tomás barking from the doorway. 'What the fuck are you doing?'

'I'm making a big turd pie! Come on over and wipe my ass!'

He didn't answer and stalled for a minute before I heard the door close. How long before he roused his boys to check me out? Yakov *should* have taken that call, he knew this was the night and his Russian muscle team were up from Dublin ready to handle Hamilton once I had double-crossed Artie and Brigid. It was wrong. I tried to force myself calm and work through this logically but it was twisting away from me. Had Yakov heard about Yana and the CIA? Maybe, but that wouldn't have spooked him, not when millions of dollars and savage revenge were a phone call away. Unless he had been tipped off that this was all a set-up. Unless the trap had already sprung and Inspector McIntyre had hauled his ass out of his luxury sheets and into an interrogation centre. He *should* have taken that call. Now all bets were off.

I tapped the number, couple of seconds before it started to ring. Almost 6.30 now, the card game could still be in smoky progress. Six rings, seven, hurry up for fuck's sake!

'Yes?! What is it at this time of the morning?!'

'Monsignor Artie McCooey, please.'

'Nobody of that name here! Goodbye!'

'Quinn!! You yellow-skinned shit!!' Kept my voice low but he still felt the menace. 'Get McCooey right now or I'll ram that phone up your ass when I get back there!'

He hesitated, the phone rattled down on the scuffed mahogany desk, and leather soles echoed in the dark corridor. The iPhone displayed 06.27, then a long time until 6.28, still no sound from the other end. Was Tomás still over there? Fuck's sake, Artie, 6.29! How long does it take to get out of bed?!

'Hello? Good morning, Monsignor Arthur McCooey here. May I be of assistance?'

'Yes, Artie, you fucking can! Get a vehicle, get a safe house ready and get your ass out here now!'

'Excuse me? I am very sorry but I have no idea what you are referring to. Who is this? Where are you calling from?'

'You know where, Artie, don't dick around! Or else ask McIntyre or Wee Joe or whoever else you play your games with! Just get out to the airport right now and wait until I contact you! Text your cell phone number to this number and wait. Make sure you are there in twenty minutes, hear me?'

'I really don't ...'

I cut Artie off. Maybe he was on the line to McIntyre right now, or McIntyre's people and everybody else's people were already listening in. Nothing I could do about any of that. I was on my own but I was getting out of this shit. Just me and the encryption key, that was the silver bullet, and that meant just me and Hamilton.

CHAPTER THIRTEEN

Tomás didn't see me come back in, wasn't seeing anything right then except for Yana cruelly teasing with all the delicious danger her long body promised. I gave her the nod. Brigid was in full flow as I pulled the door to the cell. Hamilton's curled lip had earned another bloody nose. PJ started to usher me out...

BOOM!!

Brigid and PJ froze, open-mouthed and stunned like rabbits in headlights. Hamilton was already pushing through, I grabbed his collar and hauled him to the door. Tomás and the muscle were at the outer door, in that twilight vacuum between fight or flight.

'Get out there and put that fire out!!' I screamed.

The van had gone up like I expected but maybe I had poured too much fuel over the floor. My fire roared right along the back wall of the barn and then another **BOOM!!** – plastic barrels I hadn't seen but the wrong place for volatile chemicals, a blue flamed tornado curled and twisted up through the roof to breach the early morning sky.

Yana heaved with me, shoulder to shoulder, Hamilton crouched behind, we tunnelled our way through them. The second van was safe where I had pushed it but the fire was spreading quickly. One of the guys had better reactions than the rest and ran to cut us off. I pushed Yana and Hamilton aside, punched as I ran, no time, just steamroll over him – but he wasn't there, dodged me, like it was slow motion, he clipped me with a lucky right hook that must have caught me off balance and put me down. I bounced up straight away, no mistake this time, I shouldered into a straight right – but he landed a right left right before I could fire. I was on my back, could lift my head but the rest of my body wasn't there, could feel the heat of the fire on my cheek but couldn't move. He angled above me, seemed like he was far away at the wrong end of a long thin telescope. Yana cracked him with a lump of scaffolding iron. He folded over on top of me, she dragged him off and yanked my weight over her narrow shoulders. Hamilton pulled me into the van and Yana jumped in to hit the gas. The barn door buckled but didn't break, Yana reversed back into the fire, then jolted forward with Tomás hanging off the hood. The barn door split and Tomás bounced off into the yard. She nearly lost the van, tyres skidding over the frosty grass lane, then we hit the tarmac and she floored it.

'Which way?! Where we go from here?!'

'Doesn't matter!' I shouted from the back. 'Just get away from here!'

I puked in the corner of the van, the gyroscope that was my brain rocked around my skull.

'Was *that* your famous battle rage?' she laughed. 'That green kid took you down like you were a tired old man!'

'You hit him pretty hard with that length of iron back there,' I said. 'You maybe killed him.'

'Nah, I hope not,' she breezed, 'he was a sweet kid, the one who loaned me this warm sweater.'

The sun ebbed a drab slice of gray over the distant hills. The further we ran from the barn the higher and fiercer the flames streaked into the sky. PJ's top secret hideaway was screaming its GPS co-ordinates across every security screen in the country.

'You know how to get to the International Airport from here, Hamilton?' I said.

'I do,' he said, 'but that wouldn't be such a bright idea. One approach road, one way in, one way out. I don't know about you two but I'm not terribly confident that the local guardians of law and order are all that well disposed toward me, not just at the present.'

'Better ideas?' I said.

'A small village near here, just enough early morning traffic that we won't be the only vehicle on the road.'

'Sorry boys,' Yana said, 'but we aren't going anywhere except back to last night's orgy house. We have a package to collect, Mr Hamilton, don't you agree?'

'What package?' I said.

'Mr Hamilton here left his calling card in that shit hole,' she said. 'Why do you think we were there? Think we were just along for the ride?'

To the murder scene? The left half of my face was numb but maybe Yana had been hit hard on the head also.

'It's important, Maknazpy,' she said. 'American lives will be at risk if we walk away.'

American lives were always at risk according to these people and that was mostly because these people needed an excuse to feed their power. None of those fat white rich people last night looked like they would be much of a risk to America – no more than our own fat white rich people.

'They won't find it,' Hamilton said. 'It's turned off, no signal, invisible to any scanner. We can retrieve it later, when the situation is less fraught. They *won't* find it.'

'No! We go now!' Yana was in control. 'They'll find it if they look long enough, if we give them the opportunity. How do we get there?'

I slid along the back of the van, the numbness was slowly being replaced by a throbbing pain.

'Forget the house,' I said, 'we're going to Hamilton's village right now.'

Yana was a real pro. She glanced back at me in the rear view mirror but didn't react otherwise. She knew it was a Glock pressed beneath her ear.

'That sweet kid,' I said, 'you got his warm sweater, I got his firearm.'

Hamilton's village was big enough to have its own Fire Department, their blue lights charging down the street giving us cover as we slipped into the quiet spot Hamilton had promised. It was a municipal recreational area, a path leading up into the forest above to the right, a quick flowing river ahead and to the left, and a small toilet block and spaces for maybe twenty vehicles. A silver SUV sat close to the path. A dog walker, Hamilton suggested. Yana rolled as far under the bare trees as she could.

'Unless this thing can drive on water I'd say this is the perfect area to set a trap,' Yana said. 'One vehicle is enough to block our exit, a river that doesn't invite swimming and a pretty dense forest above. This is about the last place I would select to hide out.'

'We won't be here long,' Hamilton said, 'isn't that right, Maknazpy? We can expect your Russian boss soon?'

I shouldered Yana aside and pulled the keys from the ignition.

'Your family aren't *in* Russia,' Yana said. 'You really going to fuck with their good life on Long Island? And there will be no way back to your girlfriend in Rio. Sure she will follow you to Siberia or wherever the fuck you end up?'

I wedged Yana tight against the door and stretched to twist her shoe off, collapsed the heel and slipped the blade out. I tossed the shoe between her legs and licked a wet kiss across her cheek. She lunged to stab my eyes when I released her but I parried her fingers and was out the side door before she could get at me. I tapped Hamilton's window and motioned him to follow me.

'Where is this place?' I asked. 'Would Artie McCooey know how to get here?'

'McCooey? Are you serious? You're still in contact with that slippery shitbag McCooey?'

'You prefer Yakov?' I said.

'Is that supposed to be a choice? You aren't going to say my well-being depends on Artie fucking lying bastard McCooey, are you?'

'Yakov has a team in place in Belfast right now to go to work on you,' I said. 'Your call.'

Hamilton even thought about it, self-preservation in conflict with his pride, like being obliged to McCooey would induce some sort of fatal allergenic shock.

'Tell McCooey it's the mosque in the forest,' Hamilton said, 'McIntyre and his listening crew won't know where it is, most of them these days hardly know where Belfast is.'

'There is a mosque in this place? Sure Artie knows where?'

'It was that papish perjurer that told *me* about it,' he said. He saw the question in my eyes. 'I used to meet McCooey in all sorts of secret places in the old days, and I didn't trust the lying bastard then either!'

The dog shit and squashed beer cans dotted along the track were a sure marker that we couldn't expect to be on our own. A casual dog walker would take no notice of me or Hamilton, but Yana's long black-stockinged legs in heels and short dress would lodge in anyone's mind anytime, and especially anyone on an early morning winter's walk on this rough forest track. Hamilton led the way, I kept Yana close between us, stepped back when she slipped and reached her hand out for support – too dangerous, too smart. The track was steep at first, punching out short sharp clouds of frosted breath, the roar of the swollen river somehow even louder in my ears up here, then the path evened out and followed a ridge, further into the forest. Yana kept her head up, taut, alert, primed for danger from the dark trees.

The cell phone jumped in my pocket. I tugged Yana's shoulder and edged her against a tree. My numb fingers were slow and clumsy on the tooled iPhone.

'Well?' Hamilton said. 'Is his Lordship riding to our rescue?'

'He's out at the airport. How long will it take him to get here?'

'Fifteen, twenty minutes for ordinary people,' Hamilton said. 'In Super McCooey's mind that would equate to about five minutes for him.'

I tapped the message, mosque in the forest, then stalled without sending. Artie McCooey was the worst kind of liar, the sort that thinks his lies are actually a higher form of the truth, that his manipulations are preserving the greater truth that mere mortals can't see, can't hope to understand. I hit the send button.

'I hope you know what you're doing,' Hamilton said. 'You wouldn't be the first to rely on McCooey only to be found in a ditch with a hole in your head.'

'Yeah,' I said, 'like if I rely on you and Yana to call in your people then all my problems will be over, right?'

Hamilton shrugged, didn't waste his breath trying to convince me otherwise. Yana pushed off from the tree and marched off in front.

'That kid caught you good, Maknazpy!' she snapped over her shoulder. 'Your face is swelling up like a pumpkin. I wouldn't have smacked him so hard if I had known he had done such a good number on you!'

He *had* done a number on me, a real good number. I cupped one side of my face then the other, my left jaw felt like I had had a coconut surgically inserted. I caught up with her, dropped a couple of steps back, but close enough to see the smirk on her face. I waved Hamilton in front, saw the grin on his face also.

'Let's hope I don't have to do a number on the two of you before this is finished,' I said.

I checked the Glock in my waistband. I knew it *was* there and didn't need to check, it was a reflex, a kind of reassurance, it was there and I would use it if I had to.

'That's it,' Hamilton said. 'Here is your mosque.'

The mosque was some sort of viewing point, lodged into a tight turn in the path where it started to descend back to the river. A fun architectural feature, a crazy little gray stone hut in the woods, like a tower from a castle copied here in small scale, somebody's idea of a joke. The bare stone walls and ceiling trapped the moisture rising from the river below. The rough floor was littered with dumped beer and cider cans, packaging from strong pain-killers and plastic water bottles, and smelled like it was sprayed daily with stale beer and rancid piss.

I smashed a boulder down on the phone, hammered and banged until it splintered, ripped out the battery and launched it high and spinning, watched it plunge into the white water. I hammered the body of the phone some more, then flung it into the river.

'You say this is a mosque, Hamilton?'

'According to the story Monsignor Artie McCooey told me, yes, it is a mosque.'

Hamilton's grin was irritating me now, big time.

'McCooey says there was a man of the Islamic faith brought over here by the big landlord who owned this whole area. Some sort of servant. McCooey said he was an Indian, but that's probably just McCooey's cultivated ugly ignorance. Anyway, he was a Muslim man, found himself here in this Christian backwater with nowhere to say his prayers. They say the landlord built this place for him, he worked out which direction Mecca was and that was him as happy as a piper. Could pray away to his heart's content.'

'Don't folks around here get a little red neck when it comes to religion?' Yana said. 'What did the Christian God fearing Irish think about it?'

'They didn't think anything about it,' Hamilton said, 'they thought the man was up here saying his prayers. If the landlord said it was okay, it was okay. Interfered with nobody up here, and nobody interfered with him.'

'So, these folks aren't really wrapped up in 17th Century religious wars after all, right?' Yana teased. 'What about all these racist attacks I see reported in Belfast then?'

Hamilton and Yana yakked on about tolerance and weakness, generosity and insecurity, patriotism and xenophobia. Artie should be here by now, I sent that text fifteen minutes ago.

'I don't know about...'

A dog barked. We froze, it was close by, a big dog and getting closer. I drew the pistol and craned my head around the doorway. The river was louder out here, and the trees and wall above and around the hut meant a snatch squad could be right on top of us with no warning. The German Shepherd bounced around the corkscrew turn in the path and was almost on me before I jerked the gun up. The dog brushed past me, still barking, hurtling down the path toward the river. The old lady appeared out of nowhere on the path above me. I think I wrestled the gun under my sweater before she saw it but the look on her face said she knew I was up to no good.

'The dog scared me,' I said, trying my best with their accent.

'He'll not touch you,' she said, 'as long as you are behaving yourself.'

She marched on past me, hesitating just to take a quick look back before she disappeared around the corner below. She made me, no doubt about it, any search party around here would get precise directions. I backed into the hut, still watching the path below.

'Fuck you Maknazpy!!' Yana went for it. Smacked me hard right on the swollen jaw, bundled past me and bolted back up the path.

The pain punched right down to my knees but it was like it was somebody else's pain, like the pain was on the inside and I was on the outside. I gripped the rough stone doorway, steadied, staggered, on the cusp of the black implosion – McCooey's Ríastrad, the brain quack's amygdala freak show. Not this time, I had come too far to fall now. A man, not an animal. 'Don't fucking move, Hamilton! Without me you're a dead man!' Hamilton saw it in me, no wise cracking grin, submitted to the primeval juice sparking my every sinew, he hunkered down with his hands up in surrender.

Yana should have been ahead on the path when I made the corner but the dark corridor ahead was empty. I slowed down. I tasted her body and breath on my tongue, could smell her hate, the real presence of her violence. She was close in these black trees, pumped high with the kill lust, ready with rock or club or her bare teeth and hands. Then a crack and ripple through the tangle of undergrowth below. I dived into the trees, fought through the jungle, stumbled over the rough ground. She could hear me on her heels, no way she would make the car, kept going in desperation. She was right ahead and I was going to take her. THUMP!! The branch broke across my back, keeled me to my knees, bounced straight up, punched her hard, buried my fist below her ribcage, momentum carried her forward, my knee rocked her head nearly off her shoulders. She lay sprawled at my feet among the black roots and green sludge moss. I stood over her, the animal urge probing for my weak spot, a chance to infiltrate its old supremacy.

'What the fuck are you doing down there!?'

The voice from above, the black figure pushing through the trees.

'Con Maknazpy!!' It was Artie's voice. 'What the fuck are you doing with that girl!?' It was Artie's dark shape. He barged and waded his way through the bushes, stood between me and Yana.

'How'd you know I was down here?'

'How did I know?' His bloodshot eyes burned into me. 'I could fucking hear you screaming from down in the car park! Screaming like the wild man of Borneo! Howling like a fucking mad dog!!'

What screaming? He jutted his whiskey and cologne head into my face. I was screaming? I sucked the cold air, deeply, slowly. The forest was silent except for my breathing and the German Shepherd barking in the distance.

'She's with Hamilton,' I said, as if that explained everyting. 'She's CIA.'

'Is she dead?' Artie knelt beside her like he was about to start his prayers. He fingered her neck, found a pulse. 'Thank Christ! Help me with her, you fucking head case!'

Artie wrapped his arms around Yana's waist and hauled her off the ground, her clothes gathered under Artie's hand, exposing her back. He saw it, froze, then looked at me. Even in the biting cold of this dank forest Yana's skin shimmered with a golden sheen of vitality and health. Golden, except for the ragged red scars gouged along her lower back, fanning out from the epicenter below her ribs and disappearing under her skirt. This woman had taken a big hit sometime in the past. Maybe hit by somebody like me, maybe hit by the same people I had fought because "American lives were in danger". I pulled her sweater down and took her off Artie. I cradled her weight with respect, like the coffins I had shouldered in another life, because fallen comrades and shared loss were never far from people like me and Yana, and that shared blood bond meant I owed her.

Artie scurried along behind me, out of breath and blowing hard. He was shouting something but I couldn't hear him, wasn't slowing down to listen. The roar from the white water below funnelled up here to be amplified off the rock face framing the path. An invisible chopper was in the air, its staccato merged with the river backbeat. That German Shepherd was going nuts somewhere. Artie caught up and tugged my shoulder.

'Where's Paddy the Brit?' he shouted in my ear.

The sharp turn down to the mosque hut was right ahead. 'He's in here,' I said, turning sideways to carry Yana in the doorway.

But he wasn't. The hut was empty, Hamilton gone. Artie puffed out his cheeks, his marker of disapproval and disappointment. I had failed him again.

The chopper was over the car lot, hanging close to the trees.

'Well done, Artie,' I said, 'you were followed. Where does this path lead to?'

'Keeps going along the river, then a bridge and an exit to the road on the other side of the town. What about this girl? What are you going to do about her? What happens now?'

I laid Yana down gently, propped her head up with my jacket, wrapped my sweater around her legs, draped Artie's heavy coat over her. She was breathing easily now, softly, as if she was asleep. Artie's cell phone was back in his car.

'If Hamilton wants to be seen by that chopper we're fucked, the war's over,' I said, 'but something tells me your Paddy the Brit doesn't exactly trust his own people. He won't get far on his own, not far enough to escape me.'

The path tumbled down to the river's edge. Artie slipped on the frosted moss and I left him planted on his fat ass. The path ahead opened up along the river bank. The old lady came into view first, standing on a big stone with her cell phone pressed to her ear. Then the dog, holding Hamilton's right forearm in its jaws, the heavy shoulders and flanks pinning Paddy the Brit to the black river earth, his screams drowned by the river's thunder and the dog's deep throated growl. I dodged back behind a tree and waited for Artie, shoved him ahead to display his priest collar and calm the old woman. She was shouting something. Artie moved forward with authority, knew he could take her deference for granted. I slipped along behind him.

'I can't get a signal on this silly phone down here!' she cried. 'We need the police, Reverend. There was a terrible howling going on and then this scoundrel came running up behind me! Thank the Lord my Kaiser was here to protect me!'

Artie pressed his hands together in a prayerful pose and touched his fingertips to his lips. She waited for him to take control. Artie angled around to keep the old lady between himself and the frothing Kaiser. I kept Artie between me and her.

'He's a wicked terrorist!' she said, 'no doubt about it! I saw him up at the wee Cockle House and he had a gun! We need the police straight away!'

She still didn't notice me or, if she did, the fleeting imprint of a terrorist assassin had been transferred from me to Hamilton.

'The police sent me here to get him,' Artie said. 'You can relax now, everything is in order. The police inspector is waiting outside with his men. The arrangement is that he surrenders his weapon to me and I hand him into police custody. Nobody gets hurt and the police have their man.'

The old lady looked at Artie with wary suspicion. She was unconvinced but *wanted* to be convinced, wanted to take Kaiser and get the hell out of there. She looked at me then, studied me up and down as if she had seen me before somewhere but couldn't quite put her finger on where and when.

'This man with me here is a social worker from the Prison Service,' Artie said. 'He was taking the felon to his anger therapy when the prisoner escaped.'

'Hmmph! Social workers!' The old lady loaded all her disgust on to me. 'Taking this parasitic wretch to some holiday camp my taxes are paying for, I'm sure. It's a good riser up the arse these boys need, never mind a useless social worker!'

Artie empathized, his world weary eyes in communion with her outrage.

'Well, there you are,' he said, 'it's an appalling vista when a respectable lady like yourself has to countenance these sinners in broad daylight.'

She was warming to Artie now, a fellow bulwark against the encroaching tide of low manners and high crime.

'You can call off Kaiser now.' Smooth Artie. 'Once you are safely in your car and on your way, the police will come out from their hiding places and seal the place off.'

The chopper buzzed further along the river. She looked up at the sky and then down at Kaiser. Hamilton looked pathetically helpless, squirming beneath the dog's jaws. She barked a sharp order to Kaiser, the hound hesitated, she hissed, he released Hamilton, pissed quickly on a rock, and nuzzled against her thigh, waiting for her praise. Artie ushered her off, assured her the situation was under control and the guttersnipes would be kept in place, at least for now.

'Appalling vista! Very good, Artie, very good!' Hamilton rubbed his right wrist but didn't try to get up. 'Good job you're such an exquisitely sublime liar, that fucking mutt nearly had my arm off!'

I hopped forward, stamped my foot on Hamilton's arm and jammed the pistol into the back of his neck. Hamilton screamed, I shoved his face into the ground.

'Nice try, Hamilton!' I said. 'Now we'll go get that fucking encryption key and you'll transfer the funds!'

Hamilton didn't struggle, lay face down with my knee on his neck.

'I wondered what it would be like, Paddy, seeing your ugly face again,' Artie smirked. 'Paddy the Brit and scourge of the dispossessed! Listen Con, maybe we should just tie a rock around this dirty bastard's neck and dump him in that river! Fuck the money!'

The chopper would see us soon. The old lady would have a signal on her cell phone as soon as she got out of the trees. I pulled Hamilton up by his collar, kicked him on the ankle as he staggered, and shoved him forward.

'We'll leave your car back there, Artie,' I said. 'Take our chances this way. Get out the other exit and boost a ride.'

Artie shrugged, gestured me to lead the way. Hamilton trudged along in front, head down, in no particular hurry, like we were on a therapeutic recreational stroll. Artie followed, hands in pockets, his tuneless whistle lost below the river blast. Their forced nonchalance didn't fool me. The tension generated its own force field, crashing between them like the raging river against the rock face. The chopper was almost teasing us now, just behind the naked trees, as if the pilot was hiding from us, as if he thought he didn't exist if we didn't see him. The bridge to the other exit appeared ahead. I nodded to hunker down behind the thick shrubs.

'We'll wait here,' I said. We would be across the bridge and under cover on the other side in about two minutes, but better to stall here until the chopper buzzed off.

'Wonder who tasked that whirlybird, Artie?' Hamilton said. 'Not your police chum McIntyre, anyway, that's not his style, too much attention, too much light for the Dark Side, eh?'

Artie levered himself up with one hand on my shoulder and popped Hamilton straight in the mouth with the other. It was a good shot, surprisingly good, and I saw Artie in a different light, maybe what he was like in his prime. Hamilton took the shot and slumped back against the earth. He wiped his mouth, cranked a forced grin.

'Artie doesn't like that, Mr Maknazpy, you see?' Hamilton sneered. 'Likes to be seen as the defender of the oppressed, righter of wrongs and champion of the poor. Doesn't like it when the stone is lifted and his dirty friends on the Dark Side crawl into the light.'

'How many innocent people *did* you set up for the triggermen, Hamilton?' Artie said. 'How many Loyalist death squads did you direct?'

Hamilton belched a snorted laugh.

'You've heard of the Dark Side, haven't you, Mr Maknazpy?' Hamilton said. 'The tragic rump of the Securocrats still fighting their war against the IRA because that's the only way to hide their dirty past. Artie here, of course, has joint enterprise with them, he can't afford to have *his* dirty past exposed either.'

Artie started to move but I figured smacking Hamilton was my job so I eased the punching priest back down beside me.

'Have a look up there,' Hamilton said. 'That doesn't look like a military or police chopper to me.'

I bent forward, couldn't see get a glimpse of the helicopter.

'Who could put a private chopper in the air?' Hamilton said. 'Not Brigid and PJ, that's for sure, not unless their Provo pensions are performing miracles. But Yakov? I'd say a day's helicopter hire wouldn't break his bank!'

'It's a Brit helicopter!'Artie said.

'Of course, *Monsignor*,' said Hamilton. 'The Brits are always to blame and you're always the victim.' He pronounced the *Monsignor* with an exaggerated reverence.

The chopper drifted into view, hanging like a hawk right about where the stone hut was. The tail floated slowly around toward us. The crew were facing the opposite direction, toward the parking lot. I pulled Hamilton up by the collar and pushed him ahead. Artie half-jogged behind me. Hamilton paused at the mouth of the bridge. I thumped him between the shoulder blades, he jolted forward. The helicopter still buzzed over the stone hut. Maybe the foot soldiers had found Yana in there, or maybe the old lady had roused the cavalry. I made Hamilton and Artie walk, no running, no panic. The ground on the other side fanned up into a steep hill with plenty of tree cover. Artie scrambled up like a dog, on hands and knees. Hamilton angled his head so he could keep an eye on me, ready to run if I gave him the chance.

The early morning sun was waiting on us when we emerged from the dark tree ravine. The path skirted behind some houses and ended at a security gate. A guy had just arrived and was unlocking the gate from the other side. He swung it open as we approached, nodded, and stood aside to let us past.

'Our car is waiting,' Artie said.

It was an old Merc, chugging blue diesel fumes into the crisp morning air, two wheels on the sidewalk, nose fronted to the street ahead. Only the driver, as far as I could see.

'What a priest!' Hamilton said. 'He even brings his own getaway car!'

I held back until I made sure there was only the driver, then rammed Hamilton into the back seat and piled in beside him. The thick cigarette smoke choked a reflex cough from me. The oily black head in the driver's seat didn't move, didn't look in the mirror. Artie clambered in the front passenger seat, twisted to throw me the wink.

'Father Quinn very kindly offered to give us a lift, God be good to him!'

Yellow faced Quinn dragged a couple of heavy puffs on his cigarette before flicking it out of the window.

Artie held his hand up. 'Ah, ah, Father Quinn! Keep Ireland tidy!' He hopped out and skipped around to scoop up the glowing cigarette end, then plopped back into his seat, dowsed the cigarette into the overflowing ashtray between him and Quinn.

'Christ! He even tidies up the forensics!' Hamilton laughed. 'What a priest! What a joke!'

CHAPTER FOURTEEN

Quinn peered ahead with the jerky concentration of a man who had learned to drive in the 1950's and hadn't been behind the wheel since, his yellow face screwed up like somebody had smeared a moustache of sour shit under his hairy yellow nose. We were headed back to Belfast. Away from the small town, down a narrow country lane, meeting locals on the way to work or the school run. Artie pulled a plastic bag from beneath his feet and tossed it into my lap.

'Put this gear on, boys,' Artie said, 'never know when you'll need it.'

I emptied the contents, a couple of priest shirts, complete with regulation dog collars. Hamilton laughed and slapped his thigh.

'Expecting police roadblocks, Artie?' I said.

Artie shrugged, but Hamilton answered for him, 'Don't worry about last night's little mishap. Nobody here will ever hear about those gentlemen. I expect you'll see a brief paragraph in the papers in Germany and Holland in a couple of days, tragic loss of noble philanthropists and captains of industry. An automobile accident, or boating tragedy, maybe a skiing force majeure on the Lauberhorn. Not death by gunshot, anyway. They were never here, you see.'

Quinn strained to keep the car between the hedges and make sense of Paddy the Brit's words at the same time. If ears could squint, that's what Quinn's were doing.

'That would need some high end protection,' I said. 'You saying you're the good guy, in there to nail them with your secret recording?'

Hamilton pouted that stupid grin again.

'No need to call me a hero,' he said. 'Just doing my job. But you should ask yourself why all your friends are so desperate to protect those devils you saw last night. You should ask Artie there, or McIntyre. And Yakov, especially ask Yakov why he needs to get in on that action.'

Quinn gripped the wheel even more tightly now, approaching the big roundabout, spinning with traffic in a hurry to reach the airport. The third exit signposted Belfast. Quinn hesitated, then decided he was trapped in that lane and couldn't pull out now. Two gray Land Rovers perched at the lip of the exit. A young male officer waved the traffic herd on, staring out the drivers, culling the vulnerable. The older female was less demonstrative, thumbs tucked into the shoulder straps of her Kevlar vest, seeing everything without looking. The rookie raised his hand in front of Quinn, motioned for him to pull over. I slipped the Glock beneath Artie's plastic bag, made sure Hamilton knew it was aimed at him. The female officer slapped the young guy's arm down, stepped in front of him and waved Quinn on, according us all the deferential respect the priest uniforms deserved.

'We need somewhere quiet, Artie,' I said, 'somewhere Brigid's crew don't know about.'

Artie screwed his lips into a silent caution and jerked his eyes at Quinn.

'Don't worry about Mr Quinn, here,' I said. 'If he opens his ignorant mouth to anybody I'll see to it personally that he goes through his own very painful Calvary before he goes to hell.'

Quinn sank a little lower in his seat, his foot a little heavier on the gas. Artie nudged Quinn's elbow and mumbled something under his breath. Quinn touched the brake, started to signal turning right, slowed again, looking for the turn. Artie pointed ahead, Quinn slowed, the traffic behind became impatient. The road eventually arrived, Quinn fumbled the wheel though his fingers, clipped the grass verge as he made the turn. Hamilton sniggered. About a mile down this narrow road, Artie declared this was it. A run down concrete block with no windows that looked like it had been empty for fifty years. The car slipped back as Quinn tried to hold it steady on the slope, Artie's door caught him on the shoulder.

'Sorry about that, Monsignor!' Quinn called out as he jolted away. The three of us watched Quinn disappear back the way we came.

'Bastard did that on purpose!' Artie said.

We were on one of the country lanes etched into the hills curving around west Belfast. On the other side, urban streets tightly packed with lives supervised by history and security cameras. On this side, a rural oasis of green fields, stone walls, ancient trees and pure mountain streams. As if the intensity of their passions could only be stirred and purged and then capped in the crucible on the other side, leaving this quaint scene innocent and cleansed.

'You remember this place, Paddy?' Artie said. 'I was dragged up here one night to administer the Sacrament to that young fella, the one your death squad dumped in this ditch. You remember, surely? He used to be an altar boy, served the Mass for a couple of other funerals you bought, isn't that right?'

Hamilton stamped his feet and rubbed his hands under his armpits. 'Cold, isn't it?' Ignored Artie's venom. 'We'll need *two* quiet places, and this isn't fucking one of them. Quiet and secure, a decent fiber-optic connection, and not too close together. And Brigid's people will be no problem. It's Yakov and McIntyre we need to worry about. Isn't *that* right, Artie?'

Artie turned his back on Hamilton and braced his weight against the wall to shift carefully over the icy surface. A rusty gate into a lane beside the concrete block was open. A slime green corrugated roof jutted out. An old Audi Quattro waited. Artie creaked as he stooped to pat the ground behind the front driver-side wheel, then hauled himself up with the keys in his fist.

'Quinn will crack,' Hamilton said, 'they'll have this car tagged as soon as we hit civilization.'

'Quinn *won't* talk,' Artie said. 'The two-faced bastard would dearly love to sink me but that's under control. Don't worry about Quinn. Anyway, he doesn't know this car was made available for my use.'

That figured, fitted exactly into my idea of how Artie operated, things and people were always controlled and always made available for his use, and he sure knew how to use them. He crunched the gears on the Audi, pumped it along a deserted track road, made a truck brake hard as he swung it back on to a main road. The truck driver gave the universal gesture, and then we were just another link in the chain of ordinary commuters, being sucked down the mountainside to the waiting work stations below.

The mountains thirty-odd miles to the south were blue and sharp in the morning light. A thin silver haze crested the sea horizon to the north and east. The flatlands in between prepared to take another mundane day for granted. Somehow, mundane and ordinary didn't work for me anymore. Now Artie and Hamilton were my natural fellow-travellers. The sea in the distance sparked an image of Yasmin on the beach, and I knew the blackness in my soul meant I couldn't go back. Artie and Hamilton were my real kin. Yasmin deserved better.

Artie pulled in to the yard behind a bar. A no-frills three storey red brick. The back door was open, a guy throwing buckets of water over the sick on the doorstep saw us coming and retreated, left the door open. Artie led the way up the stairs. Last night's beer hung in the air like a salute to the good times badly remembered. The first floor was another bar, up again led to a corridor piled with tables and chairs and cardboard boxes. Artie pushed a door open, then stalled – two young women changing into their work clothes, one with her skirt around her ankles and the other unbuttoning her blouse. She glanced at Artie and kept the buttons popping.

'Sorry, dear!' Artie coughed. 'Wrong room, please excuse us.'

He slammed the door closed but the handle was broken and it bounced open again. One of the girls shouted something, I guess it was a smutty one-liner, and they both cracked-up laughing at us.

'Shit! More Russians! Just what we need right now!' I said.

'They're Polish,' Hamilton said. 'And who says that's the wrong room? From where I'm standing a room never looked righter.'

Artie was flustered. He tried the next door, a gray-haired guy hunched over a cluttered desk, dwarfed by boxes and crates of spirits, hammering away at a keyboard. I nudged Artie toward the door at the end of the corridor. It opened to a store room, with a ladder reaching to a square gap in the ceiling. Artie went first, struggled to get through the gap. Then Hamilton, I tapped the Glock off his skull to keep him docile.

A dim glow from the naked light bulb. I ducked below the exposed wooden roof joists. A pigeon took fright and flurried above my head to escape through the missing roof tiles. The bare floorboards were strafed with droppings, mostly birds. Black plastic bags jammed with old paperwork piled up against one end wall, a couple of mattresses lay against the other.

'You must be fucking joking!' Hamilton laughed.

'What else do you expect at such short notice!' Artie fumed. 'It'll have to do until I get the chance to talk to some people.'

'Well I'm fucking not staying here,' Hamilton said. 'I'd rather be back getting punched by Tomás!'

Something scurried across the floor behind the plastic bags.

'Alright! Alright! I'll go now and make alternative arrangements!'

'Will you fuck!' Hamilton turned to me. 'You let him walk out of here and the two of us will be carried out in body bags!'

'Don't listen to this Brit liar, Con,' Artie said. 'It's safer if you lie low here. I'll make arrangements and be back as soon as I can.'

I nodded to Artie to get out and get to work, held the ladder steady for him as he backed down through the gap. Hamilton couldn't believe I was so naive. 'If you knew half the things that treacherous self-serving bastard has done you wouldn't trust him to go to the shop for a pint of milk!'

I didn't trust him. I didn't trust Hamilton either and, full house, I didn't even trust myself.

'We need to talk,' Hamilton said. 'But not here. You'd be surprised who is listening, even in a flea-pit like this.'

I trained the gun on him as he climbed down.

'You can stop with the macho shit now,' he said. 'We're in this together and neither of us is coming out in one piece without the other. So stop with the slapping and pushing me around, okay?'

I slid down the ladder and pushed him hard against the wall.

'You're a miserable fucker, Maknazpy!'

The law said the dingy bar at the back shouldn't be open so early but lawyers and policemen wouldn't ever be drinking in there. The barman with the sick bucket nodded us to the little side room, through the main bar. A race track from Australia on the satellite TV, a dozen rough faced drinkers hinged to the bar counter, and a better dressed guy at his own table, thumb counting a fistful of notes. The cash guy stared us out, the rest dropped their eyes.

The Polish girl came to take our order.

'Oh! Didn't recognize you there, *mój maly skarbie*, with your clothes on,' Hamilton winked.

The girl bent to wipe last night's scum off the table, the thin cotton of her blouse strained against the heavy breasts.

'I see you got your shirt on, just about.' He stroked her ass as she stretched across the table. 'A pint of your worst Guinness for me, *slodziutki*, and a black coffee and a packet of painkillers for my old uncle here.'

She rewarded him with a fake smile and a flick on the ear.

'Okay, so you know a couple of words in Polish. I'm impressed even if she isn't. Now make your pitch before McCooey gets back to me. I haven't decided what to do with you yet, and Yakov is still an option.'

He put his hand on my wrist and shushed me. When the girl came back with the drinks and two bowls of yesterday's reheated stew, he motioned me to move into the main bar area.

'Never sit where you've been directed to,' he said. 'They are always listening, bclicve me.'

The bookie didn't like it when we took up a table at the far end, behind his back. He called out to the barman and thumbed toward us, 'John Boy! What the fuck?!' John Boy shook his head and put a finger to his lips, the bookie shut up, didn't look around at us again.

'Why are you here, Maknazpy? And I don't mean in a metaphysical sense. Why are you *here?*'

'I don't know, but Yakov keeps getting more attractive the longer I have to listen to your shit.'

'You are here to kill me, that's why,' he said. 'They didn't tell *you* that but that's the game plan. Or, more to the point, you're here to take the fall when *they* kill me. You're here on fake travel documents, I presume. You took over my lodgings in Sandymount Street. You kidnapped me from that party. That helicopter could have had us surrounded in five minutes but they were happy enough to get us on camera. You took me through a police roadblock. When they find me with one in the head, you are the easy answer.'

He fired it out quickly, without a breath, like he had rehearsed it until word perfect.

'And it will be easier still if you don't make it either. The two of us, all neatly packaged and forgotten. Two birds with one stone. End of story.'

'I'm just a curious Yank,' I said, 'stumbled into somebody else's shit, wrong place, wrong time. They have nothing on me.'

'No? They have Inspector Swansea on you! You were there when he was wasted down in Armagh a couple of years ago. I know they know that. I even know on which desk the forensics file is sitting right now, waiting to be lifted and opened. They know Swansea was revenge for the ambush on those McCooey scumbags. You know? The uncles of your good old friend and blood brother, Ferdia McErlane? They can pin Swansea on you, believe me. And now me. I was duty Military Liaison when we hit the McCooey's. Now you're back to finish the job on me.'

I was prepared to churn Hamilton's shit through my head without listening. Just like taking in the false smiles and winks that peppered Artie's lies. But Swansea's blood and brains *had* seeped through my fingers. They knew, in this town nobody ever forgot anything, all the hits, all the blood scores, they kept it all close to their hearts.

'I heard what you did in Portugal,' he said. 'Creamed off a few million dollars and they let you walk? You really think they *ever* let anyone walk?'

My brain started to swell and my skull to shrink. Steel bands coiled around my lungs, a black hole with no way out. That's why I always blocked out even dreaming of a real future, kept Rose and Yasmin and everyone else at a distance.

'Why kill you if you're such a hot shot?' I said.

'Exactly because I *am* such a hot shot! Because they know I have it all stashed away, all their dirty secrets, all the disgusting deals, the corruption, all the holier than thou sharks on the take. I know where the bodies are buried, going way back.'

'But they've always known that,' I said. 'That's always been your job. Why the big deal now?'

Hamilton blew out his cheeks, then sucked in the stale air like it was a sweet Habana corona.

'Because some deals are so dirty that nobody can know about them. Because Brit Security got jumpy when I started to freelance for you Yanks. Because they started to bust my balls. Because I told them to fuck off and give my head peace. Because I have been fighting for my country for over thirty years, when the new desktop warlords were still at their mammy's tit.'

'So, you've got the encryption key?'

Hamilton exploded. 'Yes!! I've got the fucking encryption key!! That's how we're getting out of this shit!!'

The bookie and the drinkers shifted uneasily in their seats. They wanted to hear but knew they shouldn't, wished Hamilton would keep his voice down and save them the worry.

'And what else? Recordings of the killings you planned here, down in Armagh?'

'Fuck off, Maknazpy!' Quietly now. 'Nobody's interested in that shit except for a few looneys like Brigid and PJ that wish the Troubles never ended. Yes, I have it. I even have stuff nobody has heard since the 70's, stuff MI5 and Special Branch thought was wiped years ago. Well, the fuckers *did* wipe it but I got copies they didn't know about.'

'What else then? What's so hot that they need to keep you quiet?'

'Look, there's stuff even *you* don't want to know about, right? Supercop McIntyre might be interested in McCooey's ancient history of Armagh, but fucking Yakov isn't, and neither is he a fucking option for *you*, unless you see your scalded balls in your mouth as a viable option, I'll tell you that for nothing! Now I'm going for a piss. Order me another Guinness, put it on the Monsignor's tab.'

I grabbed his wrist as he started to get up.

'If I tell you, I'd only have to kill you,' Hamilton grinned. 'Just make sure Artie gets me a decent place to do my thing, I'll make the encryption fucker work. And the pint, tell her that last one was stinking. Tell her to whip it up with her big Polish tit this time, I'll be back to lick it off for her.'

Sometimes you have to believe a liar. It doesn't mean they aren't telling lies, just that somewhere in their dirty swill there's a little husk of clean truth, maybe they haven't choked on it yet, haven't spoiled and twisted it, but it is there, even if it is true only for you.

I let him swagger off to the toilet. I would shake the truth about Yakov and McIntyre out of him later, without an audience, but at least now I knew for sure that Paddy the Brit had the encryption key, and for sure there would be no escape window out of that smelly toilet.

CHAPTER FIFTEEN

Artie hit the up market button for our next safe house. A chrome and glass pod spliced into a Victorian gentleman's villa near the university, shielded by its own defensive greenery and the lime trees that flank that exclusive street from top to bottom. A self contained executive apartment for short term business or conference trips, separate entrance, neighbors relaxed about strange faces. The residential property below was vacant. Artie said the owner was in Rome. Perfect for a couple of passing high powered business execs to kick back after a hard day's dodging and dealing. Perfect for a couple of killers.

Artie thought he could drop us off and disappear in his latest 'made available' car but I took the keys and bundled him along in front. Hamilton inspected the laptop and web connection straight away. He wasn't the type of guy to get ecstatic but he said it was okay, he could work with it.

'The house in Sandymount Street will be under surveillance but the encryption key and everything else is there,' Hamilton said. 'We'll have to risk it.'

Artie's beefy face drained to ash gray when I clamped my hand on his neck and told him it was time to get his hands dirty. Sandymount was right across the road and up the hill. Artie coaxed the small Renault along with extra care, like he was afraid any passing police vehicle would somehow sniff out his guilt.

'Maybe we should just drive past so you can see if it is all clear,' Artie said, 'then the two of you can come back later when nobody's about.'

This *was* later, after midnight and enough action in the student area so we weren't the only ones roaming the streets. I told him to drive past smooth and steady and without touching the brakes. It *looked* dead, nobody sitting in any of the parked cars, no sign of any snoopers at the windows. But if they were there that's exactly what it *would* look like. Artie rolled on down Sandymount and around the corner, took the first right to bring us back to the main road. A guy with an armful of fast food lumbered into the car waiting at the end of Sandymount. Artie stalled long enough to take his vacant space. The alleyway along the back of the houses was right there.

'I'll wait here,' Artie said.

'Will you fuck!' snapped Hamilton.

I pulled Artie's door open, held his elbow as if I was helping an elder out of the car, took the keys, and steered him to the alleyway.

The narrow alleyway was dark, no lights and the black bins and discarded debris didn't help. Hamilton found the bin with the house number painted on the front, and motioned for me to climb over the wall. I hesitated, it was like that old riddle of a guy with a fox, a hen and a bag of grain having to cross a river. I always wondered why that guy would even have one fox but now I had two, both more cunning than the average fox and about as merciful as a couple of starving wolves, so leaving them on their own for even a few seconds had its own danger. I went for it quickly, hauled myself up over the wall, hopped down and cranked back the rusty bolt.

They were both still there, watching each other. Three good boots opened the back door without too much noise in an area where neighbors kicking their own doors in wasn't so unusual.

No light inside, the supply must have been disconnected. Hamilton hustled about in the cupboard below the sink and came up with the torch and screwdriver he had planked in there. Artie's natural need to know everything was overtaking his anxiety, he jostled past me to follow Hamilton into the small living room.

'Why didn't you find the key when you were here!' Artie scolded. 'Now we're beholden to Paddy the feckin Brit!'

'And what would you two Luddites have done with it even if James Bond here had found it?' Hamilton sneered.

He was in the cramped cupboard below the stairs now, on hands and knees squeezing into the darkness. I crawled in, barely space for both of us to lie flat, I twisted up on my elbow and took the torch. He tapped the wood panel below what would have been the bottom step of the stairs, nudged my wrist to direct the torch, found the screw on top right, got to work.

There were six screws holding the panel in place, he had four out when the front door burst open and heavy boots came running. Artie stamped the cupboard door closed behind us before they reached the living room, at least two voices, sounded like two more charging straight up the stairs above us. This was a shock and awe squad, screaming in Artie's face, throwing the cheap furniture around. Artie took a couple of hard slaps in silence. They screamed louder, some in English, mostly in Russian. Artie was one tough old priest. They were kicking him now, and laughing about it.

'Hold on,' Hamilton whispered, 'nearly finished here.'

I edged myself back so I could crouch at the cupboard door. The two from upstairs came back down, one went out to the front door and the other joined in the kicking game. It sounded like they had Artie pinned in the corner. I hit the cupboard door and lurched out, Glock first. Three of them had Artie nailed against the fireplace, with their backs to me and too pumped up on their own power. Three big men, very big, in their forties and with ugly shaved square rock heads displaying their criss-crossed scars as trophies. The first one saw me, wasn't fazed, nodded to the others. The three of them looked at me and then each other, started to laugh, nothing humorous, just proving their scorn for my pathetic attempt to intimidate them.

I took a step back and plugged the first one above the knee, right smack in his fat Russian thigh. He went down on one knee and squirmed to grab me, right hand clutching. I let another one go, his hand dissolved, the round hit the floorboards between the other two.

'The next one goes between his eyes,' I said, nice and quietly, no panic, under control.

The other two shrugged, went down on their knees with hands behind their heads, the shot guy lay on his side, convulsed between shock and pain. Hamilton struggled out of the cupboard, holding a plastic bag tight to his chest. Time to go, but there was at least another one out front, maybe more at the back. I corralled the three Russians up against the cupboard door and ordered them inside. They wouldn't budge, so I fired two rapid rounds, hit one in the ankle and the other behind his knee.

Out the back door, me and Hamilton hoisting Artie between us, Hamilton with a death grip on his bag, me half turned, waiting on a shooter to come out behind us. We made the end of the alley, scrambled to the car, shapes outside the house, heard the sirens coming fast. We pushed Artie into the back and took off, down to Stranmillis roundabout and then right up the hill.

'Yeah, Artie,' Hamilton laughed, '"*And unto him that smiteth thee on the one cheek offer also the other*", hope your Fenian ribs aren't too sore back there.'

Artie struggled to breathe, yanked himself up straight and got close to Hamilton's ear. 'Don't worry about me, Hamilton, "*But now you must rid yourselves of all such things as these: anger, rage, malice, slander, and filthy language from your lips!*"' Artie was angry. 'And fuck you too, Hamilton, you two-faced Brit cocksucker!'

CHAPTER SIXTEEN

Hamilton fingered the pile of disks and drives like a miser finding a long lost hoard, pouncing on one he had forgotten and pressing it to his lips, recognizing a better one, nearly sniffing the booty, and getting high.

He was like all the big time operators. Nothing special when he wasn't at his business, just a regular guy when he was busting Artie's balls or trying to hit on a young Polish waitress, but when he got down to it, like this, when he *really* got down to it and was in the zone, then he was something to behold.

Artie lay on a couch, wincing each time his curiosity forced him to turn his head.

'How do we know what all that mumbo-jumbo is?' Artie said. 'Maybe he's selling us out right now.'

Maybe he was, lines of code advancing up the screen, stalling, then launching into hyper-drive before exploding into a snow-storm of squiggles and hieroglyphs, he could be crafting any sort of message he wanted, safe in the knowledge myself and Artie were 100% ignorant and helpless.

'They'll be tracing this,' Hamilton said, 'we'll need to move on, keep one step ahead. By the time they realize what hit them it will be too late.'

'So you've used the encryption key already?' I said.

'Give my head peace, son,' he said. 'I'm hacking into the server that'll let me "*use*" the key.' He tapped the black box wired to the laptop. 'That dark bank is hanging in no man's land because they can't access the funds in it without my code. They have half the code, I have the other half. But I left the back door open the last time I invited myself into their little nest, first I just need to check on any mantraps they think will make them safe.'

Artie coughed up a glob of bloody phlegm. His ribs and back were black and blue. Good chance he had a couple of cracked ribs, I hoped there wasn't a jagged rib-bone about to puncture his lung.

'You have somewhere else fixed up, Artie, right?'

'Feck off!' he wheezed.

'You fucking better have somewhere sorted out, McCooey!' Hamilton said. 'Once I roll this baby the chase will be on. I've laid a false trail of proxies but that will only delay them. We need a new base to finish the job.'

Finish the job? What else was there to do? Didn't that encryption key decrypt some squiggly shit and open the bank vault?

'Patience is a virtue,' Hamilton smirked. 'First of all I have to get to their server hard drives. All drives have firmware, that's what makes them work. I left a nasty little Trojan on their firmware. It's invisible, none of their nerd security will ever know it exists. I'm going in now to activate it. *Then* I'm going to use the encryption key. But that's only the start. When they get the message created by *my* encryption code, they'll respond. Then I'll capture their code and hijack their side.'

'Don't trust him!' Artie's breathing wasn't getting any better. Maybe something inside *was* ruptured. His spine was badly bruised. I knew a guy once who damaged his spinal cord and it started to swell. A couple of hours later his lungs stopped working and he drowned in his own juices.

'The dickheads think their encryption is foolproof,' Hamilton said, 'and it nearly is, to be fair. It works like this. Say I am A and they are B, okay? My A sends a message to their B using our pre-arranged code, this encryption key, right? B gets the message, confirms the code and then he knows I'm a good guy, I'm A. So then B sends a new message to A with a new code, a new key, the one we will actually use to do our business in secret, right? We keep doing that, and B keeps changing the code so that only A and B will understand it, so nobody else can listen in and work it out, it keeps changing, understand?'

I understood it as much as I was ever going to, as much as I needed to.

'But here's what's going to happen,' Hamilton said, 'I'll start it the way they expect, my A sends a coded message to B. When that happens those Russian bastards will shit themselves! They'll think they have me. They know we're in Belfast for starters so they'll think they can track the IP address for this machine easily. It's not as if Yakov has to search the whole of Europe!'

Yakov worried me. I had winged a couple of his heavy squad but he would replace those quickly, bringing as much backup from London as he wanted. Hamilton worried me also. The way things sat now meant I was at his mercy, and he knew it, this was what he had been waiting for, when he called the shots and I was a passenger.

'They'll think they have me beat,' Hamilton said, 'but plenty of people have thought they had me cornered before. That's when I'm most dangerous. Isn't that so, McCooey?'

Strangely enough, I was worried about Artie. He shipped a lot of damage in those few seconds when I was hiding in the cupboard. He could have diverted the attack away from himself and sold me and Hamilton. That's what I would have expected him to do but this time he didn't, he took the punishment and gave me the chance to escape. He called me over and asked me help him to the bathroom. I lifted him off the couch and took his arm. He seemed older now, and weak. I had been roughed up enough times myself to know the psychological bruises take a lot longer to heal than the skin deep ones. Artie looked to me now as if he was a beaten man, ready to capitulate, throw in the towel.

Hamilton waited until I came back, looked over his shoulder to make sure Artie was out of earshot.

'Once they activate their B code and start communicating with my A, our sleepers on their firmware will start to take over their servers. We'll capture their source encryption, send it to good friends of ours in the United States and they will take it apart and reconstruct it, send us the new code, our firmware sleepers will infiltrate the new code on to the Russian servers, and we will control both sides of the communication. We'll be A and B at the same time. They'll be locked out of their own system.'

'Then what?'

'Then we take that dark bank out of suspended animation. Then we transfer the cash. Then we fucking disappear!'

Hamilton had that trick of using "*we*", "*us*" and "*our*" to lure his prey into a brothers-in-arms illusion. Not this time, we shared our enemies but that's where the alliance stopped.

'We split 60:40, five mill, American,' he said, 'we move $2m to any bank account you want, anywhere in the world. You keep me free and alive, no McIntyre, no Yana, no fucking Yakov, you get me out of this shit hole and you're $2m richer. McCooey has all the right contacts but the hoor would hand me over. You use *his* contacts, get me as far as Paris and I'll be good.'

'What about Artie?' I said. 'What about his friend Beikle you suckered in Rome?'

'Beikle? He's as guilty as sin! It was the Vatican tipped us off, for fuck's sake! The new holy regime looked at the books and found that bastard was rinsing dirty money through the Vatican Bank for the Mafia Capitale. Been at it going way back!'

That probably wasn't as unbelievable as it sounded.

'Well? What about Artie?' I repeated.

'McCooey? He's a priest! What the fuck's he need money for?' Hamilton twisted his face to mime disgust. 'You can sub him out of your share if you like, brother, all he can expect from me is a boot in the hole or a nine mill behind his ear!'

'That's $5m taken care of,' I said, 'what about the other $25m?'

Hamilton snorted, made like he had an important sequence of code to inspect, tapped away at the keyboard, finished it off like a piano maestro in a hurry.

'You've been listening too much to McCooey! Another $25m? Yeah, sure, it's in there somewhere. Twenty five million *virtual* dollars, that's true. But that's gone, may as well be paper money thrown in an incinerator. That system is broken, completely and irrevocably. There's just no way to convert that digital shit back into real cash anymore, forget it! The $5m I'm talking about was *already* converted and is sitting pretty and alone in a legit bank in Vienna, a stone's throw from the Sigmund Freud Museum. We'll take control of the dark bank and send instructions to the legit bank.'

Artie called me from the bathroom. His right leg was numb, maybe a trapped nerve. I helped him along the tiled corridor and into one of the two executive bedrooms.

'What's that lying bastard doing out there?' he said.

'He's being a lying bastard,' I said, 'thinks he can palm me off with two mill, tells me there is only five million in total.'

'What? What did you say?'

'You know me, Artie. Sometimes I act stupid and let lying bastards think they're so smart and superior that I'll be no problem. You know that, right?'

'I know, son,' Artie chuckled, 'I know well.' He chuckled even though it ripped a pain across his ribs. 'You're not as stupid as you look. Sure I always knew that.'

I took the other bedroom, left the door wide open to keep Hamilton in my view, stowed the pistol in my waistband, and settled into the designer bed. A triple-bolt deadlock secured the apartment door, and the key was in my pocket. The balcony outside my room opened to a spiral fire escape. Not ideal, but if Yakov's people got that far we would be fucked anyway. Or McIntyre's people. Or Brigid's. Or Yana's...

Glass smashed. I jumped out of bed. Hamilton's screen was still punching out code but he wasn't there. I listened. A woman laughing. A door slammed. She laughed more. I leaned over the balcony, a light in the room below. If our host family had come home early Artie would have to keep them sweet. I went down the spiral staircase like a ghost. A neighbor two doors down burned an outdoor light, everything else was dark and quiet. She laughed again, having a lot of fun, sounded high or drunk. Three more steps and I was at the window.

Hamilton, pink and plump, racked naked on the bed with the young Polish girl astride him. He was grunting some shit, she laughed *at* him, knocked back her drink, tossed the cocktail glass over her shoulder, slapped his fat gut, pinned his hands behind his head and smothered his sweaty face with her prized breasts. She laughed, Hamilton drowned, still grunting like a pink pig.

The gun was cold and heavy in my hand. I could have shot him there and then. I descended carefully, the metal steps glazed with a film of ice. He must have come down here, smashed a window somewhere, bundled her inside and up the stairs. I felt my way around the back, found the iron framed conservatory, the door window broken.

It would have been bad enough if the girl had made her own way over here but if somebody had brought her and was waiting outside that would be a total screw up. So maybe there was more to Hamilton's split with Brit security than he had said, like maybe his behavior had become so erratic and reckless that it had triggered the burn notice. I knew these old guys were prone to go like that in the end, panicked into freefall when all those years of being an Untouchable hit the tipping point and the only promise they have is the nosedive to the finish line and the end of the blank IOU with no repayment date. If I couldn't shoot the prick I was sure going to kick his sorry wrinkled ass when I got back in there, but first I needed to check Cinderella didn't have a handsome coachman waiting out front.

I could see eight parked cars from behind the front gate. No red cigarettes dancing in the darkness, no car radio or a/c setting a control panel aglow. I climbed over the fence to the next garden, moved further down, more cars parked, no sign of life. A set of headlights turned into the street, a taxi, rolled down the hill and stopped a few doors away. A couple got out, left the taxi door open, went into a house, a young girl bounced out and into the waiting taxi. They took off. Half way down the street the brake lights pulsed red, he pulled into a gap to let another car come up the street.

This new car stopped about five doors up, pulled in to the space on the other side of the street. He turned the lights off, and waited. Five full minutes before the driver door opened and a man stepped out. A wiry middle-aged man. His shaved head gleamed purple even in the orange glow of the streetlamp. Fucking PJ! He stood in the middle of the road and looked up and down. I crouched low behind the hedge. He swivelled about as if he was expecting to see something. Didn't look as if he was paying any particular attention to our house, it was still sitting easy in the dark like all the rest, except for Artie snoring, Paddy the Brit grunting.

Another car came slowly up the hill, a London style black taxi. PJ hailed it, pointed to a parking space. Six men got out of the taxi, one of them sporting Tomás' neglected gray beard. They huddled around PJ for a moment, then the rest followed Tomás up a driveway while PJ stepped back behind a lime tree. I could see they were armed from their body shape and movement, cloning the SWAT teams and bad cops of American movies.

The house they were interested in was the only one in the street with a 'For Sale' sign hanging over the pavement. They had been tipped off that we were here, 100%, but I figured somebody had mixed up our empty house and the empty house for sale.

When they traipsed back down the path after ten minutes they were depressed and crestfallen, like pumped up kids when their vision of glory has been snatched away by some spoilsport adult. More looking up and down the street, as if they knew what they wanted should be here in plain sight but they just couldn't see it. Another couple of disappointed minutes, then the pack sloped off quietly in the taxi.

PJ slumped back into his car and lit a cigarette, thinking it through, retracing his steps, working out his next set of moves. If that was all there was to it, and he was going to move on soon, that would be fine. But if he had the kill scent, if he knew we were close and was prepared to sit it out, then that wasn't so good. Then I would have to walk up behind that car and remove the danger. I liked PJ. I hoped he would move.

Five minutes dragged into ten. I started to negotiate with myself, I'd wait fifteen minutes, twenty, twenty-five. But it was too cold, the gun was clumsy in my fingers, and he would have to move. Another car arrived, PJ flashed his lights, the car stopped parallel to his and they started to speak. It was a sleek sports model, idling its low growl in the dead street. I could just hear the weird ding dong drone of their speech but couldn't make out what they were saying. Another taxi came along, forced the sports car to move down the street and pull in to a space. The taxi passed, dropped the couple, picked up their baby-sitter. The driver of the sports car waited for the taxi to disappear back into the night before he climbed out on to the sidewalk. Artie's Inspector McIntyre, plain clothes, smart casual, sauntered back up to PJ and slid in to the passenger seat. I moved like a cat, over the fence, kept behind the trees, very close, could have plugged them both, and thought about it, but then McIntyre emerged into the lamplight, PJ's cigarette end splintered across the black road, McIntyre rapped PJ's windscreen, went back to his own car, and they drove off in opposite directions.

PJ would work out the mistake. They would be back. Hamilton's grunt work for the rest of the night would be in front of that screen, and before morning we would be gone.

CHAPTER SEVENTEEN

Hamilton was wasted. He had cracked open the family drinks cabinet and treated Alina to a rampage of Stolichnaya and Hennessy XO. And she didn't come to the party empty handed either – the party pills still rattled in her throat when I held her down for Artie to wrestle her clothes back on.

'It's no problem! It's no problem!' Hamilton floundered in front of the screen. 'I can handle this shit! No better man! No fucking better man! No problem!'

It *was* a problem. The code still inched up the screen. Hamilton said it was ready to go, just hit the button when the code had emptied its guts.

'Just hit the fucking button! No problem!'

He had already admitted the Russian mafia would be tracking us, doing their best to make it a *big* problem, and I knew from experience how good those guys were at taking a minor squall and twisting it into a megastorm of shit and blood.

'I'll give you thirty minutes to clear your head, Hamilton. If you're still seeing two screens doing somersaults in front of your eyes then we're all done. Me and Artie are out of here and you're on your own. You and Alina can stay behind and hit all the buttons you like.'

'No fucking problem!' He nuzzled his head close to the screen. 'No better man!'

And I didn't see how a problem like Alina *could* be solved. If we left her behind, and she didn't choke on her own vomit, she would open up to the first glass of vodka or promise of a ride home. And we couldn't take her with us. The vomit choking looked like the best option.

'I told you not to trust him!' Artie hobbled out of his room to remind me. 'No moral core, no sense of decency. Takes what he wants, does what he wants, takes himself off, no consequences, no responsibility. It's in their DNA, Con, their imperialist mindset.'

'He says the Vatican blew the whistle on your friend Monsignor Beikle. He says Beikle is a middleman for the mafia in Rome.'

'Bullshit! There is no mafia in Rome! He's trying to wipe your eye. He took advantage of poor Johannes' naiveté so now Paddy the Brit thinks he can do the same to us.'

Hamilton wouldn't be taking advantage of anybody for a while. His puckered face mirrored into a repulsive reflection on the black glass table top, frothed with his thick slime drool. Alina had taken Artie's place on the couch but she wasn't so hard to look at, even in her own open mouthed blackout.

'We'll need to see what else he has in that bag,' Artie said. 'See the way he holds on to it, even now when he's blind drunk?'

I eased the bag out of his grip and emptied the contents out on the couch, below Alina's delicate feet. It was all computer junk, I knew that much, but the mess of cables and wires didn't look like anything I could hope to work out. About ten little black boxes, color coded with tape, some had initials labelled also. *Sb 95, Bg 12, RDI 1&2,* and other scribbled labels too faded and difficult to read. Artie flicked through them, holding a box up close, mumbling the jumble of letters to himself, tossing it down, picking another, until he found one lettered, '*SSU/E4*'.

'How do you work this thing?' he said. 'Can you get it up on that bucking screen?'

There was a cable attached, and I guessed it was just a question of finding the right place to plug-in but the dark bank code was still running.

'What is it, Artie? What do the letters mean?'

'Is it possible to make a copy before he wakes up,' he said.

'Yeah, sure, but we can't do it while this other shit is running,' I said. '*I* can't, anyway. I might do something to crash this code he's running.'

Artie wrapped the cable around the box and stuffed the bundle deep into his pocket.

'What is that shit?' I said. 'SSU whatever, it means something to you, I can see the hate smoking in your eyes.'

'It's Hamilton's insurance policy, his "*Get out of gaol free*" card. Recordings of shoot-to-kill, collusion and state sanctioned murder. I don't know what the other ones are about but I'll bet you a pound to a penny it's not good news for somebody.'

I scooped the rest back into the plastic bag, twisted the top so I could form a secure knot.

'Get a bowl of iced water from the kitchen, will you?' I said. I pulled Hamilton's head up by the hair and slapped his face. 'It's time we got him to work again.'

A couple of Alina's happy pills boosted Hamilton from inert carrion to manic Lazarus in a wink of his bloodshot eye. Thrashing the keyboard and screaming like the mangled code had to be wrenched from his fingertips. Then the screen would stall, pulsing like a heart monitor, and he panted and sweated like he was shackled to an executioner's chair. The cursor pinged to life again and whacked him like a cattle prod.

'This is it! This is fucking it!'

He slowed down, each keystroke dragged out to prolong the agony of his ecstasy, until the final '*Enter*' prompt slaked his craving.

'That's it! I've done it! I've fucking done it!'

He went down on his knees, folded over on his side and curled into a foetal ball, shaking and retching like a Preacher's con sidekick at a hoax exorcism gig.

'I don't know what he's supposed to have done,' Artie said, 'but this man has serious issues. He's cracked up. The weight of such guilt is too much, even for a black hearted devil like this.'

The screen went black for a second and then erupted into a firestorm of code and symbols, as if all Hamilton's stabbed keystrokes were being consumed and reeled back in time. The screen disappeared into a miniscule pin of light at its center and then burst back to life. The cursor shuffled across the screen, dragging a message in its wake.

'Russian?' I said.

'German. It says *Initiation acknowledged. Awaiting confirmation protocol,*' Artie said, 'or some bucking thing like that.'

So far, so good. That's what I thought at first. Then it hit me that maybe this was all some three card trick, like Hamilton had created the illusion that there was life on the other side of that screen, or maybe Yakov was close by working his levers, or McIntyre was yanking his chain.

'Ach, Jesus, Mary and St Joseph! Now look! The dirty dog has pissed himself. Paddy the Piss! I'm sorry, Con, but you'll have to deal with that yourself. I don't do piss! Paddy Piss In The Pants! I can't be having that!'

Artie swerved into the bedroom. The thick pile carpet sponged Hamilton's acrid piss. I gripped under his shoulders and dragged him out to the bathroom. He wrapped himself around the toilet. I didn't really do piss either so I left him there and went back to see to Alina.

The vein in her neck throbbed under my fingers, she moaned from deep in her throat, the faded scar on her forehead crinkled into a hashtag. At least she was alive. There must be a guy somewhere back in Poland pining for her, wishing she had never left him behind, wondering what she was doing and who she was doing it with. I wished she had stayed there too, or wished I could call the guy up and have him whisk her away to his lost Polish paradise. My wish was as futile as his because she *was* here, she would wake up, and she would have a problem.

Artie also had a problem.

'So, Artie, the point of no return,' I said. 'From here on in people get hurt, hurt bad or hurt dead. I need to work out how much of your bullshit is down to your usual pompous bravado and how much is part of the plan to nail me.'

Artie sat on the edge of his bed. He was cornered and knew it but his bloated ego and natural cunning were usually enough to handle the likes of me.

'Okay, who made the first contact? If it was your idea to bring me into this shit then I really should break your neck.'

Artie rolled his fingers like he was playing with imaginary beads. I stood over him, one hand on his shoulder, my thumb testing for his carotid.

'It was essentially all true, just as I told you,' he said, 'there was no point in making it too complicated. I just wanted to protect you from any unnecessary difficulties.'

That was the Artie bullshit I expected. I placed my other hand on the other shoulder.

'This can be very easy, Artie, or very hard. Your call.'

'I suppose maybe I did let my concern for you cloud my judgement a little,' he said.

I squeezed, felt his soft neck compress.

'It's true about Monsignor Beikle. Don't let that Brit Hamilton lead you up the garden path on that one.'

Tighter, he reddened, his voice struggled.

'The only thing I maybe glossed over was that I got the tip off about Hamilton from PJ in the first place. He contacted me out of the blue. He said he had heard from his sources that it was Hamilton that conned Monsignor Beikle, and that Hamilton was back in Belfast, in the MI5 compound.'

I pushed him back on the bed, my knee pinning his gut, his big hands pulling at my wrists.

'That's all, Con, for God's sake! How does it matter how I found out about Hamilton? It's all true anyway!'

'It's bullshit! How did I get roped in? Who told you to bring me in?'

The pressure pumped through his skull, his face was purple.

'Colin McIntyre heard Hamilton had been disciplined and sent back to Belfast. He knew PJ had told me about Hamilton, so he came to see me. I knew I could trust him. He said he would help where he could but he said we needed an outsider. Somebody with no baggage here, somebody who wouldn't stir up repercussions for the Peace Process. Not PJ or Brigid or anybody with their sort of history. He suggested you.'

McIntyre? A cop I had never heard of and who shouldn't have heard of me?

'He's a bit more than an ordinary policeman, Con, to be fair to him,' Artie spluttered. 'I'd say he gets more orders from the Security Service than he does from Police HQ. But Colin McIntyre's a good lad, all the same, you can depend on him. His word is good enough for me.'

Trustworthy Colin and PJ's sources, and the two of them outside in the street, tracking us down.

'What about Yakov, Artie? His word good enough for you also?'

'Ah, Yakov the Russian character? But I thought you brought him into the mix, Con? Didn't you contact him as soon as I left you in Rio? And he sent his nephew over there to see you? I don't think you can rightly pin that one on me or anybody else, can you?'

I let go of Artie's neck and flopped on the bed beside him. He rubbed his throat and coughed the fear out. I clapped his back to get his lungs working again, wasn't thinking of his bruises, he squirmed away.

'How come you took that kicking from the Russians, Artie? You could have saved yourself a lot of hurt by telling them me and Hamilton were trapped under the stairs.'

He rubbed his throat, I could see the superiority flood back into his eyes, his voice, his broad shoulders.

'We look after our own, Con, old son,' he said, 'I would never sell you out. You know that. Don't let Paddy Piss the Pants twist everything in your head so you turn against your own people. Say what you like, but we look after our own, always have, always will. And the Russians can go fuck themselves!'

The computer screen kicked into life, I pulled Artie up off the bed.

'*Encryption code confirmed and accepted,*' he mouthed the words robotically, '*Standby for Phase Two Encryption.* What the hell are we supposed to do now?'

'It means you are going to start doing the piss thing, Artie. It means we both are. We need Paddy Piss the Pants back in the saddle.'

We couldn't risk kickstarting Hamilton with any more of Alina's pills. We stripped the clothes and dignity off him, and dumped him under the outsize square showerhead, with its rainfall effect and freezing cold water. Hamilton stumbled, slipped around on his ass, the soft pink flesh blanched white, then purple, swallowing without reflex. We hoisted him out, rough dried him with the thick bath towel. He couldn't stand so we took an arm each and walked him to the computer. He couldn't sit up straight so we slapped him.

'Give him a brandy,' Artie said, 'and make mine a double.'

A little brandy and plenty slapping snapped Hamilton back into this world. His hands quivered and he squinted at the screen to pin it down. Slowly, shakily, he started to move.

Phase Two Encryption activated.

Hamilton found autopilot and started to click. The Code Tic-Tacked back and forth between Belfast and Vienna, or maybe St Petersburg, or Odessa or wherever they decided the bank would be this night.

'It's nearly four in the morning. What time is it over there?' Artie said.

'Extraneous question!' Hamilton snarled. 'It is an automated response. But an alarm will be activated by now. The chase is on.'

Hamilton was pulling himself through, still shaking and gray faced, but he was pulling through.

'What next, Hamilton?'

'I've downloaded the second phase of their encryption,' he said. 'Now I'm sending it to the United States. They'll turn it upside down and send it back to me. Then we attack the bank servers and lock the Russians out.'

I wondered who or what in the US it was being sent to but, right then, with no other option, that would have been an extraneous question also.

'How long have we got?' I said.

'Not long enough to sit it out here,' he said. His voice was getting stronger. 'They will trace this machine to this address within hours. Maybe two or three days before we get that encryption code cracked. We better move on, quickly.'

Artie puffed out his cheeks and did the Italian shoulder shrug he had picked up in Rome.

'Don't look at me,' Artie said. 'I have just about used up all my favors. People I thought I could trust aren't taking my calls. I don't have anywhere else left to run to.'

'I have a place,' Hamilton said. 'A nice quiet spot down outside Dromore. Nobody knows about it. All prepared and 100% guaranteed.'

'I'd jump out that window before I'd trust you!' Artie curled his lip, shook his head. 'I'll work something out, Con. We'll take our chances down in Armagh. Not very comfortable memories for Paddy Piss the Pants here but there you go.'

'What about switching the vehicle?' I said.

Artie did his Roman shrug.

'Then let's go now,' I said, 'if we're lucky PJ's crew are back in bed and McIntyre hasn't got a surveillance team in place yet.'

'What about this unfortunate wee girl?' Artie said.

'Leave her sleeping where she is!' Hamilton said. 'What's she going to tell anybody they don't already know? Except I gave her the best ride of her life and it's sore when she walks!'

I didn't know what to do with Alina. She probably hadn't heard or seen much, and would remember less, but McIntyre or PJ could coax out details she didn't even know were lying dormant in her head. Taking her along wasn't an option. Hamilton and Artie were bad enough, I sure didn't need another complication waiting to go wrong.

'I'll have my disks back now as well, thank you very much!' Hamilton said. 'You two have both burned whatever bridges you had, no going back. Your only way out depends on me working my magic. The disks are part of the deal. Not negotiable, compadres!'

Artie felt the disk and cable deep in his pocket. The rest were stashed under the couch.

'That's your problem, Paddy,' Artie said, 'you believe you can seal away all your sins and evil acts in your wee black boxes. And who ever said you weren't going to be held accountable? I'll have to pray for guidance and search deep in my conscience before I accede to that.'

'Dickhead!' Hamilton laughed in Artie's face. 'You think I've been a pioneer in surveillance for over thirty years and I'd have anything incriminating *me* on those disks? Wise up! It's yourself you need to worry about, you old bollocks! Perhaps you turn up in there somewhere, and perhaps folks will be surprised when they hear what McCooey the great Rebel Priest was up to back in the day!'

Artie flinched like that was a major kick in the balls. I could read it in his eyes, scanning back through all the occasions of sin, his betrayals and compromises, clicking through them in his mind like rosary beads. Or worse, maybe he knew *exactly* what Hamilton had on him.

'And I know that big lump in your trouser pocket can only be a certain disk,' Hamilton teased. 'Only Troubles fetishists like you are actually interested in that crap, you know, the rest of the world has moved on.'

'Oh really?' Artie snapped right back at him. 'Then why have you gone to such lengths to keep it hidden on these tapes for so long?'

'What? You think that's what Yakov has been sent to recover? You fucking haven't a clue, you dick! The real predators, the big dogs, *they* know I have the dirt to spin their world upside down but *you're* still creaming yourself about insignificant parochial shite that happened on a rainy country lane in Armagh thirty fucking years ago!'

Yakov had been *sent* to recover something *else* in the disks? Not the encryption key? Not the cash? What if there was no dark bank, just Hamilton's big dog predators and their secrets, and me in the middle?

'Fine! You can keep that shite as a memento of our time together, how's that?' Hamilton was practically foaming at the mouth. 'Not that it'll do you much good, like, since it's triple encrypted to fuck and you'll never read it. Never mind, I have copies of all this stuff planted with friends and colleagues around the world.'

Hamilton was still manic, and that was dangerous. The coolheaded Hamilton would play it safe, and that meant recognizing that I might still hurt him bad. This psycho Paddy was forgetting why fear was a necessary precondition to our relationship, and that meant his perception of risk was impaired.

A cell phone ringing stopped us dead. The tone was muffled so we knew it was here in the room but couldn't see it. Alina stirred on the couch, still with her eyes closed, she groped underneath the cushions and produced her phone. It was still ringing. She looked at it, then at us as if she didn't know where she was or who we were. The ringing stopped. I had searched her purse when we carried her up here, must have missed it. She blinked at us, the cracked memory slowly panning out, getting worse the more she remembered. The phone rang again. I shouted at her to ignore it, let it ring. She thumbed '*answer*', inclined her head to listen. I could hear the voice from here. She was startled now, and frightened. I took the phone and listened.

'You are there, Con Maknazpy, I can smell you.' Yakov's voice cut me like a razor. 'Enjoy the little Polski bitch while you can, my friend, because now you are dead. You must know this. For you it is finished. But I still give you a choice. Hand over Hamilton now and I will permit your Yasmin to stay in Rio. But you help him run and she will be back in Lisbon working for me again as a very busy whore after you are dead. Her little daughter also, and you know that beautiful little one will be *very* popular with my clients, very, *very* busy. When they cry, and they *will* cry, I will remind them, every day, Con Maknazpy did this to you. This is how little he cared about you.'

No mention of the encryption key being activated, or the dark bank, or the missing cash. It was Hamilton he wanted. I slipped the phone into my pocket.

'Maybe you'd like to use the bathroom, Alina, get yourself cleaned up,' I said. 'You're coming on a trip with us.'

CHAPTER EIGHTEEN

'This house stinks!' Hamilton hammered the jammed window frame. 'Just like the rest of your stinking Armagh!'

'What's stinking about it?' Artie sniffed his nose in the air and inspected the ceiling. 'It's as dry as a bone. The sister is looking after it while he is away.'

The house was damp, colder in here than outside, a bad smell choked the air. Alina pulled out a mould-crusted mop and bucket from the kitchen cupboard and threw them into the quagmire that was once a garden. Hamilton leaned out the kitchen door to survey our new refuge. A green brown film sponged on the concrete yard. Three steps led up to the deserted garden. Kids play equipment rusted in knee length grass.

'See up there?' Hamilton pointed to the low black hill that cradled the house and now skulked below the gray cloud. 'That lane running behind us? That used to be a rough track with a drainage pipe sticking out underneath. I had a camera in that pipe. Covered this house for eighteen months. McCooey's cousin. Bastard never knew a thing about it.'

Artie joined us, still sniffing the air.

'Of course they knew about it!' Artie scoffed. 'They let you *think* you were getting something when the real business was happening elsewhere!'

'Your cousin?' I said. 'Ferdy's uncle? One of the guys hit in Swansea's ambush?'

'No, not one of the golden McCooey boys!' Hamilton gloated. 'This one took his own life. Guilty conscience, wouldn't you say, Monsignor?'

'That Coroner was a disgrace,' Artie said, 'he only said what his paymasters told him to say. The memorial stone says "*Murdered by Forces of the Crown*", everyone knows that's true, and you most of all, Hamilton.'

'Of course! The Brits did it! Of course!' Hamilton laughed. 'The Brits did *everything!* That sheep in the field farted, but the wicked Brits made it fart!'

'Your crowd murdered him,' Artie said, 'and they crippled his son's business. That's why the lad is in Australia now.'

The lad was in Australia, and all the neighbors knew it. This house had been mothballed for five years and now it wasn't. People would notice.

'There must be lots of eyes on us here, Artie. Is it safe?'

'How many homes can you see from here, Con?'

Two above and behind us, three more on the hill below, maybe a dozen scattered along the hill on the other side of the river.

'All those *eyes* you're worried about,' he said, 'they aren't a risk, they're a safety net. They're either related to me or I've baptized their children or buried their parents. Nobody will venture down this road without me knowing about it.'

I recognized this river. Off to the north I could see where the dark and bright waters met and clashed together, churning and coiling into one, then spilling along down below. The McErlane house must be somewhere behind these hills. That's where I set off from, with Artie at my side, the night Swansea was gunned down in Armagh city. I didn't believe in fate, didn't believe much in anything, but it somehow felt like I had always *known* something would drag me back. I couldn't go back to an innocent time because for me there was none. The oily hands that pulled the levers in my world had tilted that game away from me. I could only go on, and hope the chips would fall in my favor, just this once. Maybe swim against the current right back along that river and be baptized in the bright salvation water, or maybe be sucked into the smoking cauldron and be drowned in the dark. It really wasn't my call, I accepted that now, never had been, never would be, and that was cool.

'Let's rack up these disks, Hamilton,' I said, 'time to see what all the fuss is about.'

But Hamilton wasn't playing. He folded his arms and stuck his chin out in an "*I'm not doing it and you can't make me*" scowl. I sorted through the disks as if I knew what I was looking for. Artie had sparked a few sticks and sods of turf into a pyramid of smoke and barren flame. I tossed a disk into the fireplace.

'Fuck!!' Hamilton dived to fish it out, I gripped his wrist and held his hand over the flame until he dropped the disk.

'McCooey! Get this mad Yank bastard under control! You've been after this stuff for years and now you have it this fucking header is destroying it!'

Artie twitched his lips, didn't know what to do. I flipped another disk into the fire.

'Okay! Okay! For fuck's sake! I'll do it!'

I released his wrist and pulled the disks away from the flames.

Hamilton jacked the laptop into life, started to untangle the wires and cables in the bag. I took Alina into the bedroom that adjoined the living room.

'Alina, listen to me. It's better for you right now that you don't hear or see any of this stuff, okay?' I said. 'Now, you could climb out that window and run away but where are you going to run to? There is nowhere to go and the Russian Mafia are hunting us down. If they catch you they will hurt you, you know that, even if you give them all the help you can, they will *really* hurt you.'

Alina nodded, and sat down on the edge of the damp mattress. There was nothing else in the room except for a picture of a mournful Jesus exposing his thorn-crucified heart. She folded her hands together as if she was about to pray. I left her and closed the bedroom door behind me.

Hamilton scrutinized each disk like a savant DJ priming his A-game playlist. He pulled one and clicked it into the drive wired to the laptop.

'No, you're going to play this one,' Artie held the SSU/E4 disk out in the palm of his hand.

'Ahh, yes! The Holy Grail for professional Fenian victims,' Hamilton laughed. 'Law and Order when it suits you, right?'

'Play it again, Ham,' Artie said, 'and be forewarned – if that tape happens to get accidentally wiped I'll call in the neighbors and tell them who you are. Even Maknazpy here won't save you then.'

The static and crackle spiked and faded, then settled to a low hum. A car door opened and closed. Muffled sounds of movement, pages shuffled, a match scratched into life, a deep inhale, a smoker's rasp.

'Who is he?'

'A Fenian.'

'A Provo?'

'A Fenian! Isn't that not enough?'

Two throaty cackles.

'It's your man! You know the cunt! Your man! Fucking Taig buying land? Around here?'

'When?'

'Sunday night. It's all in the file.'

Rustle of papers, rasping cough. A car door opened, a throat cleared, loud cough and plumed spit, summer birds singing in the background, door closed.

'Roadblock?'

'Our boys will be there til ten o'clock. Roads will be cleared for you. You get there a quarter to. Your man gets home about quarter past.'

'Have you anything for me? That fucking piece jammed the last time.'

Movement, crackle, metallic clank.

'In there, two Brownings and an SMG.'

'Clean?'

'As a fucking whistle! Straight out of King's Park last night.'

'Just your man? Nobody with him?'

'His cuntin' hoor of a wife. She'd be better off at home to clean their pigsty Fenian hovel!'

'Aye, her? They'll find her with her fucking rosary beads stuck up her rebel gee when I'm finished with the Fenian bitch!'

The crackle faded until the timer on the audio file fell over the line. Artie peered at the black laptop screen but I knew he was staring straight back into history.

'That's the only recording we have of Weir and Jackson,' Hamilton said, 'two Loyalist paramilitaries up to their necks in Fenian blood.'

'Loyalist paramilitaries and serving members of Her Majesty's British Army at the time,' Artie said. 'Also foot soldiers for British Intelligence, weren't they, Hamilton?'

'Dunno about the British Intelligence bit,' Hamilton said. 'That was long before my time, that recording was made away back in the seventies, I was still at school.'

'They were both in the Brit Ulster Defence Regiment, Con, the UDR. King's Park was the UDR depot in Lurgan. Her Majesty's local militia had the unfortunate habit of '*losing*' weapons that were then put to use in the Loyalist murder campaign. Very careless they were, '*lost*' hundreds of weapons.'

'Well, I suppose they didn't have the coffers of Irish America to fund arms shipments,' said Hamilton, 'unlike your friends and relations in the 'RA.'

Artie's glassy eyes told me the recording was genuine, but I knew it was useless.

'Interesting stuff, Hamilton,' I said. 'Got anything better? Like, faces to go with voices? Reliable identification and proven linkage to actual events?'

Hamilton sneered at the outrage against his dignity.

'Here's a nice wee film,' he said, 'wait a minute, here it comes, just for you and Artie.'

A grainy video, blurred, more gray and gray than black and white, the screen flickered, disappeared, came back with a better focus. No audio, video only.

A car chugged up a steep driveway to a low house, a clumsy maneuver to reverse into the space at the side, failed, abandoned the car at an awkward angle. A man gets out, dark clothes, a big man, waving at somebody inside the house. A boy hops out of the car, about ten years old, kicks a ball against the gable wall and jumps high to catch the rebound, taps the ball to the man, takes the return pass and smashes the ball high over the roof of the house before running inside.

It was this house, it was Artie McCooey, and it was my lost comrade brother Ferdy McErlane.

'Had you worried there, didn't I, *Monsignor*?' Hamilton goaded. 'Never know where you might turn up in my archives, never know who I caught you speaking to, eh?'

Hamilton dragged the short video back to the beginning, then clicked Ferdy alive again, playing ball and running free.

'A long way from the streets of Yonkers and the Bronx, isn't it? Mind you, if the cub had stayed here he probably would have followed his bloodthirsty uncles to an early grave anyway, wouldn't he?'

Hamilton's words burned into me, my chest coiled tight, my skull throbbed.

'No matter, that wee child on my film is more maggot than corpse now, I'd imagine.'

I levered myself off the seat, head spinning, like I was trying to escape my own body. Artie stood up to steady me.

'That mouth of yours is too big for your own good, Hamilton,' Artie said. 'You'll live to regret saying that, by God you will!'

'Ahh, come on now, boys!' Hamilton cranked the pressure. 'No point being squeamish about it! Ferdia McErlane was no angel, he got what he deserved, pity a few more of you didn't do likewise!'

I pushed past Artie and stumbled my way into the bedroom. The fear in Alina's eyes made me think I was the Devil. She was on her knees against the bed, Artie's rosary beads threaded through her fingers. She lowered her head now to whisper her prayers, jumbling the words all together like it was a race to get finished, like time was already up. She looked up at me again, carved a quick sign of the cross against her breast, and kissed the beads to her lips.

'It's okay, Alina. Keep saying your prayers. Pray for my friend. Pray for all of us.'

She froze at the sound of my voice, like she could hear something that wasn't there. Her eyes flashed in wide-open shock, and a shiver shook through her body, like something had just walked over her grave. I sat on the bed beside her, stroking her fine hair with my shaking hand until my heart slowed and my breathing came easy again.

'You really have nothing to fear, Alina. I haven't come for you.'

Alina prayed and cried, and I sat there in silence, stroking her hair and wondering what mournful Jesus would do about it.

CHAPTER NINETEEN

'Maknazpy! Get out here!'

Hamilton barged into the bedroom. Alina squirmed and rolled away from me.

'We have a problem,' Hamilton said. 'McCooey's guard dogs say we have company.'

'Okay! Okay! Get out of here! I'll be right there!'

Alina turned her back to me and pressed against the wall. Artie's rosary beads hung over the end of the bedpost, the gun was on the floor. I took the beads and folded them into her fingers, then stretched under the bed for the Glock. Alina threw the beads against the wall and buried her face in the dirty mattress. I lifted the beads and draped them over the frame of the Jesus picture.

'Maknazpy! Hurry up to fuck!'

I stopped at the door. I was going to tell her not to worry, not to cry, to promise her that everything would be fine. I was *going* to, and *knew* all the right words, but that "*pay now, enjoy later*" paradise warranty wasn't really my business, that was more Artie's gig, or

God's. I closed the door behind me. The Jesus picture smashed against it.

'Don't forget, big lad!' Hamilton said, 'if they get their hands on me then you don't get *your* hands on the cash!'

Artie was out on the porch with two other deep voices. Hamilton hammered the laptop, doctored his history, snarled the encryption path into a dead end.

'There are two cars down below,' Artie said, 'blocking each end of the road. The boys say there are six of them, and they're not local. They look like trouble.'

A black SUV swung into our lane, revved over the pot-holes, not in a particular hurry, not in a chase. I figured I could make it out the back and over that hill. No way Artie or Hamilton could keep pace. I could make it if they hadn't posted cover at the back.

'Time for you to walk the big talk, Maknazpy! You do a runner and swear to fuck I'll give them every bank account you have stashed away! I'll open them like a wet lettuce and both your hoors will be back on the game this time next week!'

The SUV crawled closer. A broad shouldered minder driving, the smaller figure framed in the back. They stopped, he got out and nosed around in a casual routine, like he was a passing tourist scoping out a rest stop. Not like he was here to kill or be killed. He nodded, she stepped down from the SUV, limped behind him, held the neck-brace as she looked the place over. I opened the door nice and easy so they could see the Glock, no panic, keeping it cool. I motioned her forward and him back to the car. She nodded, he stepped back, folded his thick arms and hoisted his butt against the driver's door.

Yana brushed past me, didn't speak, planted herself in the middle of the room and inspected her nails, like she was the boss and we were her anxious underlings waiting to hear if we were already fired.

'Christ!' Hamilton said. 'What animal did that to you?'

Yana looked through him as if he should wait for her permission before opening his mouth next time. Her face was swollen, the thick make-up couldn't hide the purple bruises. The neck-brace forced her into an awkward pose.

'Like I said, we want that recording. We are going back to get it. You will retrieve the disk and hand it to me.' Yana spoke without looking at us. 'No deals, no negotiation. You will give full and effective co-operation. Anything less will be construed to be contrary to the security interests of the United States of America, and you will be held fully accountable before the due process of the law.'

'The *law*?' Hamilton sneered. 'You sure about that?'

'How did you people know we were here?' Artie said.

Yana snapped out of her robot mode.

'I'm sorry, Padre,' she said, 'no miracles required. Your congregation here sent a code to the US to be cracked. Of course we knew where you were. We simply followed you from Belfast.'

'What about Yakov?' I said. 'And the others?'

Yana held the neck-brace as she twisted her body to look me in the eye for the first time. She was about to say something but then stalled, took a deep breath and blew out her anger.

'Put that gun away, Maknazpy, you're out-gunned and out-muscled. We don't need you anymore, so don't push your luck.'

'Don't need him *anymore*?' Hamilton said. 'So what *did* you need him for? To take the rap after *I* was murdered? You're fucking in this with McIntyre and the Brits! You fucking whore!'

Yana reverted to the blank canvas face.

'I have no idea what you are talking about. Now get your shit together and move out.'

A car horn blared down on the road. Yana's driver kicked the door open and pressed the Remington 12 Gauge tight to his shoulder. 'Incoming! Incoming!' This guy was freaking out. He swung the shotgun from side to side, trying to cover us all at once. He was too slow, and Yana too shackled by the neck-brace. She lifted up on her toes as I cramped my forearm around the neck-brace, the Glock screwed tight under her right ear.

Two men came in the back door. Four more appeared at the front. Artie signalled to one of them, he relieved the driver of the Remington. Yana had a pistol holstered under her left arm. I told Artie to take it, slowly. Down on the road, another black SUV was squeezed from both sides by two builder's work trucks and surrounded by ten or twelve men.

'This is South Armagh, dear,' Artie said. 'You would need more than the US Cavalry to subdue the natives around here. I suggest you go back to wherever you came from and take your cowboys with you.'

The SUV raced down the lane, the trucks backed off, both SUV's screeched away. Artie waved down to the men on the road like he was the Pope, and the men outside the house lined up to shake his hand like he had just said a funeral mass for their grandmother, then they slipped back into the hill mist, taking the Remington and Yana's shortarm with them.

'Did you tell those bastards who I am?' Hamilton said.

'Do you think you would you still be standing there if I had?' Artie answered.

'Well, I'm not hanging around here any longer. Get me to Paris and I'll finish the job. You'll get your blood money, Maknazpy, and you'll get the tapes you *really* want, McCooey. We'll say au revoir and disappear.'

'We'll have to move again, Artie,' I said. 'Somewhere Paddy the Piss here can get to work on that encryption before Yakov or anyone else nails us.'

'You're talking through your arse, Maknazpy!' Hamilton said. 'They'll be back! Get me to Paris now and I'll finish the job!'

'You can hit Paris all you want later, Hamilton. First you're going to jack the cash out of that bank.'

'Why? What difference does it make where I do it? You'll get the money in Paris and we won't have Yana's goons on our necks.'

'That might not be such a bad move, Con.' Artie nodded in agreement. 'Maybe you could take him to Rome and clear poor Johannes Beikle.'

'He will do the bank thing here,' I said. 'Then we are going back to get those recordings.'

'Ach, Holy Fuck! Did you get a knock on the head? How am I going to get that gear now? Yana and McIntyre and all the rest of them will be waiting on us!'

Artie screwed up his face and scratched the back of his head. 'Sure that's a good idea, Con? You can't trust Hamilton to go there on his own, you'll have to go with him. What if they are waiting for you?'

'Somebody will be waiting,' I said, 'we'll just have to manage that when we get there. One thing for sure is those recordings are our bargaining chip. That's how these things work out. They want it bad enough, we do a deal. That's our free pass out of here. Our only way out.'

CHAPTER TWENTY

Another room, another town, over the border, a bar with accommodation upstairs for stranded tourists in the summer. Artie was running out of friends, had to pulld out his wallet to fix things. The guy didn't look him in the eye when Artie tried to shake his hand.

But Hamilton was in his zone, big time. Punching keys, nose against the screen, eyes popping, feet tapping. A junkie cooking crack. A hustler hot rolling the dice. A wino locked in a bar.

'How long is this going to take?' I said.

'As long as it takes! Why? Do you want me to balls the whole thing up and send personal invitations to Yakov and Yana?'

The cursor stalled, marking time, Hamilton held his breath, almost choked, like this screen was his flat-lined heart monitor. A jumble of code bounced back. He gulped air and crashed his witch doctor script into the dark.

'Let's see the bastards work this one out!'

Hamilton was on the edge. Burnt out or freaked out, there was no way the boss spooks could risk this maverick on the loose. He wasn't the cold schemer from the Swansea ambush days, not the functional apparatchik tilting their truth filter. The life had won. These power guys all started off anointed in the credo that they were their God's gift to civilization. They were at the top because they were entitled to be and the lowlife scum were only down there because that's as much as they deserved, and the smelly jealous bastards weren't even grateful that the real citizens were so generous and tolerant. This was *their* natural order, their right, their rules, and the only way to protect the rules was for sanctioned apostles like Hamilton to operate outside the rules, detached in their own bubble, parallel to the real world but not subject to it, and the only rules were to not get caught and to not become a risk to the bubble. Right now, Hamilton was their worst nightmare – the disaffected insider gone rogue, paranoid and reckless but still with the ego to fantasize his final victory.

'So, you're still on top of this thing? Yakov won't be able to warn the bank or some shit like that?'

'Yakov can ring as many alarms as he likes, they can't do anything about it. It's like I shake your hand and come away with your fingerprints, and then anything I touch it's your prints I leave. That's what I've done to them and they won't even realize it until after I have cleaned them out.'

'Sure, but how come Yana was able to intercept your contact to the United States and then tag us?'

'Bullshit! Absolute bullshit! Nobody intercepted anything! They haven't a clue!'

'No? She knew you had sent a code. She knew where we were. How could that be?'

'Dunno. Don't ask me. But it wasn't because anybody "*intercepted*" my wire. Somebody leaked. Ask McCooey. Or maybe you're not as smart as you think. Maybe you broke cover. But it sure wasn't from my end.'

Artie rumbled his prayer mantra in the next room. Then Alina's voice, maybe making her confession. I pressed my ear to the adjoining door. Silence, then Artie warning her about Hamilton.

'A young woman like you sees only excitement and glamor but this is an evil thing, not even a man, not like anything you could know. *"And no marvel, for even Satan himself is transformed into an angel of light."* He is a predator, he will devour you. We will pray to Our Lady of Czestochowa and ask for her succor to fight your female weakness.'

I tapped the door, silence, then Artie opened it just wide enough to stick his nose out. I shouldered my way in, kept the door open so I could keep eyes on Hamilton.

'Listen, Artie, this is important. Did you make *any* contact with anyone at all, even with anybody you thought was 100% safe?'

'I've been with you the whole time,' he said. 'Has Hamilton said I was in contact with anyone? And you're listening to *him*? You know every word out of his mouth is engineered to manipulate, to bend you to his will. Do you not trust me? Who knows what Paddy the Brit is doing on that fecking computer?' Artie tugged my collar. 'He could be emailing or snapchatting or whatever to hell else they do on those things! Get it into your thick skull, Con, once and for all – Hamilton will say and do anything and everything to get what he wants. Start from that premise. Every word is a lie. His life is a lie. He won't change now.'

Hamilton rattled away at the keyboard. I didn't know shit what he was doing except what he told me.

'And what about this girl?' Artie whispered close to my ear. 'Is it really necessary to keep her here?'

'It's not ideal, no, but you think her life would be a bed of roses and Polish honey if Yakov's heavy crew get their hands on her?'

Artie rubbed a hand over his bruised ribs, he sucked air through his teeth and clicked his tongue. The kicked ribs were still sore, I knew that, but I knew even more that his real pain was his helplessness. That network of power and influence that insulated him from the real world was being untangled quickly, but Artie's pride was slow to keep up.

The phone beside the bed vibrated before it trilled. Alina was closest. She looked at it, then at me. She wanted to scoop it up and scream for help. Artie looked at me. Hamilton stopped, and cranked his head to listen. Artie lifted it, answered softly. A quick message, Artie's eyes bulged. He signalled at the TV hanging on the wall. Alina hit the buttons, the news had already started. Two police vehicles blocked a country lane. Figures in white forensic suits trawled around a distant red car.

"Local sources have identified the two men found shot dead on the outskirts of Belfast today as Thomas McEvoy and Joseph McEvoy. The men are believed to be related, and security sources report that Thomas McEvoy was a prominent Belfast Republican ex-prisoner."

'Holy fuck!' Hamilton said. 'That's the start of it! Didn't I fucking tell you we needed to get out?!'

'Tomás and Wee Joe?' I said.

Artie bowed his head in prayer, blessed himself, kissed the crucifix.

'Was Tomás the informer, Hamilton?' I said. 'The one you told me about?'

'Tomás was no bloody informer!' Artie punched his right fist into his left palm and twisted his hands together. 'No matter what this conniving dog tells you, Tomás was no informer!'

'I didn't say he was an informer, did I?' Hamilton smirked. 'I said their own people *believed* one of them was an informer. That's hardly my fault, is it?'

Artie moved toward Hamilton, I took his elbow and guided him back.

'What do you mean, "T*he start of it*"?' I said. 'The start of what?'

'Obviously, I mean we're next. *I'm* next, anyway, but probably you also, Maknazpy. Easier to pin a murder on a dead man, know what I mean?'

'Don't listen to him, Con, he would kiss a lie to his dying grandmother.'

'Actually, most of the time I don't need to say anything,' Hamilton said. 'Most of the time I just play back the words from other people's mouths. The recordings are true, it's their words, truly. Whether they are telling the truth or telling lies, if you want to limit yourself to that sterile binary code of morality, isn't my business.'

Hamilton pulled the disk and plugged it into the laptop. A new screen appeared, he jumbled up some passwords, and a new audio file started

'Here, listen up. You too, McCooey, see if your curated lies get anywhere near my objective truth.'

A man yawns, clears his throat. A long, drawn out fart. A snort. Footsteps, a door opens.

'Are you sure? 100 per cent?'

'No bout adoubt it! 200 per cent!'

The first voice was PJ, long ago but unmistakable.

'How are you sure? I need to know. Your word's not good enough.'

'His handler fucking withdrew five grand, PJ. I saw the requisition slip. The boys were talking about it in the canteen. Everybody knows. Ask him where he got the five grand from. Ask him what he was doing at Kilkeel Harbor Sunday week ago. Ask him who he was meeting in the Jag, British Racing Green.'

The second voice was familiar, I had heard it before.

'He'll be interrogated,' PJ said. 'Will he say anything about you?'

'No way. He doesn't even know my name. But don't encourage too much dialogue, you know, get it over with quick - never know what a wee rat like that will throw out to save his neck. But sure when he sees you he'll know he's fucked anyway, won't he?'

The second voice was Superintendent McIntyre, a younger McIntyre, less composed, not so confident, more strident, edgier.

'What about his handler? Will he be trouble?'

'Aye, he'll be fucked off he's lost a good tout. Back to square one for him. But I'd say he cares more for the dog shit he's walked on his wife's white carpet than he does for this bollocks.'

'How much has he told them already?'

'I'd postpone it for a while, if I was you. The FBI know the dollars have been transferred but don't know the details of the shipment. That's what the Yanks tell us, anyway, not that you can believe everything those bastards say!'

'What about you? Anybody looking at you funny? No worries?'

'No worries, PJ, absolutely not!' Clapping hands, chair scraping on tiles. *'So that's it then, gentlemen? Time for a drink? Just orange juice for you, PJ, I suppose?'*

Rattle of glass and bottle.

'A wee drop of water for your whiskey, Father McCooey, is that enough?'

Hamilton clicked the audio off, swung around in triumph, challenging Artie to deny it.

'You and PJ worked for the Brits, Artie?' I said. 'All that shit about Ferdy's uncles and you were working for the Brits the whole time? You better tell me you didn't set them up for that ambush, Artie, you really do.'

Artie gazed out the window, a million miles and thirty years away, as if he was in the room on his own, as if he was in his own sealed confessional cell. I poked a finger in his chest and he jumped, like I was a hypnotist bringing back a victim with a click of my fingers. Artie blinked, stroked his cheeks with both hands, then stood and walked off to the bathroom.

'You're hearing that arse about face, Maknazpy, my good man!' Hamilton was having a lot of fun. 'It's not that PJ and Artie worked for the Brits. Detective Sergeant McIntyre, as he then was, was your man flying two flags. Except, of course, he wasn't a spy for the

Brits, no, that treacherous bastard was a spy *for* the IR fucking A. You've just heard him sign the death warrant of a high value asset that RUC Special Branch had invested a lot of time and resources in. And Saint Artie McCooey, in there now taking a leisurely piss for himself, blew the ink dry. You know, the bastard even had the audacity to turn up at the murder scene and mouth his spurious prayers into the man's ear, what was left of it. He may as well have been the trigger man himself, just as culpable in any man's catechism of right and wrong. You heard it yourself.'

I had heard PJ, undoubtedly, and a guy that could have been a young McIntyre. Hamilton was telling me what their words meant. I hadn't heard Artie's voice.

'So, McIntyre is taking care of old business? Except it *is* old business, very old. Why now? Why Tomás and Wee Joe?'

'He's an opportunist! Like all of them, sociopathic opportunists! He has his eye on a big retirement package, I hear, and a jackpot consultancy job waiting, Bahrain or Qatar or some other estimable reification of human rights married to police accountability. He was sanguine enough about it when he knew he would always be here to put his boot on somebody's neck. Now, he doesn't like the idea of what the vermin could get up to when he is away, and this confusion is the perfect smoke screen for him. He'll clean up his mess and nobody will notice.'

'Two bodies found shot dead on a country lane? Somebody noticed.'

'Like I said, you're the big time torpedo, you're the convenient receptacle wherein the shit will duly be shitted. But nobody else cares, that's what I keep telling you. Nobody except the antediluvian Troubles junkies like McIntyre and McCooey and Brigid and fucking PJ! The rest of the world has moved on. There's real things to worry about, right now and right under our noses.'

Artie came out of the bathroom and opened the door to the corridor. A figure appeared, handed over shaving cream and a disposable razor. Artie had his priest collar off, his wet face dripping on the carpet. He turned and went back to the bathroom.

'Keep an eye on McCooey, that's all I'm saying,' Hamilton said. 'He acts the big mouth windbag because he is one, but he's nobody's fool either.'

'What's the real thing to worry about?' I said. 'Like, the thing you and Yana have cooking up in that house?'

'You don't think the Yanks are here to rake over ancient Irish history that means fuck all to anybody, do you? But look, I just don't know what or who they have in their sights. They needed that place rigged up. I'm the best in the business, I was here, and they knew I had good reason to be pissed off with my own crowd. I don't fucking know what will be on those disks. I don't think we should go up there after them, either. I have everything almost set up here. As soon as the codebreaker gets back to me I'm ready to go. Maybe tonight even, maybe tomorrow.'

'What else do you have on McCooey? Did he sell out to the Brits? Did he betray Ferdy McErlane's uncles?'

'Ach, it's not just one big thing with McCooey,' Hamilton said. 'He is shitting himself because he has his fingerprints on so many dirty subterfuges and hypocritical somersaults that he just doesn't know what I might have on him. Let the bastard sweat! I'll lay Artie McCooey's grubby ass out when I'm ready, when it will cause the smug bastard most grief. In the meantime, why don't you fuck off out of my face and let me get on with the task in hand?'

Artie was right. I had no idea what Hamilton's real task in hand was. His computer code was king and I didn't speak that language. I *knew* he was fixing the bank cracking routine but everything else was up for grabs.

I pulled Alina's cell phone and clipped the battery in place. He hadn't withheld the number, I was supposed to phone him back. I sent Alina in beside Hamilton and hit the call button. He didn't answer. I knew he wouldn't, and knew he would let me stew before calling back. I flipped the phone down on the bed. Five minutes, then I would pull the battery out again.

Artie planted himself in front of me, stretched to his full height, dabbing his shaving nick with a scrap of tissue paper.

'I'm leaving, Con,' he said. 'I'm getting out of here and I'm taking Alina with me. This is no place for her. I won't allow it anymore.'

It was the full Artie bluster, authoritative delivery, stern faced, all his black robe dynastic rights asserting their jurisdiction.

'Well, I don't know if that's such a good idea, Artie. How will *you* keep her safe? What if she walks out on you and walks straight into Yakov?'

'She will be safe. I can guarantee that, absolutely.'

Artie licked his finger and pressed the tissue to the cut. The tissue stuck to his fingertip instead of his face and a trickle of blood zig-zagged down his cheek and bulged over his lip.

'Okay, okay, that would be fine, Artie. Alina's well-being is a responsibility I didn't ask for or want. But there's the thing, Artie, what about *your* responsibility? To me? To Johannes Beikle? In fact, fuck Beikle, just what about me?'

'In the name of Our Lord and His Holy Mother! Such ingratitude and insolence! I ...'

'Hold it there, Artie, hold it there!' I was on my feet, pressed my finger against Artie's purple lips. 'You're mistaking me for one of your naughty altar boys again!'

'For God's sake, Con! If you won't trust me who will you trust?! What can I do for you when I'm trapped in here like a convict? I'm walking out that door now and the young woman is coming with me. Then I'll do what I can for you – if you don't get yourself killed in the meantime. I can get you on a boat, France, or maybe Spain. That's if you don't get yourself killed.'

'What about Hamilton?' I said.

'Fuck Hamilton!' Artie licked the blood from his lips. 'Paddy the Brit is on his own. Get the money, get the recordings, then fuck him!'

The cell phone pulsed into life. I put it to my ear, Artie sliced a quick sign of the cross at me and backed out the door.

First the heavy breathing, then the brutal voice.

'The great American loser! Why waste your time calling me? Don't you want to hear the voices of your beautiful loved ones just one last time? My associates in Brighton Beach and Rio are on their way now. Call them, quick, they deserve to hear from your own lips why you have done this to them!'

'Maybe you should make a couple of calls yourself, Yakov. Like, maybe you should call your darling Valentina at her nice college in Paris, warn daddy's girl to look over her shoulder for any bad Irishmen on her tail. I hear that UPMC is a fine college but you know that Latin Quarter is full of mad Irishmen. Tell her to be careful, very, very careful.'

Yakov's heavy breathing was real now, I could almost taste the white fury down the line, and it gave me a kick.

'Then call your younger daughter, Galina. She's doing some sort of Chemical Engineering shit at Imperial College in London, isn't she? At least that's what your nephew told me when we were having our long chats in Rio. Pyotr's very proud of his cousins, you know, I could hardly stop him talking about them – all those details, where they were, what they're doing.'

'I will fucking tear your heart out and eat it, Maknazpy, I'll fuck you and all your fucking Irish bitches ...'

'No you won't, Yakov. You'll remember those Irish bitches dropped a mortar bomb on fucking Downing Street! You'll remember the Brit Prime Minister hid in a cupboard when those Irish bitches were outside dropping mortars! You'll remember those Irish bitches blew up a fucking hotel right underneath Margaret Thatcher and her whole fucking Party. They got to Margaret fucking Thatcher, Yakov! Think you can keep your sweet Russian Princess safe?'

'I'll fucking kill you with my bare hands!'

'No, Yakov, you won't kill me. You'll put the phone down now and then go think about it. You'll think you made a bad mistake by taking this thing personal. It was a mistake to threaten my people, Yakov, you know that. That's what you would call a two way street. Nobody wins that way, that's what you'll be thinking.'

Yakov was already thinking, I could feel it, but he was still thinking about how much pain he could tear out of me, and how he could make it last longer.

'Go ahead, Yakov. Put the phone down and think about it. You aren't stupid. You're a businessman at heart. This is business.'

'American prick! I'll cut your balls off and you'll watch me feed them to my dog! That will be our business!'

'No, you *know* how business works. Like, how much do you want something? What are you prepared to trade to get it? *That's* business, Yakov, that's business right fucking there.'

Still the heavy breathing.

'So, tell me, Yakov, just how much do you want Hamilton?'

The phone went dead, but the echo of his bear's growl rumbled deep down in my gut.

CHAPTER TWENTY-ONE

Hamilton's eyes fried like his eye drops were habanero sauce. He wanted vodka. I said he needed water. The barman brought up a pot of bitter lukewarm coffee. Hamilton gulped without taking his eyes off the screen, still pounding out his sacred language, trance dancing to ecstasy.

'Thank fuck McCooey's gone!' he said. 'Now I can breathe!'

His breath was sour. Bad air churned around him. The sick smell curdled from his pores as if his gut was digesting itself, a sac of pus fermenting and crawling the canker under his skin. I opened a window.

'It's fucking freezing! Close that!'

The window was just wide enough for me to squeeze my shoulders through. The street below had been busy all day - double-parking delivery vans, school buses, farmers in bull-torqued SUV's towing trailers or picking up their uniformed kids. Now it was dark and quiet. It looked like people didn't live in the town, maybe scattered to those housing projects pushed to the fringes. Artie said the barman would ring if any strangers happened to pop in for a quick drink. Stray American or Russian faces would be no problem, I knew the guy had been paid enough to buy that call. Irish faces, though, would be a different ball game. I figured any Irish "*strangers*" wouldn't be strangers at all, not in here, not to this bar guy, and that even Hamilton couldn't scare up enough cash to make it worth his while to make that tip-off call.

I told Hamilton to sit tight and I would bring him his vodka fix.

'Tell him to make it Stolichnaya, not some cheap shit he's poured into a Stoli bottle.'

The barman didn't want any chit-chat, the customers looked the other way. I paid for the vodka and took two glasses half full with ice.

'That's not Stoli!' Hamilton nearly choked. 'That pirate down there has wiped your eye! I hate swindling bastards like that!'

'You're about to shift millions of dollars out of that bank account, right?'

'And what? Are you going to try some moral equivalence shit on me, Maknazpy? Really? You know the difference between me and that little weasel downstairs?'

'He sells vodka, you rip off banks?'

'Fuck off! I've sacrificed thirty five years of my life serving this country while thieving bastards like him have been robbing the people blind! He takes cheap vodka and sells it in expensive bottles. Does the same for whiskey, gin and brandy. He probably has an extra cash register down there that the tax man knows nothing about. All cash, in the back sky rocket and fuck the system!'

Hamilton slugged a chestful of the cheap vodka and held his breath until it had seared into his gut. I didn't tell him that I hadn't even asked for Stolichnaya, and I didn't remind him that he was over the border and the barman was ripping off a different taxman, because this was more fun, more instructive.

'I could have been a rich man, you know, very rich. The dirt I have on those recordings? I could have screwed half the smug politico bastards with their sanctimonious smiles and blood on their hands!'

Hamilton was getting himself worked up, more than all PJ and Tómas' slapping and intimidation had managed. I could see the hurt in his eyes, the jealousy or injustice cracking a tear in his armor. They should have appreciated him. They should have praised him more. He deserved better and now they would deserve all they got. This was good, more than just fun, this was an opportunity to be played smart. Act stupid, let him tell me, let the shit vodka and his cooking rage ferment and stew until he *had* to tell me. I took a sip of the vodka, knew he would swill some more in reflex.

'Istanbul was your first real taste of it, wasn't it?' he said. 'I heard the background noise that time. They were fucking pulling your strings there, alright, weren't they? They didn't think you would come out the other side then either, between the Republican Guard and the fucking Mossad! But you're a survivor, aren't you, Maknazpy?! And you're not supposed to walk away this time, aye, you're supposed to take one for the team. Fuck them! Fuck their team!'

I nodded, not too much, not too keen, but keep it coming, Hamilton, we're in it together, us two against all comers.

'It was my own fault for being so green,' I said. 'I was all patriotism and God on my side, Paddy, you know how it is.'

Shit, I called him '*Paddy*', that was a mistake! Too familiar, too cozy, he picked it up and narrowed his eyes for an instant.

'Green? Think you were green? You had an excuse, Maknazpy, you *were* fucking green! You weren't paid to be anything else but green, for fuck's sake! Cannon-fodder like you *needs* to be born green, suckled on green milk and then die in green boots!'

He laughed, knocked back a mouthful that bulged his cheeks until his Adam's Apple bobbled and he swallowed a measure at a time.

Keep quiet, sip the vodka, don't look in his eyes.

'Syria? Arab Spring? We just couldn't resist, could we? Fucking Ivans sitting pretty with their Mediterranean naval base and Assad licking the balls of Iran and Hezbollah? Fucking sure thing! Pro-Democracy and Power to the People!'

Hamilton didn't hear the floorboard creak out in the corridor and I ignored it – didn't want to break the spell.

'Guys were creaming themselves to see how much armaments we could ship in there. Fuck you, Putin! Screw you, Ayatollah! And you think *you* were green? The "*Pro-Democracy Opposition*", we called them. Then that morphed into "*The Moderate Opposition*". $500m to arm the moderate opposition, they said. Train them, they said, five thousand moderate fighters a year rolling out to fight their moderate war. What could go wrong, eh? We train them and arm them in Qatar, Saudi, the Emirates, right? As soon as they roll into Syria they mysteriously disappear with our moderate guns and moderate bombs.'

I should have bought a bigger bottle. Hamilton knocked back the vodka like it was that Irish Spring Water with added sparkle and added Irishness, and it worked on him faster than any medicine, in a good way, calming him, relieving the tension, pacifying the demons. It even improved his odor, as if his body had adjusted its natural balance over the years so that a deficiency of vodka would ignite a melt-down - he didn't exactly smell of vodka now but it somehow prickled out of his skin to produce his own personal vodka musk.

'That's what I'm telling you,' he said, 'McCooey is obsessed with history when there are more important things under his red nose. But I'll tell you this much, Mr Maknazpy, all that crap about your wired up amygdala? McCooey's Ríastrad fairy-tale shite? That's not what made you interesting, at least, not after you survived that first time. No, my old son, the reason you are called when many are not is because of your innate animal cunning. That's what you bring to the party, your unsentimental and unalloyed dedication to coming out on top, regardless of collateral damage to friend, foe or non-aligned. Some mugs may fall for your faux angst and guilt-wracked crisis of conscience act, and maybe sometimes you even fool yourself, but I don't buy it. I see you, Maknazpy, and so did Alina. You're a manipulative cold blooded killer, no remorse, no looking back. But no problem, my friend, *that's* why you are really here, and that's why I have hitched up my fortune to the Maknazpy wagon. I arrange the cash, you arrange my safe passage.'

I tossed the bottle in the air, watched it arc and spin, reach its high-point, stall, then tumble down in a confused spiral. I caught it clean by the neck and dropped it to the floor.

'You should have got a bigger bottle,' he said. 'This is going to be a long night.'

CHAPTER TWENTY-TWO

'When I was starting out we kept everything on scraps of paper,' Hamilton said. 'Couldn't read half of it, mind you - big dangerous men with a licence to kill and the handwriting of a six year old. I used to sit for hours at my creaky wee desk deciphering the infantile scrawls and transcribing it onto those little cardboard index cards like they used to have in the library.'

The street below was dead. Vehicles filed along, passing through, on the way to somewhere better but in no hurry to get there.

'Now everything is VPN this, Black Swan that, Heartbleed here, Cryptowall there. It's all empire building by the nerds, you know. If I had my way, we would just go back to the old days – pencil and rice paper and away you go.'

Hamilton dumped his bowl at his feet, then balanced my meal on his knees. The gray chicken fluid oozed under the soggy crust, he scooped it up and into his mouth with his fingers.

'We're good to go?' I said. 'We can't be traced?'

'Everybody and everything can be traced. They'll never do it in real-time, though, and that's the critical factor. At first they'll think I'm in Novosibirsk, then I'll take them to St Petersburg. After that they'll shit themselves when they think we're actually in downtown Sao Paulo. By the time they finally catch up you'll be counting your dollars and I'll be in ...'

He looked at me from beneath his eyebrows, a sly taunting look.

'We can all be traced, Hamilton, as you say yourself. You just need to make sure I don't *need* to track you down after this is over. Like, say that cash doesn't end up in my bank account after all.'

'No problem, you'll get your share!' He used a thumbnail to rake a plug of hard blood out of his nose and smeared it across my dinner plate. 'Just not straight away, like, not before my ass is far and away out of your killing zone.'

I stood up from the window and moved behind him, squeezed my hands around the back of his neck.

'What did you expect, Maknazpy? I'm going to fill your boots with cash and then leave my future life prospects hanging on the amorphous Maknazpy sense of honor? Wise up! This is a perfectly reasonable precaution.'

I tightened my hand noose against his gristle and bone.

'You'll get your fucking money! I'll transfer it, you just won't be able to touch it for ten days, that's all! But if I'm not still alive and in corpore sano enough to hit the confirm button after that ten day quarantine period is up, your share reverts to one or several of my hiding places.'

This was one of Hamilton's black swans and I hadn't seen it coming. His quarantine stunt would turn my own plans upside down, *if* I let it happen.

'It's the only way I'm doing it,' he said. 'If you refuse, well, then I'll know you are acting in bad faith and you may as well whack me here and now! Be a pity, though, all that cash more or less already in your pocket, you fucking the whole thing up just because I'm too smart to leave myself vulnerable.'

He wasn't stupid, not at all, but he was just a little too smug about how smart he was, about how much smarter than me he was, and about how he would always be one step ahead. His limbo idea was a sucker punch but I would ride it, something else would come up, and I would get my chance again. I released his neck.

'Stick your bank account details down on that sheet of paper,' Hamilton said. 'That's where it will end up but I'll lay a decoy trail to shake them off first.'

What details? I poised the pen over the paper as if the mechanical act would spark the details to magically appear. Shit. I never did know the details. The last big pay off worked pretty much like this one – a computer geek invoking the net gods to voodoo the cash from one place to another. I didn't need to know. The Cayman Islands were part of it, as far as I could recall, and then it had filtered through to regular bank accounts in Rio for Yasmin and in Manhattan for Rose and young Con, or was it New Hampshire? Fuck it! I could find out by calling Yasmin and Rose but that wasn't going to happen. Anyway, since Hamilton was so hot on trust and precautions, what was to stop the slippery bastard siphoning everything that was already sitting in those accounts to fuck out and into his own bank if I did give him the details?

'Forget it,' I said, 'Set a bank account up for me. Is that enough trust for you? Enough to prove I'm acting in good faith here?'

Hamilton squinted his surprise, suspicious eyes examining my face, trying to chisel out what my angle was. A big smile broke on his vodka veined face. I had no angle. *He* had all the angles covered.

'I'll probably go for the Caymans. You can work it out from there when you get home.' Up close like this his eyes were bloodshot and yellow but somehow faked a charisma he didn't have. 'But perhaps you've decided you're not going home?'

He could have been speaking Yasmin's words, or Rose's. I ignored him, told myself I hadn't decided anything beyond how to get out of here. Rose, most definitely and especially Rose, would be wise to that cop out – my feigned indecision, playing for time until I could plead that the luxury of choice had been removed from me. Long before the end, she had become just too pissed off to care anymore. Yasmin wasn't quite at that stage yet but she would get there eventually, if I were to go back.

'You sure about this?' Hamilton nudged me. 'I'm putting it in one of my own spare accounts in the Caymans, okay? I don't want you coming whining about it afterwards, you hear me?'

I heard him and, through him, heard Rose and Yasmin also.

'How much?' I said.

'McCooey agreed $5 million, didn't he? I know, I'm a fool to myself, you don't have to tell me, but forget the wire in that fucking house, get me to Paris and you get your whole five mill. I'll send the Account Log-in and ID anywhere you want. Ten days from now you can open the piggy bank, as long as I am still alive and free.'

'So it's not only the real cash in the legit bank. You're hitting the digital shit as well. How much?'

'You have your five mill, Maknazpy, take it and run! You don't want the grief that comes with the knowledge of how much and who from, believe me, I'm doing you a big favor here.'

'Does Yakov know yet?'

Hamilton sniggered like a school boy getting one over on the teacher.

'Not yet, probably. They were already locked out from making any fund transfers without my encryption code. Now I've taken the code from their side and changed it so they are completely screwed. They'll soon work out their code is redundant but won't know for sure how much I have hi-jacked or where it has gone.'

'So it's finished? Nothing more to do here?'

'Aye, more or less.' Hamilton's eyes changed again, not fearful, exactly, but primed for action, like prey suddenly alert to the ghosting shadow of its predator. 'A few minor procedures I'm waiting on, that's all. But you still have to wait for the ten days before you can touch it, don't forget that, and if anything happens to me in the meantime then you can forget the whole thing. Not that I don't trust you, like, I do the same with all my own accounts. Once a month I check in with a confirmation code, keeps my assets safe, so even if some bastard gets in there they won't be able to touch it.'

'Then get your shit together,' I said. 'We are going back for that wire.'

"A police spokesperson declined to comment on reports that the men were targeted as part of a drugs war between rival criminal gangs."

'Wankers!' Hamilton sneered at the car radio. 'Reports from who?! Some half-pissed hack that McIntyre has tamed?'

"Police say the Ligoniel Road at Wolfhill Road will remain closed for the rest of today while a forensic examination of the murder scene is conducted.'

'Conducted is right!' Hamilton laughed, 'and give big Colin McIntyre the baton!'

'Wolfhill? Will that be a problem for us?'

'Nah, miles away,' Hamilton said, 'and we're coming from the south. We have enough problems but that won't be one of them. Might even be a good thing, might keep the ordinary decent policeman out of our way.'

Hamilton was buzzing. He had just dumped thirty something years of loyal service irrevocably down the toilet. That alone would have been enough for his ego to bask in the endorphin high but, even better, he had cracked his freedom by knocking over a prime plunder hub of the underworld clans – any fears he had about returning for the wire were flushed away in the adrenalin rush.

'There's a wee lane runs more or less parallel with the back of the house,' he said. 'We'll pull in there, cross two or three fields on foot and come at the house from the back. If there's nobody there to give me grief I'll be in and out in five minutes. If there *is* anybody there, then that's your province, okay?'

He spoke quickly, without drawing a breath, and I started to wonder if he had stashed some of Alina's happy pills.

'And we'll need another vehicle. Fuck knows where McCooey got this wreck from but it's bound to have been tagged by now.'

Artie had left the keys with the barman before being picked up by a retired priest from Finnis. Hamilton avoided the regular gas stations and their security cameras, asked around until he found an illegal diesel operation up a dark lane, then criss-crossed the side roads going north.

'They have cameras monitoring all the main roads, all the time, don't even need to have manpower tasked to watch for us, you know, just input our licence plate into the system, it does the rest. And that's not me being paranoid, by fuck, that's a fact.'

'What about the two perverts blown away by Tomás' crew the other night?'

'Those two? What about them? A Whitehall warrior in the section that hands out the licenses to arms dealers and the other bastard a broker with a Section 5 certificate. The two of them over here raping and brutalizing young boys that were trafficked on demand. Think anybody wants to open that can of worms? Doubt it! Doubt it very muchly!'

Hamilton gripped the steering wheel so hard it looked like his white knuckles would rip through the red parchment skin. Flecks of white spit foamed on his lips. His eyes were sore to look at. His MI5 bosses must have detected a change in him. The cool disinterested observer losing his cool and in danger of letting his emotions usurp his duty. And there is always someone waiting to pick up on the hazard signals, noticing a stray word or unexpected reaction, homing in, alert now for the one off lapse to smoulder into a pattern, threatening deviance, chaos, even exposure. In that herd the weak get culled, and quickly. Hamilton was getting out just in time.

'A Section 5 certificate entitles the arms broker to deal in otherwise prohibited arms – assault rifles, explosives, combat gear. I happen to know that the Whitehall wonk approved your man's Section 5, and I also know Her Majesty's Revenue and Customs were on his tail over an unlicensed shipment of arms he brokered all the way down to the Congo - £8 million and enough Blood Diamond money to pay an extra bounty, with Whitehall Willie getting his cut. Like I said, there's no investigation into their killing because they were never here. End of.'

Hamilton was more volatile than was good for this job. Sick sweat purged his vodka bloom. He sucked air into his chest then held it before rasping some words deep in his throat on the exhale.

'Fuck them. Maknazpy! Fuck them all sideways!'

CHAPTER TWENTY-THREE

The runway lights behind us throbbed an orange halo like sunset on a new horizon at the edge of the known world. Hamilton splashed rank piss against the car and over his ankles and claimed he wasn't nervous. The house was dead ahead, somewhere in the darkness across the black fields. The back of my neck tingled. It felt good to be alive again.

I poked Hamilton ahead, he clambered over the frosted steel of the gate and into the field, stumbling, down on his knees and then splaying forward saving himself with outstretched hands and rolling over on his side. He whispered his curse, dragged himself up, picked his way over the deep ruts in the dark. Heavy wheels had scraped through this earth before the ice numbed it into cement-hard grooves. I took his wrist and guided him to the edge of the field. The drainage ditch was invisible below but the airport glow outlined the jagged hedges above our heads. I stopped to listen. The night was still, the black space ahead without sound or shadow to give direction or scale.

Hamilton jerked sideways to belch a throatful of vomit into the ditch. A creature bolted into the hedge and clawed its way through to the other side. I hunkered down and waited. No movement, no torches, no red dot dancing to the sniper's tune across my torso.

'Keep going to fuck!' Hamilton urged. 'It's over the next field!'

We kept going. Over the next field and then into a third. Still no house, only more ditches and hedges to crawl and scratch through. This was too far. If I had to run this would be way too far with a snatch squad on my heels.

'There! I told you!'

There was something at the far end of the fourth field, not exactly a shape but another kind of blackness, a black void in the black sky.

'There's a gate in here somewhere leads to the lane at the back.'

Hamilton tripped over the rough ground again and banged his knee. I placed my hand on his chest, felt his thumping heart and pumping lungs. The heat from his soft body was like a furnace. We were about 100 meters from the house, if they had a thermal scanner pointed this way he would be red hot on their monitor. He rested his elbows on his knees, then sunk down and curled into a ball.

'You go ahead,' he gasped, 'I'll catch up when I get my breath back.'

I squatted down behind him. No movement ahead but I knew they wouldn't be seen. I blanked out Hamilton's panting and strained to listen - no movement, no sound. I waited.

'What the fuck's that?!'

A low growling noise far away, coming closer, a chopper with red and green lights, rotating red beacon at back, skimming over the house, banking around, hovering like a hawk, the white search light erupting to split the black night in two.

'Holy fuck! We're too late, Maknazpy!'

I eased Hamilton down to his knees again. Wait. Watch. The fields off to our right blinked and ignited into their nightshow - the approach lights for the International Airport. A passenger jet coming fast. The chopper was too close, he killed his searchlight and spun away from the house, away from the airport. I dragged Hamilton to his feet, pushed him forward. We were at the gate as the aircraft angled over the hedges and aimed for the runway.

'Move it!' I screamed over the jet roar. 'They wouldn't send a chopper if they had men inside waiting for us!'

'Ballicks! How would you know?! They could have a hundred fucking men in there!'

He was right, I didn't know, and mostly I really hoped the place would be deserted but, deep in my core, there was a fragment of gleeful battle hunger howling to be unleashed. I pushed Hamilton through the gate. The black shape was even blacker now, burning runway lights bleeding all particles of light from the house, bartering synthetic day for depraved night.

I kept a hold of Hamilton's collar, guided him to the gable wall. The door would trigger the spotlight at the front. I waited. Steam swilled from Hamilton's head, his face glistened with sticky sweat. The crack of breaking glass splintered through the still air. I dodged down, waited some more. The low drone of a far away engine rose and fell, then silence.

I shouldered Hamilton in first, let him creep along to the end of the corridor. No sound, no reaction, in through the window and tight to Hamilton before he opened the door. He hesitated, I nudged him forward, he prised the door open – the sharp chemical tang intensified in the perfect dark silence. He tapped the wall to find the switch, the light tube choked and stalled, the harsh light blinked into life.

'The cleaners have been here,' he said, 'hard to get good staff these days.'

The room appeared bigger than before, carpet and furniture removed, the floor scoured and scrubbed. The fumes from the cleaning fluids stung my nose and eyes, and detonated Hamilton's jagged breathing into a ruckus of cough and splutter. A large circle of the tiled floor marked where the two men had been shot, the surface purged by a heavy duty scrape and polish routine.

Hamilton stood in the center of the room like a ring master and turned a slow circle as he surveyed the walls and ceiling.

'No problem,' he said. 'Wait here a minute.'

He brushed past me and opened a small storage cupboard screwed to the wall in the corridor, rummaged around until he found the screwdriver and wire-cutter.

'Just where I left them,' he said, 'now let's see how smart these whizz kids really are.'

He popped the cover from the light switch to expose a jangle of wires and a thumb-nail sized box. He flipped the box out and twisted it open at the base.

'They have the SD Card from this one but I would have been majorly pissed off with them if they had missed it – that was easy.'

He was buzzing again, moving with speed and efficiency to unscrew the electric socket on the far wall – the spy camera was gone, he moved on to the curtain fixing, stretched up to examine the decorative stopper at the end – gone.

'Lucky you hid them so well, isn't it?' I said.

Hamilton did his patronizing smirk, started the tuneless whistle of a man at work, pulled himself up on the window sill and peered up at the corner.

'MI5 had me set those up. I installed them first, then Yana's extra set up. I had to fill in requisition forms and get them signed off. Things would be badly wrong if the Brits couldn't find their own gear, wouldn't it?'

He clambered down from the window sill and crossed to the diagonal corner. He stretched as high as he could, again squinting up at nothing.

'Tell you what, Maknazpy, if the safety of the realm is in the hands of these so-called fast-tracked whizz kids, I fear for the future!'

I stood behind him. The plaster where the walls met the ceiling was old and a little cracked.

'Up there, exactly, where the new breed of MI5 super kids *should* have looked!' he scoffed. 'But, no, no, once they found what they already knew was there, that was them! Back to Loughside for a serious debrief and a bout of report writing – another super successful mission and something for their next promotion board – except I reversed the motion sensor on them, they stopped recording as soon as anyone entered the room! Wee wankers!'

I peered closer. Hairline cracks on the ceiling, little gaps where the plaster had flaked and fallen away, rough edges where the walls met.

'The units are in both of those corners,' he said. 'You'll see insulation foam between the roof rafters. Lift that up and it'll look like the plasterboard of the ceiling,' he shook his head, 'that's a false bottom. Take this screwdriver, poke the board up and the camera units will be underneath, little plastic box about the size of your thumb. Just lift the whole thing, right, but be careful, the camera itself is at the end of the wire, don't snag it when you are extracting it, okay?'

Access to the roof space was through a small square hole in the ceiling close to the window we had come in. I knocked off the light in the room and opened the front door just enough to scan the yard outside - all quiet, the spotlight would trigger if anyone was moving around out there.

'You're going up to get it,' I said. 'I'll keep watch down here.'

'What? How? Like, if I had known we were coming I would have brought my ladder with me, you know?'

'Is there a light up there?'

He flicked the switch beside the door.

'No problem, you can't see the light from outside, believe me, I checked.'

I braced Hamilton against the wall and used his soft gut to lever myself up against the square lid, pushed it open and away, wedged my elbows in the gap and pulled myself up. It was like an ice-box up here, freezing and damp at the same time, no space to stand straight, the bare bulb leaking just enough dim light so I could make out the rafters breaking through the pink insulation fiber.

'Go straight across and then follow the wall to the right,' Hamilton's voice echoed from below. 'It's in that corner, be careful how you remove it!'

'Fuck off, Hamilton!'

I teetered across the rafter like a tightrope walker, except I was crouched double by the low roof. Scaly claws scratched in the darkest corner, a clunk like a small book being dropped, then another, and more scratching and squeaks. Edging along to the corner. Shit! I forgot the screwdriver!

'Hamilton! Throw that fucking screwdriver up here!'

No answer, but the sound of wood splintering down below. What the fuck was he doing down there? I started to turn back, saw the shape in the corner. The pink fiber formed a small mound where Hamilton said a thumbnail sized camera unit would be. On my knees, scrabbled over the rafters, pulled the insulation back, a carpet rolled up, like a bag. More splintering down below, wood tearing, Hamilton's footsteps running across the corridor. The carpet bag was heavy, wedged in tight against the roof. I dragged it out, scaly claws shuffled off.

A purple and red scarf, twisted and stretched around her pale throat, tangled in the long black hair, soft and glossy even here, in this squalid vermin cave, in her tawdry carpet body bag. Her jaw hung detached from her face and black blood crusted her nose and mouth. She had bitten through her tongue. I felt her neck for a pulse, her head rolled over, saw the rats had already started to open that side of her face. Brigid should have been laid out like Queen Méadhbh, not discarded here like a piece of worthless shit. Her killers knew that, intended this as a wanton insult, their ritual to demean her and us all, a "*fuck you*" message delivered with a sneer. Hamilton was getting away but I wouldn't ignore this affront to our dignity, she was one of our own, a human being.

I hauled the carpet bag across the rafters. Sweat ran into my eyes despite the freeze, must have prickled the tears that bubbled down my face. I sat on the edge, my legs dangling, and pulled Brigid on my lap. Her head nestled softly against my neck, scented hair smeared against my wet cheeks. Her divine perfume lingered, the warm musk of a living woman not submitting to the creeping stench of death, so it felt that she wasn't dead yet, or that she was dead but that dead and not dead couldn't be *that* simple – now a live and intense presence, now a dead and phantom memory. I clasped her tightly against me with my right arm, sure she sighed in my ear, the last gasp of breath squeezed from her lungs, the last murmur of the dying queen, the dead queen. My left arm strained as I lowered us down, dropped to the floor without letting her go.

The front door lay wide open, the security light creating a false day outside. I cradled Brigid in my arms and carried her out, Hamilton disappearing around the corner of the big house as I laid her down on the icy ground. I unravelled the scarf noose from her neck and draped it around her face, covering the rat bites and smoothing her hair back. Her perfume melted around me in the bitter night air. I kissed her. Her cold lips tasted only of death.

It *was* that simple.

CHAPTER TWENTY-FOUR

Crystals of ice crunched under my pounding boots. No need for stealth and caution now, and Hamilton would find out what that amygdala Ríastrad shit was all about when I ripped out his black heart and rammed it down his throat. I was breathing hard in the cold air, starting to ghost in and out of my own body, me and the other in parallel, nature overtaking nurture – no pretending anymore. Reached the corner of the big house, brake lights down below, exhaust fumes dancing red, Hamilton half running, half staggering.

A black shape jumped in front of me, I kept running, launched high with my knee in his chest, crumbled beneath me, stamped my boot on his face as momentum carried me on, stumbled, caught my balance and came upright, took a heavy crack across my back but no pain - not now, not like this, the demon didn't know pain. The car was still there, Hamilton almost safe. Two more dived on me from the side, taking arms and legs, crashing me over, kicking, twisting, biting, clawing, one on top of me now, crowing some Russian shit to the others, thought he had me, stabbed two fingers in his eye socket, right up to the knuckle. Three more were coming fast. I could see it all from down there and up here, gliding above the pain, hovering outside the squirming bodies, like watching a dog fight, only I was one of the dogs, happening to me but I wasn't there, over-ruled by the Ríastrad.

BOOM!!

Hamilton's car went up, blast wave like a tsunami quaked through the ground, knocked the Russians off me.

BOO-OM!!

A second one, the car spouting a white fireball rocket into the black sky, spirals of flame surging upwards until it could rise no further then fanning out above us, a last pulse of orange blue tornado and it was gone.

Their nervous systems were fucked, the brain rocking inside the skull, the limbs disconnected like the spinal cord had snapped. I saw myself emerge from beneath them, two hands deep into a thick throat, squeezing his Russian life to pulp. A shaky hand fumbled a Makarov – tore my left thigh, still no pain, I saw it, and saw him, he fired again, scorched across my hip. I caught him on the way down, teeth deep in his face, one hand on the pistol, the other crushing his throat. I saw the big one coming behind me with the half plank but wouldn't let this one go. He swung the plank and knocked me sideways, I was on my knees with his throat in my hands. Their boots rained down on me but I had this one and was never fucking letting go. Screaming and spitting Russian shit, one stuck the pistol in my face. More screaming, I don't speak Russian but I knew what was happening, the boss man shouting I was to be taken alive and the rest screaming at the guy to blow this Amerikanski motherfucker away. Fuck him, I wrestled a better grip on his throat and squeezed. The guy with the gun could wait no longer. I squeezed harder. They whacked me with the plank, my head spun, Brigid's perfume on my lips, her soft hair against my face. He cracked me with the plank. Brigid sighed her death kiss into my mouth. He slipped away from my fingers, and I was in darkness again.

The brain doesn't function like an on/off light switch unless there is a total and catastrophic shut down. Even when they were dragging me over the frost crusted stones and throwing me into the van like a condemned carcass there was a pulse of action in there somewhere, hanging on and looking after business until I came back. And when I did come back it was slowly, strings of transmitters blinking and flashing life across the gaps but cracking up under the strain, faltering, then sparking up again. Everything I knew or felt or thought I knew jumbled around in a crazy gyroscope, no anchoring filter, not even the normal veneer that I was somehow in control or that this mish-mash of sensations, this life, could only exist as I decided.

The testosterone marinated banter seeped through the fog first, macho talk in any language, beefing up their schizoid brothers-in-arms brouhaha, stoked with raw spirits in the bottles they guzzled and shared. I had been there myself, done that, brutalized through choice and accident so that sucking the corps de esprit con job offered some comfort when I had been excluded, excluded myself, from genuine human intimacy. I guessed they weren't even talking about me, had better diversions like women, drink, sport.

It was only when my eyes opened for normal business that the real pain erupted. It wasn't only that my legs were painful, it was as if I had no form below my waist at all except for a new limb called agony. When the shock hit me and made me shudder the movement cranked the pain to even higher intensity, unbearable, and I think I passed out again, only to emerge back into my new pain world knowing that this was it forever, things would never get better. A dirty frayed blue nylon rope strangled the blood supply to my thighs, their token effort to bring Yakov his living trophy.

One of them noticed I was alive and stamped on my chest. Fuck! Damage there also, ribs for certain, my right shoulder was screwed, maybe dislocated or smashed altogether, my right arm dead. My mouth and nostrils foamed with blood but I could breathe if I nipped shallow bubbles of air that didn't require my chest to move. The stamping man pulled his pants down and pissed straight into my face. I couldn't move my head, it was like being waterboarded with his stinking piss and contempt. I couldn't hold my breath and reflexed into a coughing splutter that cranked the pain from head to toe. I knew the body can't sustain this torture for long before heart failure, and right then I didn't care.

They thought the piss waterboard was hilarious and, as always happens, another one thought he could do even better than his pal. He was already high and unsteady on his feet and had to bounce from side to side to move up the van before making a big deal of dropping his pants and squatting his shit crusted ass in my face. The rest roared, he grunted and strained, I closed my eyes and heaved as much air into my lungs as my crushed chest would allow. They chanted 'Maxim! Maxim!' Maxim farted in my face.

CRUNCH!!

The van hurtled sideways with the impact, something heavy and fast crashing into us from the right. We tipped over on two wheels, kept skidding forward, out of control, smacked into a ditch and tumbled over on our side, sliced down off the road and into a field, rocked and rattled, then slewed to a halt. Maxim's hairy ass smothered my face, he floundered like a beetle on its back until another one hauled him to his feet. I could see the rebound of blue flashing lights, heard the Irish voices screaming at them to come out slowly, one at a time, hands up. They scrabbled out of the van as a fighting unit, aggression and firepower their only tactic, ready to fuck the police or anyone else in their way. Shots fired, shouting, fighting, the police squads flooding into the field, catching some, chasing others.

I lay there, twisted on my side, struggling to breathe. My brain was starting to work out this pain crap so, instead of my body being just one giant mass of pain receptors, it was beginning to analyse and shelve the damage and distribute the slivers of pain to its rightful owner. My right arm asserted its suffering with sharp stabs, then the ribs on both sides, and my left fist was not far behind. Okay, if that's how it was I could take each one and work with it, no problem. The big problem, though, was the fact I couldn't feel my legs at all.

A young cop clambered into the van, wearing the usual paramilitary black uniform of a tactical unit. He shone a torch around the skewed interior, calling a running commentary into the radio mic attached to his helmet. He was thorough and careful, took his time to scrutinize the debris, reported slowly and clearly to his superior. I tried to call for help but my throat wouldn't work. He worked his way along methodically, reached me eventually, shone the high-powered torch in my face and then twisted his mouth in disgust.

'Ach for fuck's sake! This cunt here's shit himself!'

CHAPTER TWENTY-FIVE

Belfast, May 22nd

Artie's God moves in mysterious ways. He moved me out of the hospital and into the big red brick house with Artie, yellow-faced Quinn and the other blackballed men of collars. I was advised to consider it as a type of quarantine, a limbo to be endured until somebody somewhere decided it was safe to release me back into the general population. A couple of gray faced policemen had arrived at my hospital bed late one bleak afternoon to say I wasn't under arrest, wouldn't be under arrest and, in fact, had never been under arrest.

The driver who brought me from the hospital directed me to a small room on the ground floor at the back as far away from the others as possible. Artie kept himself very busy doing nothing most days, made sure to either hide in his own room or be out of the house altogether. The little round housekeeper gently passed on Quinn's instruction that I should stay out of sight as much as possible and must stay in my room when any visitors called. I soon realized that the house was some sort of open prison for Quinn and the rest and that nobody *ever* visited. I could move about pretty well by now with the aid of the aluminum walking frame and shuffled around as much as I could so that Quinn was forced to adjust his daily routine if he wanted to avoid me.

Rain hammered off my bedroom window for the first two days and the room pressed in on me like the prison cell I had been denied. On the third day the rain stopped and summer started. Suddenly this was another country - blue skies, birdsong, sweet smelling earth, and warm sunshine on my face. Early morning was best. It was bright here at 4.30 a.m. and I would hobble into the garden before 5 a.m. when the birds worked themselves into their song frenzy. I did one circuit around the long lawn on the first day before I had to sag into the garden bench below the hanging yellow tree. I added a circuit each day, hoping it would make me stronger and speed my recovery. On the good days it was almost too much to bear, on the bad days I knew I would never recover. On one of the bad days I was stretched out on the bench when his voice came.

'Well, Con, how are things?'

PJ and three big guys standing over me. I struggled to pull myself upright but PJ lifted his foot to press my thigh back down on the bench.

'What do *you* want?' I said. 'You should have called to say you were coming. I would have told you to keep the fuck away from me.'

'Oh? That's very hostile, Con. What's wrong? You feeling all vulnerable now?'

I took his ankle and prised his foot off my leg. It was a struggle for me to even get a grip on him and he knew it.

'We have unfinished business, so we do,' he smiled. 'I want straight answers and I don't think you can act the big lad about it.'

He took my hand and pulled me up so I could swivel around and sit upright.

'Ask McCooey,' I said. 'He knows it all. I know nothing. Anything I thought I knew was either wrong or got kicked out of me by Yakov's heavy squad. I was concussed, it's all blank.'

'You just accidentally tripped over Brigid's body? I heard they would have found your DNA all over her – that is, if they had *tested* for DNA, which they fucking didn't!'

There was real pain in PJ's voice, pain that said Brigid was more to him than just an old comrade. If I didn't feel vulnerable before I did now.

'I didn't find her by accident. Hamilton directed me up there so that I *would* find her. He knew she was up there. I don't know how he knew. He must have been messaging someone when I thought he was hacking into the bank system. And I don't know who he was speaking to but my money is on America – maybe not Yana or CIA but some branch of US security. Artie says the Brits murdered Brigid and Tomás and then double-crossed Hamilton. I don't know. Hamilton told me the Brits wanted him dead and that they planned to pin it on me. That's all I know, PJ, so now you can fuck off, okay?'

'No, as a matter of fact, it's not okay.'

He was straining to hold it together, had a job to do and didn't want the young ones seeing his weakness.

'For starters, how come you walked free? Never mind Hamilton, you knee-capped three Russians in that house in Stranmillis. I know you did, McCooey was there. Then another couple of Russians admitted to a private clinic outside Dublin, crushed windpipe and internal injuries. How come you get away with that? Maybe you're still with the CIA? Maybe you're with the Brits?'

The three big guys edged closer. One of them was that kid who punched me out when I was escaping from them with Yana and Hamilton.

'CIA pulled rank on the Brits and made them back off,' I said. 'I've got my secrets too, you know? It wouldn't be in the interests of the United States to have some prick Brit attorney tripping me up in court and maybe setting some of that stuff free.'

'What way did you find her?' The young guy with the big punch squeezed my shoulder. He sounded very young and his voice was choked in his throat. 'What way was she?'

'Michael!' PJ stepped forward. He nodded at the other two to take care of Michael and flashed a warning look to me. 'Michael is Brigid's sister's son.'

The kid thought he wanted to hear the truth, his shaky voice said he dreaded what I might say but he still had the guts to step up and ask for it.

'She looked peaceful when I found her. Looked like she had just dropped off to sleep, like she didn't know a thing about it. She looked just like she was dreaming and about to wake up at any second. She looked at peace with herself.'

PJ knew I was lying through my teeth and I think the kid did also but it was what he needed to hear right then. Michael allowed the other two to lead him away but then stopped and shrugged out of their embrace. He came back to me, took my hand in both of his and said, 'Thank you, I'll tell my mum you said that, thank you.' Then he turned and walked off. PJ stroked Michael's cheek as he passed and waited until he was out of earshot before speaking again.

'Thanks for doing that, Con, much appreciated.'

'I have seen plenty of dead bodies, PJ, believe me, but there was just something really bad about this. I can't explain it, you know, but it just seemed so demeaning, so disrespectful. It made me sick.'

PJ sat on the bench beside me and the bees buzzed above our heads.

'Hamilton told me that it was always out there on the grapevine that one of you three was an informer,' I said.

'Nobody's ever going to know now if that was true or not, are they?' he half winked.

No, I guessed not, and it was history now anyway, it didn't, *it shouldn't,* matter to anyone anymore even if it was true.

'I saw you with McIntyre you know,' I said, 'that night I was holed up with McCooey and Hamilton over in south Belfast. After Tomás and the boys left, McIntyre rolled up and you two had a meet-up.'

'And what? You trying to say I'm the informer? I had something to do with what happened to Brigid and Tomás?'

He didn't even sound angry, just intrigued to find out what I was really thinking.

'I'm not saying anything, PJ. I saw you, that's all. Like I heard Hamilton's tape with you meeting McIntyre years ago, when he was tipping you off.'

'Aye! You heard! You seen! But you still know fuck all, sure you don't?'

'I know what I saw,' I said, 'that's all.'

'So, you seen that bastard Hamilton getting blown to fuck too?'

I shrugged. Now the anger *was* starting to curdle around his gut.

'Tell me this.' He shoved his forehead up against mine, 'what height would you say Hamilton was, about my size, wasn't he? And you're about a head taller than me, aren't you? And Big McIntyre is about a head taller than you, isn't he? Then how come to fuck the forensic boys worked out the charred scraps of bone they found in that car made the body somebody McIntyre's fucking height?!'

What *did* I see? I saw Hamilton running. I saw Russian boots kicking my head in. I saw the car vaporize in a ball of flame.

'Who knows about this, PJ?'

'*Everybody* fucking knows! And everybody knows the last time anybody seen McIntyre he was being lowered into a big hole in the ground with a headstone saying - "*Here lies Paddy fucking Hamilton - now Rest in Peace, you two-faced bastard*"!'

CHAPTER TWENTY-EIGHT

I counted forty-one steps on the stairs up to Artie's room, twenty more than I could manage without stopping and cursing my legs. PJ didn't offer to help and I wouldn't have accepted. I had to stop twice more before reaching Artie's door.

'Artie! Open up! I know you are in there!'

I hammered the door with the fighting end of Quinn's blackthorn walking stick. Artie didn't move.

'Artie! Your car is sitting out front! We know you are in there!'

PJ shifted me to the side and launched his weight behind a kick that landed right beside the door handle. The lock mechanism was old, and rocked under the impact. PJ kicked again, wood cracked. One more kick would do it.

'Alright! Alright! Wait a minute!' Artie was suddenly very much at home. He pulled the door open enough to thrust his red face out. 'What the hell are you two playing at?! Can a man not say his prayers without the Jackboot boys kicking his door in?!'

Artie kept the windows shut tight and the curtains closed against the bright summer day outside. His air was heavy with dust and brandy fumes. A cheap lamp was propped against his drinking chair, the bare bulb too small and too yellow for this room.

'You let me believe Hamilton was dead, Artie. What game am I missing here?'

'Indeed, I hope he is dead, or else that Presbyterian Minister wasted some very fine words, but as far as I know that was Hamilton we buried.'

Artie rubbed his eyes and dragged out a long yawn. PJ reached down behind the chair and came up with the brandy bottle. 'Have you run out of communion wine, Monsignor?' PJ clinked the half empty bottle with his ring finger and set it up on the fireplace.

'Say it *is* McIntyre in that hole,' I said, 'what about Hamilton? You don't move the sort of money he was talking about without it registering somewhere.'

'Exactly, Con!' Artie said, 'Exactly!' He took the blackthorn stick from my hands and used it to point to the walnut carriage clock on the mantelpiece. 'It would register somewhere, but only if there was someone out there watching for it and waiting to register it.'

PJ tilted the clock forward and peeked down the back, then lifted it and turned around to show me the micro listening device attached to the underside.

'Let's go get some sunshine on our faces,' I said.

I sat under the yellow tree until my legs came to life, then joined them in the middle of the garden. They exchanged their sly glances as I approached and I don't know how much Artie had told him but PJ looked at me in a new way, as if waiting to see if what he had heard was true.

'So, what's the story, Artie?' I said. 'Let's assume that's Yana's listening device in your room, right?'

'It's not over, Con, not as far as they are concerned, and they're waiting for the next move.'

'Sure they are,' I said, 'so I guess me getting myself stomped to a pulp by Yakov's team was only a clever trick on my part, throwing Yana off my tail, that's what they are thinking?'

'Well, Con, they don't believe you could have been so naive and downright stupid as to watch Hamilton transfer millions of dollars out of that bank without making sure you got your share. I imagine they are waiting for your share to register somewhere, as you say, then they will trace it back to where it came from. They hope that will lead them to Hamilton – that's if Paddy the Brit *is* still alive, of course, which I have no good reason to believe.'

Yana should have realized just how stupid I really was, that way she wouldn't have wasted so much time waiting on that "*share*" of mine that was never going to turn up.

'They must be desperate to get their hands on those recordings,' PJ said, 'like, they're hardly that bothered about a bank robbery if it's not one of their banks or their money, are they?' They both stared at me as if they expected an answer. 'Unless, of course, it *is* CIA money,' PJ smirked, 'dirty money for dirty CIA operations. What do you think, Con?'

I didn't think anything, except that if Artie's room was bugged then mine certainly was, and probably every nook and corner in that house, also.

'I think it's time to see what Yana is thinking, and her bosses,' I said. 'I bet if we go into my room and I start telling PJ all about Hamilton and the bank job and CIA black ops we will find out just how quickly Yana can drag her sorry ass over here, that's what I think.'

CHAPTER TWENTY-NINE

'I've seen fungus with more brains!' Yana dug her nails into my shoulder. 'Your head is full of shit!'

The wheels spun on the gravel as we lurched away from the priest house. She clamped her jaw and grinded through the gears. A truck driver blasted his horn when we swung across the Antrim Road. She ran a red light before braking hard and swerving into the entrance of Belfast zoo.

'Yeah, well, you aren't the first to remark on that,' I said, 'but maybe if you had told me what the hell was going on here I could have helped. You know, like, co-operation?'

'Fuck you, Maknazpy! You were with Hamilton when he ripped off that bank! And when he pulled the tapes from that house! You were with Yakov's nephew in Rio weeks before you even got here!'

That was all a different life. Meeting Pyotr over a caipiroska or three, crunching out the details as I wandered up and down Leblon beach, bringing it all together in my big plan - I was in control back then, and the world revolved around my white Irish ass.

'So things didn't work out like I thought,' I said, 'but you *know* I was being used. I wouldn't still be here if your bosses thought any different.'

Yana forced a dry cough.

'Don't get too cocky yet, smart guy,' she warned, 'the jury is still out on Mr Con Maknazpy. Some folks think you are an insignificant piece of dumb shit and not worth wasting our time on. Others think nobody could be *that* dumb. Some of them think you are dangerous, and they're the guys you need to worry about right now.'

'What do you think, Yana?'

'You don't want to know what I think, Maknazpy, really you don't!'

She was right, I didn't want to know.

'So, Mr Big, how much did Hamilton pull out of that bank?'

'At one point he said he could get his hands on a couple of mill,' I shrugged, 'but I know there was a lot more than that on the table.'

'Two mill? Yeah, try two hundred, and then some, big shot!'

$200 million? How could it be $200 million? Artie's pirate priest was collared with a few cases full of cash, and Hamilton had piped millions more out of Vienna, but $200 million? That was too much, that was impossible. Yana laughed at me. She knew exactly what *was* possible, had been a kick ass financial analyst on Wall Street before she found her spiritual CIA home. She barked it out but I couldn't keep up. She cursed in disgust at my stupidity and then ran over it again, giving me an even more dumbed down version.

The Russian gas and oil industry was thriving until a few years ago. One of the up and coming companies was a Moscow outfit specializing in a particular niche of gas exploration. The real ownership behind the firm was vague, and a front of shell and subsidiary holding companies registered in the Netherlands kept it that way, but that wasn't unusual and it wasn't on anyone's radar. That is, not until the Russian police swooped on the company's Moscow office and put the whole operation under lockdown. They sent in a team to bag the entire contents of the office and ship it out of there. The company staff were arrested and charged with some fabricated crime. That left the door open for someone to hijack the company using the confiscated company stamps and official passwords. Within a couple of months, a new ownership was in place and they managed to rewrite the accounts for previous years so that big profits suddenly became big losses. They submitted multiple claims for refunds of all the tax they had paid over the previous years. The Moscow tax authorities were unusually generous and unusually quick to act. Tax refunds of over $200 million were paid back within weeks. Then the Russian laundry machine really went into overdrive, thousands of transfers between phantom companies that are established and then fold once a couple of million passes through their bank account. Companies based in Cyprus, Moldova, Lithuania, Latvia and probably owned by other companies registered in the UK or Ireland, Switzerland or the Netherlands, British Virgin Islands or the Caymans. Millions of dollars swilling around between fake companies and colluding banks before it came back clean to Latvia or a certain bank in Vladivostock.

'And some in the CIA's bank in Vienna?' I said.

'Even you aren't so naive as to think it's only Mafia money we're talking about here,' Yana said. 'The line where the Moscow government stop and the Russian Mafia begin is never clear but most of that cash is earmarked to attack the interests of the United States. Our operation in Vienna had a handle on the dirty Russian cash being smuggled into east Ukraine and Syria, among other places. Hamilton sold us out to the Ivans, and you were with him the whole time he was on the take.'

'What's the big deal with the tapes from that house?' I said.

'It was a meeting place for the Latvian bankers and the money people from the front companies in the UK and wherever. Hamilton recorded them. He thinks he is safe from both sides as long as he holds those tapes. He is wrong. The Russians will soon realize he doesn't have anything on us. We want the tapes before the Russians whack him.'

'And your bosses figure this insignificant piece of dumb shit is somehow going to get the tapes for them?'

'Don't over-estimate yourself, Maknazpy, nobody else does, believe me.'

Silver streamers of cloud ghosted across the evening sky above my yellow tree. Sweet honeysuckle and jasmine pumped their heavy perfume. The neighborhood kids unleashed a full-scale water fight down the street. A distant fife and drum corps claimed their share of the summer air. Artie was impressed by Yana's big numbers, PJ shook his head.

'Why is she telling you about this now?' PJ said.

'They want the money back, they want the tapes.'

'Sounds like a lot of old balls to me,' PJ said. 'Like, what are *you* supposed to do about it?'

'Same as always, do what I'm told, ask no questions, move on, don't look back – the same as all of us.'

'I heard news from Rome today,' Artie said. 'Johannes Beikle was due to be back in court next week but there has been a development. The cash he was alleged to have smuggled into Italy has gone missing. He will be released, charges dropped, no evidence against him.'

A thunderous bass drum crashed and rumbled across the roof tops. A squadron of birds dived and danced around the trees.

'Sounds like Beikle has worked out a deal,' I said. 'They'll keep him under close surveillance, Artie, so be careful, don't make direct contact with him.'

'Talking of deals,' PJ said, 'what about that Polish woman? Any word about what's happening there?'

Artie inspected the toes of his shoes, sucked air through his puckered lips and wheezed out a long sigh.

'I thought that wee girl would have been released weeks ago,' Artie said. 'It seems they are determined to make an example of somebody, and poor Alina is the only one in the frame.'

'That could get awkward,' PJ said. 'I hope she knows how to keep her mouth shut.'

'Don't worry about Alina, PJ.' Artie glanced at me. 'She knows she will be very comfortable when she goes back to Poland.'

'Sounds like a lot of old balls if you ask me,' PJ sniffed. 'Sounds like nobody knows what they're doing.'

My physio knew what she was doing, and her speciality was pain, torture and more pain. There was no way I was going to let her see she was hurting me so I clenched my teeth and sucked it up. That lasted for about half of the first session, then I screamed and cried like a child and, the more I screamed, the more she liked it.

On days when I was free from her strong arm tactics I would walk as far as I could up the Cavehill. The entrance was a few minutes from my priest hideaway, a long sweeping road led to a sort of fake castle overlooking the city and the lough. After a few weeks my legs were strong enough to carry me up to the castle, then I started to progress more quickly, a little further up through the trees each day until I could make the open hillside above the treeline. By the end of August I was climbing the whole way to the top, not as quick as I would have liked, but I was getting there.

It was one of those days when I had made the summit and back without stopping more than a couple of times and I was pretty pleased with myself about it, another small victory. Artie and a glum looking priest were waiting on me back in the house.

'This is Father Anthony, Con, a great friend of mine from Rome.'

Anthony's dark looks said he was from Rome but his twang said he was straight out of Boston. He was pleased to meet me, had heard a lot, the usual crap. Something was wrong.

'Father Anthony is from the Secretariat of Communications, it's sort of like the Vatican press office.' Artie was nervous but the Anthony guy was laid-back.

'I think we may have a development, Con, Father Anthony will explain.'

Father Anthony explained that his job in the Vatican press office was to keep on top of any breaking news stories that might prove to be controversial or embarrassing for the Church. 'Forewarned is forearmed', he quipped. He had been tipped off about rumors that some very damaging revelations were about to break on social media – damaging for the Brits, mainly, and related to their dirty war in Ireland, going way back to the 70's and 80's. The word on the tweet was that this stuff was going to be explosive and Margaret Thatcher was about to be crucified. A small trickle of old recordings was already circulating but somebody was about to hit the nuclear button.

'The word I'm picking up from the British authorities is that they are very, very concerned about these rumors,' Anthony said.

'The British authorities can go fuck themselves, Father,' I said. 'And you wouldn't happen to be a CIA sort of a priest over there in that Communications Secretariat, would you, Father? Because if you are, you can tell your CIA bosses to go fuck themselves also!'

'That's uncalled for, Con! Father Anthony is a man of the highest integrity!' Artie scolded me. 'Father Anthony believes these rumors are being engineered from eastern Europe. You see what I mean?'

Yeah, I got him. If the tapes were starting to appear now that meant one thing. Paddy the Brit Hamilton was back on the scene.

CHAPTER THIRTY-ONE

Yana picked me up one night when Artie and Quinn and the rest were at some big priest party.

'The British Conservative Party annual conference is happening in a few weeks,' she said. 'If there really are Thatcher Tape revelations coming they will be timed to cause maximum grief for the Brits.'

Yeah, we all knew Hamilton wasn't the type to disappear into anonymous retirement, and it was no great surprise that he couldn't resist some payback. I pictured him emptying Moscow Mules down his fat neck in a St Petersburg hotel, surrounded by Yakov's party girls and minders, and laughing his balls off. I hoped he was enjoying himself because it wouldn't last. I gave him about two years, tops, before that paradise crumbled to dust.

'Funny thing is,' she said, 'the material leaked so far is all ancient history. Nothing in the last twenty years, it's all recycled gossip and innuendo about political assassination here in Ireland, protecting establishment pedophiles in London, breaking arms embargoes, colluding with the security services to smear the opposition. Nothing concrete and nothing touching anyone current. He must have more material, contemporary and relevant. You were with him, Maknazpy, you must have seen the other stuff.'

'Me? I'm a dumb piece of shit,' I shrugged, 'how would I know anything?'

Yana ignored me.

'So, the rumors hit Twitosphere and straight away the Brits scale down their search for Hamilton?' she said. 'Almost like they have been warned off.'

Maybe they had, but I was still being tailed by the same four or five faces. Not all the time, but at least two or three times a week one or two of them would be waiting down the street when I went for my daily walk up Cavehill. Sometimes it was a younger guy who would follow me right to the top and take his place on that ass shaped formation on the rocky outcrop until I was ready to head back down. The others were lazy bastards going through the motions so they generally waited in the castle coffee shop. Sometimes I went in there also and we ignored each other over coffee and scones.

'It's been six months, Yana. That money is long gone and isn't coming back.'

'That type of money doesn't just disappear,' she said. 'It circulates in all the bad places paying for evil and pain. Right now it's paying Hezbollah to target the Free Syrian Army and for Palestinian terrorists to attack Israeli civilians.'

Yana was a very bright girl, too bright to allow any chinks in company doctrine, but did she really still believe that shit? She read the derision in my eyes and scowled to banish my heresy.

'Once the usual gangster roll call got their cut the remaining funds were moved through Riga to Vladivostock and then through China to Macau and Hong Kong. Right now they are bankrolling their Anti-American activities through Cyprus and Beirut. We keep closing them down, they keep moving. That's how it goes.'

'Hamilton is a clown,' I said. 'How long are you going to chase him?'

'As long as it takes.'

'Because he has the Latvian banker on those tapes, right?'

'That's right, Maknazpy, the Latvian bankers and their collaborators who are a danger to the free world.'

There was an edge to her voice like she was reading a script.

'You know my friend PJ, don't you?' I said. 'He's a pretty smart guy, you know, and he figures that crap about Latvian bankers is all bullshit. He figures there is something else on those tapes.'

Yana gave me the steady stare, no reaction, just a blank face. I knew she was rattled.

'Do yourself a favour, Maknazpy, don't bite the hand that's feeding you. And tell your IRA terrorist friend to mind his business.'

She gestured for me to get out of the car.

'Hamilton is blackmailing the Brits,' she said. 'He is threatening to release material to end current political careers if they don't forget about him. We know it, and we'll catch up with him real soon, whether that's inconvenient for the Brits or not. Make sure your head is clear when the time comes. Make sure you still realize which side you are on, okay?'

My head *was* clear, Yana, clear enough to realize that PJ was an even smarter guy than I had thought. Hamilton was smart also, and he should really enjoy those Moscow Mules now while he had the chance. I would be seeing him soon, I could feel it, and he wouldn't be getting his two years.

CHAPTER THIRTY-ONE

October 9th

It was the same ornate stairway from the photo that Artie had shown me in the bar of the Marina Palace hotel so long ago back in Rio. He had packed an extra thirty or forty pounds around his gut. The long silver hair was scraped back from his forehead. The thick white beard and heavy framed glasses hid half of his face. When Artie had slapped the iPad down on my lap I hadn't recognized the figure on the screen but I knew it could only be Hamilton.

'You've gotta admire the balls on this guy!' I said. 'He thinks he can waltz back into the Opera House in Vienna like nothing ever happened, like he won't be noticed?'

'Budapest,' Artie shook his head. 'That's the Opera House in Budapest, not a bad second choice, mind you, not bad at all.'

'That's Hungary, right?'

'It *is* in Hungary, yes, it *was* in the Austro-Hungarian Empire. I'm not surprised that's where Hamilton has ended up. There's new money there, they seem to be rekindling some of the old Habsburg glory in that city, and that bollocks has the cash now to fit right in.'

He had a woman on his arm, moneyball eyes, platinum hair stacked high, sharp cheekbones, a sparkling collar of rocks kissing her long golden neck, a shimmering dress tight like a second sequined skin, white gloves to her elbows. Hamilton looked pleased with life.

'It was the premiere of Otello, all the great and good of Budapest were there,' Artie said. 'Johannes Beikle was shown this the next morning.'

'The universal Catholic mafia strikes again, eh?'

'Not at all, Con, not at all. Monsignor Johannes says the photo came from a banker, not one of ours at all, apparently, a man with a conscience. He had been seconded to Vienna but is back now in his own bank in Budapest. He knew Beikle's story. He knows Hamilton.'

'Was it sent directly to Beikle?'

'No, don't worry, it got to him through quite a circuitous route. The Brits won't have seen it, if that's what you're worried about, nor the Yanks, for that matter. The Vatican is one place the two great apostate powers don't get their arses licked, Con, believe me.'

'Let's keep it that way. No phones, no emails, okay? Either word of mouth or ink on paper, and we're going to need your contacts, Artie, so be careful who you use. Budapest must be a big city but I guess Hamilton with money in his pocket isn't the sort to play safe and hide away in a cave somewhere, right?'

'No, he was in one of the most expensive dress circle boxes and then showed his smug face at the premiere reception in the Red Salon.'

'He thinks he has all bases covered,' I said. 'He thinks the dirt he has on the Brits makes him untouchable.'

'And the Yanks?'

'He has something big on them also,' I said. 'That's why Yana and her crew are keeping me on board. I'm one of those disposable solutions they like to keep in reserve.'

'Are you sure you're fit enough?' Artie tapped the blackthorn walking stick. 'Sure you can do it on your own?'

'I'm not on my own, Artie, no way on my own. I've got you, I've got PJ. That should be more than enough, shouldn't it?'

'Paddy the Brit still thinks he can have it every way,' Artie laughed, 'still thinks he's a modern Miler Magrath - "*Here where I am placed I am not. I am not where I am not. Nor am I in both places, but I am in each*". God help his Protestant wit! They didn't have iPads in old Miler's day!'

CHAPTER THIRTY-TWO

Budapest, Friday, October 30th

The Danube sparkled in autumn morning sunshine. Speedboats splashed and rippled between leisure cruisers and working barges. They had their own Statue of Liberty high on the other side, the usual crazy European fairy tale castles tall and proud along the green hills, and an imitation of the Brooklyn Bridge guarded by regal stone lions. This wasn't the dismal Eastern bloc jungle of crumbling concrete I had expected. The elegant boulevards were busy with dark suited men and classy women strutting their uptown chic. Big beast German saloons on the higher end of the executive expense budget decorated the streets. Clusters of policemen in baggy dark overalls and red boat-shaped caps were a very visible presence on the corners every two or three blocks.

'Zoltán Street?' The driver stopped in front of an apartment block. I palmed him the notes and stood on the pavement as if I was stretching my legs after the long journey. He was on his cell phone now. I pulled my own phone out and pretended to read a message. The driver didn't need to know I was actually staying around the corner in Akadémia Street. I didn't need to be anything except invisible to those cops on the corner. I stood in the doorway of the apartment block now, pressed the phone to my ear as if I had an important call. The driver rolled off down the street, going away from Akadémia. I watched him turn right at the end, kept the phone up to my mouth, turned back. The policemen were having a smoke and some laughs. My business suit and expensive leather holdall should work like an invisibility cloak in this neighborhood. I crossed over Akadémia, second door on the left, and stabbed the button marked *"Szabó"*. It felt like everyone on the street was watching me. The door clicked open. A policeman twitched a reflex glance over his shoulder. I went into the entrance hall as if I hadn't a worry in the world, slowly shouldered the heavy door behind me and then pressed my eye into the spy hole. The cops had forgotten about me already.

The caged elevator was an antique. The concrete stairway was wide enough to haul a Baby Grand to the top of the building. I passed an old water fountain on the first floor landing, a green copper tap and a deep curved sink stained black and purple. A young woman swilled bleach around the landing on the second floor. She stopped when she saw me coming and gestured for me to pass. A door led to the balcony walkway. The courtyard below was used for storing bicycles and children's broken play equipment. A man was singing Sinatra and frying onions in the first apartment on the left. The next door was open.

'Well? No problem?' PJ took my bag and squeezed my shoulder. 'Nice quiet flat, so it is, busy people minding their own business! An architect we know at home owns it, part of his rental portfolio. Class bit of work, isn't it?'

It *was* class, bright and ultra modern with high ceilings and big windows - like a SoHo condo transplanted to the Danube.

'Wee Michael's taking his stuff out of the second bedroom for you. He'll take the sofa.'

'Michael? Brigid's nephew? You sure it's a good idea bringing that kid in on this thing?'

'Michael? He's sound, Con, don't worry! He's smart, so he is, he's doing a Master's in Law at Queen's.' PJ grinned and rubbed his jaw. 'Fit boy, too, knows how to handle himself!'

I didn't need the reminder that Michael had dropped me that night but the kid was emotionally raw, and we couldn't risk any passengers.

'No problem! I'd trust him with my life, so I would,' PJ insisted. 'And he's not even all that young, anyway. I'll tell you some time about the Active Service operations I was on when I was younger than him!'

Michael didn't show any sign that he had heard our conversation. He shook my hand and lifted my bag into the bedroom. There was something quietly impressive about him, PJ had that much right, and I hoped that would be enough when things cut up rough.

'How much have you told him?' I asked.

'I told him the right wing media will get away with undermining the credibility of all our evidence about collusion until we bring Hamilton's tapes home.'

'What about the money?'

'He's not interested in dirty money, Con, and neither am I. You can do what you like with it, that's up to you, but that's not why we are here.'

PJ had motored down from Berlin the previous week. He was to put two teams of three in place, and to have Hamilton's routine sussed out.

'No, didn't happen,' he said, 'the other boys didn't work out. It's the three of us and another young guy, a friend of ours living in Munich, a software engineer and fluent in German - always handy having a Deutsch speaker when you're in these places, so it is.'

'He's here now also?' I said.

'No, he had to go back to Munich but he'll be back tomorrow. He'll stay at the Hilton across the river. And he's not interested in your dirty money, either, to save you asking. His father was a good comrade of ours, God rest his soul, and he's his da's son, 100%. You don't need to know his name or anything else about him and he doesn't need to know about you, alright?' PJ gripped my shoulders and looked deep into my eyes with all the earnest sincerity he had in the tank. 'I'm telling you I vouch for him and Michael without question, and I'm expecting you to respect that, okay?'

It was what it was. I might buy PJ's blarney about their devotion to some ideal or other but I wasn't biting on the "*we aren't interested in dirty money*" bullshit – I had never met *that* animal. It wasn't such a big deal, though, because if things worked to my plan they would never have to wrestle with the temptation.

'What about Hamilton's safe house?' I said. 'How'd you track him down?'

'Simples! Monsignor McCooey had a photo of him and his girlfriend in their box at the opera. Our Munich man phoned the booking office and screamed at them in his scariest German – said he had booked those tickets but they had never been delivered. The girl in the ticket office looked it up and he kept shouting until she gave him the address they *were* sent to. Paddy the Brit is holed up across the river in a luxury apartment. He's out raking about the town every night, can't burn his money quick enough. Not so much wine, women and song as heroin, hookers and Blackjack. For an ex-Military Intelligence and MI5 agent, the man's an awful prick, won't last six months at this rate.'

This was sweet. Hamilton spinning out of control was an A1 bonus as long as I could get to him before he crashed and burned completely.

'We'll have to get into that apartment,' I said, 'when Hamilton is out getting wasted and we have time to turn it over properly.'

'Why don't we just kick the door down, put a hood over his head and drag him the fuck out of there? What is it you're really after, Con? Yana's tapes from that house?'

PJ didn't need to know what I was really after, not yet.

'Yeah, PJ, we need the tapes.'

PJ was a man always on the hunt for a new nugget of information. The subject matter often wasn't as important as the process of inspection and classification itself, and he would only be satisfied after he had exhausted all the angles for probing and evaluation. Google and Wiki were his able assistants, and he had drilled them over and over until their mine of Budapest facts were exhausted.

'The Hungarian Parliament Building, largest building in Hungary, highest in Budapest. Do you know it's modelled on the fucking Houses of Parliament in London?'

That was one of the many things I didn't know and that PJ thought he should tell me. The problem tonight was that he had broken his own rule to settle his nerves with most of a bottle of wine and his voice was louder than it should have been. Right now I was only interested in slipping past the police guarding the place without attracting their attention, and one thing about PJ's wine voice was that it would always attract attention.

It was almost midnight, and there were still strings of eager tourists milling around on the hunt for a unique selfie opportunity. We crossed the road in front of the Parliament and joined the gang cramped into the walkway along the river embankment.

'The Shoes on the Danube,' PJ announced. 'The memorial marking where the Hungarian Nazis machine-gunned Budapest Jews – shot dead or drowned in the Danube, the poor bastards.'

The artist had made a line of 40's style shoes, a simple metalwork recreation of the murder scene.

'There was an exhibition like this at the West Belfast festival a couple of years ago,' PJ said, 'only they were the real shoes of people murdered by the Brits and their Death Squads. The relatives all left a wee hand-written note beside the shoes. Very upsetting, so it was, brought it all back, really emotional to walk down that line, reading all the notes about the loved ones - better than this manufactured shit, so it was.'

An older woman in the group heard him and started to mumble something into her husband's ear. The man fixed a dirty look in our direction.

'What the fuck are you looking at?!' PJ growled. 'Away home and fucking take a look at the war crimes you're committing against Palestine today, ya hypocrite bastards!'

The twenty or thirty people around us all had their smart phones or tablets already rolling. Michael took PJ's other elbow and we eased through the crowd. Two policemen above on the road could sense something was amiss, they squinted into the dark shapes, one was listening to his ear-piece, then answered short and sharp. We kept moving, left the crowd behind, quickened our pace. The policemen hadn't followed but watched as we disappeared into the darkness.

'Fuck me! Sorry about that there, boys! I don't really drink anymore, you know, that wine must have gone to my aul baldy head!'

Michael was very cool, didn't flinch, assured PJ that no harm was done, it was no problem. I admired the kid's easy grace and composure. I hadn't figured on him as a threat but now I realized I needed to be careful with this one, couldn't afford to take him for granted.

'Let's forget it tonight,' I said. 'We'll take a look at Hamilton's apartment tomorrow. Turn back and take that street up to our apartment.'

'No, it's fine,' Michael said, 'the walk over the bridge will clear PJ's head, no problem. He'll be grand. Anyway, those two cops are shadowing us, if we turn back we'll walk right into them.'

They moved ahead of me. I looked back but couldn't see the police. PJ and Michael were striding along quickly, I had to jog to catch them. The bridge was busy with traffic and waves of young people thronging along the pedestrian paths on either side. PJ stopped at a small alcove and climbed up on the railings so that his upper torso was hanging over the fast black water. I held his elbow and asked him to get down. Michael was right behind me and getting jostled by the crowds pushing through. I caught the glance between them. Paranoia? Maybe, but it wasn't the first time in my life I had picked up those warning signals, and I hadn't been killed those times either. A sucker punch from this kid and I would be in the Danube. I stepped back from the railings and ushered Michael forward. PJ was suddenly sober, the Danube air had worked its magic, and I tagged along a few steps behind them until we got to the other side.

This side of the river is squeezed by the sharp hills cresting high above the city. PJ led the way up the street, Michael hung back but I slowed so he had to walk in front of me. Steps tunnelled through the rock and into a wide open square, a church with an Apollo tower and embroidered with crazy roof tiles.

'Awesome!' PJ nudged me, 'isn't that the American word for it?'

Yeah, awesome, but I wasn't a tourist and I didn't like the vibes I was picking up right now. We walked across the square, I knew he was sizing me up, trying to get inside my skull. I tasted his anxiety starting to pulp despite his smart talk. The kid was still cool, but he was too green to know any better.

Down a narrow lane, the dim lights stopped at the corner ahead. I would take the kid first, PJ wouldn't be a problem – as long as they weren't carrying.

'Is there something wrong, Con?' PJ using his caring voice now. 'Is there a problem here?'

I didn't answer, two figures appeared out of the darkness ahead, the slow amble of guys with nowhere to go except their short patrol route. These two weren't the smoking joking cops in baggy overalls that guarded street corners across the river, both carried an MP5 and the swagger to go with it. They expected us to step aside on the narrow lane and that's what we did, then kept moving around the corner without looking back. The lane opened to another square, another pair of armed cops ahead, moving slowly on the opposite side.

'That's Hamilton's apartment,' PJ nodded, 'that building on the corner, he's on the top floor.'

A manned barrier controlled the only vehicle entry to the square, lights in the small hut showed a couple of guards inside.

'Looks like Hamilton is paying for more than just an apartment,' I said. 'Looks like he has bought himself some prime security as well.'

'It's that sort of town, so it is, pay enough and you can buy anything,' PJ said. 'Mind you, you could say that about all fucking towns!'

This was a problem. The key to Hamilton's secret world was inside that apartment but this area had its own SWAT team on the prowl. The two cops on the opposite side started to turn in our direction. A vintage Roller bumped over the cobbles to the security barrier. We angled across the square and walked under the rising barrier. The church spire was ahead.

'Let's split up,' I said, 'you two go ahead and I'll meet you back at the apartment.'

'Is there a problem, Con?' PJ said. 'You've been acting a bit funny, so you have. You had that weird look in your eyes down on the bridge - like you were ready to tear my head off.'

The look in PJ's eyes was that '*now or never*' challenge – I let it slip by.

'No problem, PJ, just think we should split up with so many cops roaming the streets. If Hamilton feels safe around here it's because he has bribed his way into the security zone. Maybe he's paid for extra eyes also. We can't afford him getting a tip off that his apartment is being watched.'

I went ahead, dodged into a dark lane, let them pass, then back tracked to get a look at Hamilton's apartment on my own. I hit the intercom, the voice inside squawked a question. I hit it again, security opened the door. I stumbled against him, felt the holstered pistol under his arm, realized I was at the wrong address and apologized as I backed out. I don't know if private security firms carry guns in Budapest but the other sort always do – state security or gangster security, take your pick. He stepped to the pavement to watch me leave the square.

I kept my head down until I reached the other side of the bridge. The apartment was left along the embankment, I started that way and then crossed the street and doubled back, skimmed through the crawling traffic and reached a green space. The bridge was behind me now and straight ahead was the spectacular facade of the Gresham Palace hotel.

A group of drinkers under a tree saw me coming and howled in my direction. I passed them, and then waited at the edge of the grass space, couldn't spot anyone on my tail and the drinkers didn't see anyone else to abuse.

The concierge pulled the lobby door, I kept moving without looking at him. Almost 1 a.m. and the place hummed with that diligently curated atmosphere unique to luxury hotels. I flashbacked to Yakov and the Merchant in Belfast. I should have known then that he would play me. I guess I did know, even then, but what difference did it make? I was still in the game, and I wasn't beat yet.

He was at the other side of the bar, spoofing some old yarn, too busy admiring his own wit to see me coming.

'Hi, Artie,' I said, 'I'll have a Moscow Mule if you are buying.'

Artie stood, squeezed my hand and thumped my shoulder. He turned to his drinking pal and started to introduce us. I already knew who this was – the Most Reverend Monsignor, Apostolic Protonotary, Doctor of Christian Philosophy, the persecuted priest redeemed by big money defense attorneys and insufficient evidence to bring a successful prosecution against him. This was Johannes Beikle, officially absolved from his skimming stigmata – and still the man with the keys to the Vatican Bank.

CHAPTER THIRTY-THREE

An elephant in steel boots stamped around the apartment above. Somebody in boxing gloves mangled a piano down below. PJ rattled the door handle but I had a chair wedged against it. The slice of sky was bright and blue through the window.

'Con! There's breakfast here for you. Are you getting up?'

Michael didn't know how to use a stovetop espresso maker so we were having jasmine tea, with dry pancakes, orange cheese, and stale chocolate pastries.

'Where'd you go last night?' PJ asked. 'I thought you were right behind us but it was after three before I heard you.'

'Taking a look around town,' I said. 'I like to get a feeling about a place before a job.'

'So? What feeling did you get?'

'Forget about pulling Hamilton out of that apartment, for one thing,' I said, 'too heavy with security. Likewise the casino. No, we'll pick him up somewhere else, somewhere easier. I'm on it, PJ, don't worry about it.'

'I was fucking worried last night when you went all weird on us, so I was. I hope you're in better form today.'

I was in *much* better form today. Monsignor Beikle looked and sounded like a genuine banker, knew the mechanics of the system and what the officials needed to hear – Beikle could carry this thing off. I was also less down on PJ. Something in his eyes had spooked me last night but now, in the cold clear light of morning, I figured it was mostly this stab-in-the-back life getting to me again.

'I'd be in better form without the jungle patrol above and Clair De fucking Looney Tunes below.'

'Ach, wise up! It's Saturday morning, so it is, the kids are doing their wee dance and piano classes. Isn't it nice to see a bit of culture about the place?' PJ's breakfast was a toxic cigarette, he narrowed his eyes as he sucked the nicotine marrow from the thin white cylinder. 'You finished, Michael, son? Here, leave the dishes, but away down there and shoot the piano player, will ye? Tell him he's getting on Con Maknazpy's nerves, and that's not good news for the rest of us when that happens, sure it's not, Con?'

We laughed, but I still probed PJ's eyes for that Judas squint, and he knew it.

I liked the tame look of the man from Munich. If I was a cop I wouldn't give him a second thought – young professional, expensive casual clothes, designer spectacles, a neat pampered black beard. It was late afternoon, getting dark, and he had no problem finding a parking space in the next street. Michael went down to the door to meet him, maybe to pass on PJ's instructions on how to handle me. He seemed the silent type when we shook hands, eyes darting around the room, letting PJ speak on his behalf, almost seemed embarrassed to be here.

He said his name was Jimmy but it wasn't, and Michael smirked when he said it.

Jimmy had been on the road from Munich since early in the morning, he was tired and hungry. PJ had sent Michael to buy food earlier but that hadn't worked out so good, he came back with a packet of brown rice, a brick of black bread, tough salami and something called Gyulai sausage. It didn't work out good because Michael had spent most of the day grazing in the kitchen so now there was basically only a packet of rice on the dinner menu.

PJ decided we would eat at one of the restaurants near Saint István's Bazilika. He thumbed through a thick wad of Hungarian currency as he led us across Akadémia and over to Freedom Square, complete with his tour guide routine. He recited his trivia about the Stock Exchange and the Hungarian National Bank, the dates and architects, the stone and style.

'And that there's the United States Embassy Building, so it is. The CIA are probably in there right now, keeping an eye on us, isn't that right, Con?'

I shrugged it off but felt the jagged edge of his tone. I wasn't telling PJ my whole story and I was pretty sure he wasn't telling me his.

'And that's the monument to the Red Army Heroes who liberated Budapest,' he rambled on, 'something to remind the Yanks and Brits that it was actually the sacrifice of the Russian people that beat the Nazis, so it was.'

Michael and Jimmy weren't listening or weren't interested, until the two of them saw the statue ahead and burst out laughing. Shit! It was a bigger than life bronze of Ronald Reagan striding manfully through the park toward us. I thought at first it was some guy dressed up to beg tourist coins but no, it really was a celebratory totem to Ronald the Right. The young guys started clowning around Ronnie, PJ said he was 'fucking *scundered*' for the people of Budapest. That was my cue to go my own way.

'Just in case there are eyes on us,' I said, 'I'll go this way and see you back at the apartment later. And don't be drinking, Jimmy, okay? We'll need you to drive later.'

Jimmy and Michael switched off the clowning, PJ narrowed his eyes.

'Drive where?' PJ said.

'To the Opera House,' I said, 'so be sober and be back at the apartment by 6.30, okay?

'The Opera House?' PJ said. 'What the fuck are we going to the Opera House for?'

'Because we've got a date with Paddy the Brit, only he doesn't realize it yet.'

CHAPTER THIRTY-FOUR

Andrássy Avenue is one of those elegant broad boulevards that are a mandatory strutting statement for any self-indulgent old school European capital built on the bones of empire and conquest. It was almost 7 p.m. and the Avenue was busy with people in a hurry. The bright lights were still burning in Gucci, Cavalli, Vuitton and the other outposts of modern empire.

'The Austrian Kaiser only agreed to pay for building this Opera House on condition it would be smaller than the one in Vienna.' PJ flaunted his superior Google half-knowledge. 'So the Hungarians shafted the old bastard, so they did, by making it smaller but even more extravagant and ostentatious than Vienna! Fair play to them!'

But PJ's spiel was more than mere show-boating. The two younger guys seemed to find comfort in his laid-back prattle, and it was way easier to bear than my own ghost voices, so I figured this was the battle-hardened vet's way of calming nerves, soothing the raw recruits, his way of attending to the business of pre-combat stress. So PJ rambled and Jimmy kept it nice and steady, no reason for anyone to notice the mid-range Audi cruising past the Opera

House, up and down Andrássy Avenue three times, then turning into a side street and running parallel with the Avenue until we came to the side entrance to the Opera House.

A line of thoroughbred black limos stretched along the street under the watchful eyes of police at both ends – not the place to double-park. I told Jimmy to find the closest legal space and to wait there until I called him.

I hopped out, waited until PJ and Michael made it to the cafe down the street, then walked back to the front entrance. A message on my phone. My ticket was waiting at the desk, the lady with a silver parting in her orange hair shuffled some papers, handed me the ticket and flashed her big black eyes at the two square-headed bandits behind me. Act III was due to start in five minutes, patrons were invited to return to their seats. I mingled with the crowd clustered at the foot of the grand staircase. The muscle took up position between me and the exit but didn't follow.

On the staircase now, in slow step with a polished couple at home in the regal surroundings, one of them heavy on the cologne. Two plump women in tight dresses behind chattered and laughed, the old guy in front enjoyed the support of a young woman at each elbow. I kept my head down, just another music lover, all of us safe in the opera bubble, because this was their world and everyone here was a diamond-cut clone - cultured, civilized and respectably rich, holding on or getting there. Places like this aren't soiled by scumbags. A tailored tux and big stone-crusted watch is the membership card and that's enough to keep the dirt outside. No need to look over your shoulder or hold on tight to your purse. So nobody noticed me and they didn't notice the silver beard up ahead beside the marble bust of some big name composer. A silver beard and hair tied back in a man-bun, peering into his phone, glasses hanging off his red pocked nose.

Hamilton didn't see me. I kept low behind the old guy in front, about half way up the stairs, Hamilton pinned his glasses back into place, turned to greet a friend, a woman's high hair blocked my view. Getting close now, tingle in my neck and balls, breathing deep, forcing my fingers steady to message PJ. The woman saw a friend above and shrieked her name. Hamilton froze, recovered, nodded in my direction. Yakov stepped forward, the round cheese head with wolf eyes, mock grinning his challenge and contempt, the bring-it-on shrug and mouthed insult.

Hamilton tugged his elbow, Yakov pretended to spit on the red carpet but slowly turned and started after Hamilton, up the next stairs to the expensive seats. Another call, Act III about to start. The crowd above Hamilton and Yakov parted, men coming against the tide. I saw Yakov's face, confounded, this couldn't be, his mouth fell open and his eyes glazed. The men closed on them, one took Hamilton's arm, three encircled Yakov, one kissed and man-hugged him and whispered in his ear. Yakov shrunk before my eyes, the bullet-proof shell cracked, he shuffled around and they led him down. I backed away before them, the stairs were clearing now, the two gorillas waiting at the bottom.

Pyotr stepped ahead of the others to shake my hand and hug me.

'My uncle realizes the position,' he said, 'there will be no trouble. We will all show him the respect he so deserves, of course, you understand?'

I understood, I moved back to let Yakov and Hamilton be led across the lobby toward the exit. The two gorillas opened the doors, scanned the street, waved the entourage forward. The ticket lady was busy searching for nothing below the desk. Yakov scuffled along like a rag doll, Hamilton like an old man.

'My uncle will come with me,' Pytor said, 'you take Hamilton.'

Two SUV's pumped red fumes at the side door. Pyotr kept his arm draped around my shoulder as I scanned the street.

'No police here,' Pyotr said. 'They were asked to move on.'

PJ and Michael crossed the street, flagged Jimmy down as he turned the corner, we crammed Hamilton into the back of the Audi, PJ stamped on his legs until Hamilton squeezed himself into the space at our feet. Yakov was in the first SUV, it took off, the driver of the second SUV waved us to pass him, then hung on our tail. Down a side street, Yakov's SUV slowing to edge between the parked cars, pulled a right, passed István's Bazilika, left at Freedom Square, the lights of the Castle district straight ahead across the Danube.

'Selling out to the Russians, PJ?' Hamilton said. 'Ah well, you already sold out years ago to the Brits and anybody else with a wad of cash, didn't you?'

I slapped Hamilton's head and pressed my foot against his neck. The lead SUV slowed, the one behind up our ass, close to the Parliament now and no police on the streets, Pyotr had pull in all the right places. We pulled right, the long Parliament building on one side, the Danube below on the other. Three dark figures in uniform stepped out, stopped the traffic and waved us across the road. Pyotr was out first, then two gorillas leading Yakov down the steps to the river embankment. Pyotr shouted his orders in Russian, four heavies from the following SUV took up position around the Audi. I slapped Hamilton and told PJ to keep him pinned down, stepped out, push and shove with the nearest guy until Pyotr grabbed my arm.

'Yakov comes with us,' Pyotr said. 'Hamilton goes to the Americans.'

Two small cruisers tied up to the jetty, dark shapes on the boats and more in uniform keeping the tourists back with the Jewish shoes.

'Not yet, Pyotr,' I said. 'Tomorrow, same time, tell them I'll bring him then.'

'Fuck! Manazpy! What are you talking about?! We have a deal with the Americans! They get Hamilton, that is why you are here!'

'Okay, okay, Pyotr, take it easy. You have Yakov, Hamilton isn't your problem. I'll fix it. They'll get Hamilton, just not yet, not until we finish our business, okay?'

'Your fucking Irish business?!' Pyotr's face was ghostly pale. 'So Moscow and Washington work out a deal but that goes down the toilet because of your shit Irish fucking blood feuds?!'

'You've got Yakov, haven't you,' I shrugged. 'He'll be in Moscow before morning, won't he? You did what you were supposed to do, the rest isn't your problem. I'll fix it. Tell the CIA to come back tomorrow.'

Pyotr's eyes danced in his head. Yakov screamed at him from down on the jetty. The dark shapes starting to get nervous, cold fingers tense against triggers. Yakov screaming my name and struggling with his minders until Pyotr broke and signalled them to bring him up. Yakov pushed Pyotr away and bear hugged me, a wet mouth smeared across my cheek.

'Con, old friend, you know how it ends if they take me to Moscow! Can you do anything for me? I will give the CIA anything they want!'

'Sorry, Yakov, too late, and I was never in control, you know that.'

Yakov nodded, defeat in his eyes, moved to kiss my cheeks again but then lunged to sink his wolf jaws into my ear, pain seared through my skull, his weight dragged me down, Pyotr tried to pull him away but Yakov was like a savage dog, we rolled on the ground, I wedged my fingers into his cheek and went for his eyes with the other hand. He worked his biceps around my throat, a front choke hold, shaking and tearing my ear like a dog with a rat. Pyotr jumped on top of us, grabbed Yakov's smooth cheese head and spoke softly into his ear. Yakov froze, I headbutted him and squirmed out from beneath them.

Three of the muscle lifted Yakov to his feet and he didn't resist, he walked off between them, only turning to shout back to me when he was half way down the jetty.

'I am sorry, Maknazpy! Nothing personal! Good luck!'

All eyes were on Yakov, I jumped back into the Audi and told Jimmy to move it.

'Fuck me! Hold it, Con, hold it!' PJ was looking close into my face. 'You're fucking pishing out blood! And where's your ear? Your fucking ear is gone! Get out there and find it! They can sew it back on if you get it soon enough!'

I clamped my hand over where the ear should have been, found the top half, felt the blood streaming down my face and neck. PJ was out of the car, yelling at Pyotr, telling him my ear was out there somewhere, telling him to fucking find it. Pyotr shouted down to the Russian boat, confusion, he shouted again, a pause, the answer came back. Pyotr opened the Audi door.

'I am sorry, Con. My uncle says he swallowed your ear, I am sorry, you know what he is like.'

'Tell them tomorrow, Pyotr, same time, same place!'

I slammed the door shut, Jimmy gunned the Audi and spun it around, the Russians scattered, two of them pulled their weapons but Pyotr screamed an order and they let us pass. The cops ushered the tourists back, confiscated phones until the videos were deleted.

'Keep going, Jimmy, down to the bridge, we're crossing to the other side.'

'What the fuck was all that about?' PJ twisted around to see if we were being tailed. 'What the fuck are we doing here in the middle of all that shit?'

'Because that's the way it goes,' I said. 'The US administration needs this done at arm's length with fire-proof deniability. They need expendables like us for the dirty work. The same with the Russians. And these places like Hungary are a little more sensitive these days about the big boys riding into town like their flag and national sovereignty are a piece of piss. It's one thing to turn a blind eye to organized crime when the pay is good but publicly taking orders from the so-called Super Powers doesn't sit well with their pride.'

'Right, so we're okay as long as we allow ourselves to be deemed fucking criminals?' PJ said. 'You need a history lesson, son!'

'You *are* a scumbag criminal, PJ!' Hamilton's voice was muffled by my boot. 'You and your Provie gang always were, always will be, and that's a fact, so it fucking is!'

PJ grinded Hamilton's ankle, Hamilton screamed.

'Over the bridge, Jimmy,' I said. 'We can't go back to that apartment. There's a place on this side of the Danube we can use.'

'Another safe house already organized?' PJ said. 'Who owns it? The Brits? Fucking Mossad?'

'Trust me, PJ, I have it under control.'

'Aye, dead on! Trust him, he says, under control, so it is, says the man with one ear!'

Just a couple of days, PJ, that's all, if I can keep it under control for a couple of days then I'll disappear, with my one ear, and you can get back to your loser's life of missed opportunities and boring trivia.

'How come your man Yakov went all docile? I thought he wasn't going to stop until he had your head off. Pit-bull to poodle in the wink of an eye.'

'Pyotr reminded him of his situation. Yakov co-operates and his two darling daughters in Paris and London are looked after, financially and every other way, Pyotr will guarantee it. Yakov cuts up rough and the girls will be home to Moscow, and not in a good way.'

'Your American friends won't be happy, so they won't,' PJ said. 'So just how expendable are we? I assume they've a back-up crew on standby to take care of us if we screwed up. Sure they don't know this new safe house of yours?'

'They don't know shit, PJ. I'm in control of the situation, trust me.'

Hamilton chugged a laugh beneath my feet. Blood flooded through my fingers and down my neck. Jimmy kept driving, over the bridge and up to the Castle District.

'So there's no hit squad coming after us? That's dead on, so it is, Con, but then who the fuck is in that car that's been up our hole since we crossed the bridge?'

CHAPTER THIRTY-FIVE

'We've already been down this street!' Jimmy said. 'We're going around in circles!'

The "Welcome to Budapest" map didn't show which streets were one-way, and the route I had planned was blocked by road works. Hamilton suggested I use Google maps on my phone but any scalphunters would be at the safe house before we were with that tip-off. The car behind flashed its lights. I got out and waved them to take the lead.

'Who the fuck is in that car?' PJ getting uptight, always expecting the double-cross, he kicked Hamilton's feet away and crouched down to root about under the driver's seat, came up with a .38 in his fist. 'I hope to fuck you aren't getting too smart for your own good, Con, because if you're thinking the three of us are expendable Mr Ruger here will have a problem with you, so he will!'

The car passed, winked its warning lights, then took a left up the hill. I told Jimmy to follow.

'We said no weapons, PJ,' I said. 'We'll never have the firepower to stand a chance in a fire fight with any of these guys.'

'*You* said no guns! But then you say a lot of stuff, so you do, mostly stuff to other people that we know nothing about. Now, no more of your cloak and dagger shit! Who's in that fucking car?!'

'It's McCooey,' I said. 'McCooey and Paddy the Brit's old friend from Vienna, Monsignor Johannes Beikle. He's a real old-school holy man, you know, believes in that "*rob from the rich, give to the poor*" idea. Well, Hamilton and Yakov are pretty rich right now, they stashed away something like $50 million between them.'

Hamilton stiffened beneath my feet.

'Shoot me now, PJ!' Hamilton yelled, 'before I have to listen to those two boring bastards!'

'Sure you're dead already, Paddy!' PJ laughed. 'Wasn't I at your funeral? Didn't I spit on the grave you already have?!'

The brass plaque on the door said this house belonged to "*József Scabó*", and he was some sort of medical consultant. Artie said József was a friend of his. Maybe that was true, but it looked to me like this wasn't anybody's home, more like a convenient address. McCooey found me a towel to jam against my ear, then served Beikle with brandy and port in the front room. PJ wasn't happy with the way Jimmy and Michael tied Hamilton to a chair in the kitchen, too loose, too comfortable, he showed them how to do it so the nylon rope bit deep into the soft skin. PJ inspected their work a second time, grunted approval, then played with the gun, imprinted barrel circles on Hamilton's skin, white on his temple, red beneath his ear. He did the Olympic rings on his forehead, and when that faded he laughed his balls off writing "IRA" in his gun barrel script. Paddy the Brit stared straight ahead at the tiled wall like we weren't there.

'Taking the hit with the CIA won't be such a bad deal,' I said. 'You'll be alive, for one thing, and I'm pretty sure you can work out some compromise with them. You won't have access to $50 million but you won't starve. They'll put you to work, maybe make you a decent payoff, but you'll get to live. That looks like a bonus for you right now from where I'm sitting.'

Hamilton didn't flinch. His eyes worked on the tile above my head, pretending I didn't exist and blanking out the pain payload he knew was coming his way.

'That thing with Yakov was never going to work out, you must have known that! A megalomaniac like him? Surrounded with too many yes-men for too long? Like he wasn't only a big dog because the bigger dogs threw him a bone? That doesn't work out long term, Paddy, not unless you really are at the top of the pyramid, and Yakov wasn't, and you aren't.'

PJ pressed steam from the iron. Hamilton forced himself not to see PJ's spit sizzle and somersault off the hot metal. PJ held the iron close to his face, close enough to singe the silver beard, turning the ends black. Hamilton didn't move, stared at the tile, more balls than I realized.

'Yakov just went too far, didn't he? He told me one time he used to be a Colonel or whatever in their GRU fucking Military Intelligence before he became a big name in the Russian Mafia. I say "*used to be*" loosely, of course, I don't think those guys are ever really "*used to be*", are they? So how the fuck did Yakov think he could rip off the GRU? That Latvian bank held their money, didn't it? Oiling the wheels of GRU operations outside Mother Russia, keeping the Kremlin at arm's length, like, if the Amerikanski can't prove it then it's not true? But how far up his own ass was Yakov to *ever* think he could siphon off the GRU's cash from their Latvian vault? And you went along with him? Fuck, Hamilton, the CIA are doing you a big favor, my man, a big, big favor! You could be sitting out your time in Vermont, the GRU would have your balls in your mouth in Vladifuckingvostock!'

A dirty smile creased out the ends of Hamilton's lips, no comment, still focused on the wall.

'What? So you have something to smirk about now? You're the one about to have your beard smoothed with that iron, Hamilton, what makes you think you get to sneer down at me?'

'Because you are a moron, Maknazpy, an unadulterated and thoroughgoing moron! Entitled to sneer? Fuck off! I'm *obliged* to sneer!'

A calculated slap. Hamilton knew the routine, pick a spot and focus on it and it alone, don't engage with the interrogator, not verbally, not any way, so this was another slap in my face, he was above the procedure because he was above me and he still felt the need to prove it.

'And you aren't in the clear yet yourself, you fucking one-eared dickwit! They know you were the matchmaker in my little enterprise with Yakov. They know I had never heard of the Slav savage until you brought him in. They know you were with me the whole time I was making my magic. So, yeah, I may have to cut a deal with the CIA but you're too insignificant to warrant that option. You won't walk away from this, you shit-brained eejit!'

Artie had warned me, Hamilton had been working things out with Yakov, and I *had* been there.

PJ pulled Hamilton's head back, I forced the blood soaked towel into his mouth and clamped the hot iron hard against his left ear.

'So tell me again, Paddy, who's the real dickwit here?'

He writhed and twisted, eyes bulging, unable to breathe or scream, smell of scorched hair and seared chicken skin. His face was purple, green veins pumping out of his skull, I didn't want a heart attack.

'Fuck's sake, Paddy! You've pissed yourself again, so you have,' PJ said.

Hamilton squeezed his eyes tight and bit on the towel, forcing himself to endure, suck it up, death before surrender.

'Don't let your ego make this personal, Hamilton,' I said. 'If it wasn't me and PJ it would be somebody else. Now, I'm going to speak to McCooey and Beikle, when I come back you're going to talk about those recordings and the Russian money.'

'Go ahead, Con,' PJ said. 'I'll look after Paddy, no problem. His wee face is burnt to fuck, so it is, wait to I see what's in this cupboard. Aye, look, this powder stuff might be the very thing!' PJ sprinkled the chili powder over Hamilton's head, slapped it around the burnt ear and cheek, thumbed it into his eyes and up his nose. Hamilton squealed and choked. 'How's that, Paddy? Better? Better like the way you looked after Brigid and Tomás?'

I tapped PJ's shoulder, gave him the look – a dead Hamilton would be a dead end. PJ nodded, he knew how far he could take it, and he was going to. I left him to it, found the bathroom and washed the blood off my face and neck. The ear stub was raw, congealed blood starting to grow a black crust but still seeping red at the edges. The bathroom cupboards were bare, no creams, no lotions, if this József Szabó lived here he did it without any of the clutter of domestic life.

Beikle offered to clean the wound with brandy, Artie said it would be a more effective medicine if taken orally. He filled me a glass, I brushed away the port mixer.

'Has Paddy the Brit seen the light yet?' Artie said. 'We have better things to do than sit about here waiting on that scumbag.'

Right now Artie looked to be doing just fine - the brandy decanter was sinking faster than the Titanic and his face redder than a well smacked arse.

'I dunno, Artie. There's too much history between him and PJ.'

'That bastard has history with everybody! Anyway, Monsignor Beikle has already done all the hard work, all you have to do is get his bank cards, or whatever it is that Johannes told you he needed. Is that too much for you? Do you want me to speak to the blackguard?'

Beikle rotated the heavy crystal in his delicate bookish fingers, dancing the red light from the music system like a ruby in the dark port brandy combo. He screwed his eyes and strained his head to the speaker, chant from a hundred ghosted monks circling the walls, using the same technique as Hamilton to make me go away.

'No, you'll only stoke that "*No Surrender*" fire in his belly. I do think it's time to fill PJ in, though. He doesn't like being left out of the loop, he's getting nervous, and that makes me nervous.'

Beikle kissed the last bead of brandy, stood, tugged his cuffs, blew out his gray cheeks, licked his lips, smoothed the silver hair. PJ's existence didn't register with Beikle when he came in, he looked through PJ, signalled his contempt with a rat-twitch of his freakily irregular nostrils – one a gaping hairy black cavern, the other a pink pin prick. Beikle didn't like this situation, didn't like the idea that we might make the mistake of thinking we were his equal just because he had stumbled so far into the shit that he needed our grubby fingered help. PJ stared him out. Beikle shifted uncomfortably, cleared his throat.

'I have already told this to Mr Maknazpy,' a curt nod in my direction, 'so perhaps it is not necessary that I repeat every tiny detail.'

His accent was almost American, like he had spent a lot of time in the US, or he spoke English to a lot of Americans in the Vatican. PJ's lips trembled as if he was printing the words and the voice inside his head. So Beikle repeated, more or less, what he had told me in the Gresham Palace, slowly, at first, with pauses to allow PJ to try to understand, but Beikle quickly realized that PJ's brain was sponging up his every word with plenty to spare. That made him a little uneasy also.

Beikle painted himself as the scammed victim, his innocent nature exploited by Hamilton's evil criminal mind. He quickly got down to the aftermath, the "unfortunate episode" that saw him penned up in his Vatican apartment.

From what I could make out, it sounded like he would be in for a ten stretch by now if the Italians hadn't decided they had bigger pizza to bake. Beikle's disgrace over-lapped the Mafia Capitale scandal still rocking Rome, and the National Anti-Corruption Authority plucked him out as a weak thread in the fabric.

A team of Anti-Corruption investigators travelled to Vienna, met their counterparts, discovered that Hamilton was indeed known in Vienna but all the Austrian authorities wanted to know was that Paddy the Brit was certainly a British security agent, and even, perhaps, an American asset. The Vienna boys dragged their feet at first, but, eventually, and with a little added pressure from the Vatican, the Austrians got busy.

Routine surveillance on "friendly" agents had recorded Hamilton as a frequent visitor to Budapest, sometimes by air but almost always by rail – less than three hours from Vienna Hauptbahnhof to Budapest Keleti station. Red tape let the Austrians off the hook at the Hungarian border but the Italian squad knew a little bribery would go a long, long way in Budapest.

They were signposted to a particular bank, GMC, in the financial district, right around the block from our apartment. Since the US had started putting the squeeze on secret Swiss bank accounts, GMC had been pulling in new clients – a lot of them familiar to the Italian squad. The fixers and consiglieri of Italy's black economy were especially welcomed by GMC and they even developed a new and ultra-secure safety deposit box offer to cater for the new customers.

'Hold on, hold on there,' PJ held his hands up to interrupt, 'I can see where this is going and no way am I setting myself up to rob a bank! I'm not doing twenty years time in this dump, so I'm not!'

Beikle hoisted his eyebrows, cleared his throat.

'That won't be necessary, PJ,' Artie said. 'Other arrangements have been made.'

PJ glanced from Artie to Beikle, tilted his head to examine my eyes, then looked Beikle up and down.

'What? You're doing it?' PJ laughed. 'Serious? Sorry for laughing, and with all due respect, Monsignor Beikle, but how many fucking banks have you ever blagged before?'

Beikle squeezed his lips so tight it looked like he had a mouthful of puke in there about to explode.

'Now, PJ, I really don't think that sort of language is appropriate, do you?' Artie smoothed the rough edge threatening to erupt between Beikle and PJ. 'There is no question of Monsignor Beikle *blagging* anything, let alone a bank.' Artie smiled, invited Beikle to see the funny side, Beikle wouldn't. 'There are other parties involved, certain other customers of this bank, and they are sympathetic to the unfortunate difficulty we find ourselves in. Representations on our behalf have been made to the bank to find a way to facilitate our needs, to see justice is done.'

'Fuck my baldy head!' PJ pressed a hand to his mouth to cushion his laugh. 'You've pulled in favors from the Italian fucking Mafia to lean on the bank?! Is that what they call Divine Intercession these days? What's that? An Invocation to Holy St Fat fucking Tony?'

Beikle's face burned crimson, he gripped his shaking hands behind his back.

'We have many friends, PJ, and this service has been offered, and accepted, with the purest of intentions,' Artie's diplomacy working overtime, 'you know, "*There is only one Lawgiver and Judge, who is able to save and to destroy; but who are you who judge your neighbor?*"'

'Aye, dead on! So how come people like you and your mate here have been judging me all my life?'

This was more common touch than Beikle could tolerate. He turned his back on PJ, splashed brandy into his glass and rattled the decanter across the glass table.

'Look, PJ,' Artie said, 'what you *do* need to focus on is convincing Paddy the Brit in there to be more helpful. He has an entry card for this bank, like a credit card, with a magnetic strip on it. I know how persuasive you are, so have a wee word with Paddy and *get* that card. Okay?'

'Aye, okay, okay. You and St Hypocrite listen to your holy music and drink your brandy, that's okay. Turn the music up a wee bit, just in case the sound of screams disturb you, like.'

PJ waited for me outside in the corridor.

'Hamilton's a tougher nut to crack than they realize,' he said. 'He knows he only has to hold out for less than 24 hours. I dunno if I can break him in that time. I dunno how much he can take before it's lights out for good. I mean, I can kill him, so I can, and the bastard might be stubborn enough to make me do it, but I dunno if he will break.'

'He hates your guts, PJ, and that's plenty extra motivation for him right there. Let me try it for a spell. He hates my guts slightly less than yours.'

PJ called Michael and Jimmy out of the kitchen, the kid hid his shame-faced look as he edged around me. Hamilton was in a bad shape. He shook like he was in a freezer, his eyes and nose pumped a steady stream of yellow and red mucus and a clammy skin of sweat glistened on his forehead. Three fingers of his right hand were broken or dislocated. The music system on the window sill was loaded with a Franz Liszt CD, I hit play and turned the volume up, took the blood soaked towel from his mouth and held a glass of water against his lips. He sucked the glass, coughed, spit on the floor, and drank the rest before it spilled down his chin.

'It's the end of the road, Paddy. PJ knows he only has until tomorrow night before I hand you over to the CIA. He will either break you or kill you, and I don't think you will let him break you. Is it worth the trouble? Tomorrow night you will be on your way to a new life in the United States. You can make that work good for yourself, maybe better than you ever could here.'

'It was *you* burnt my fucking face with the iron, not PJ, so don't work the good cop shit on me. The two of you can go fuck yourselves, and take McCooey with you!'

'Look at yourself! You're too old for this. You should be looking forward to a nice easy retirement. The CIA will interrogate you to find out exactly what secret recordings you have stashed around the world but they don't want to get heavy. All you have to do is co-operate and they will fix you up with something, you'll see, you'll be back in business in no time and without spending the rest of your life waiting on the Russians to catch up with you.'

Hamilton gestured for more water, he gulped it, then spat the red swill on the floor. He strained his neck forward to whisper into my ear.

'You're a stupid bastard, Maknazpy, you really are! Didn't I tell you the Brits wanted me dead and you with me? What do you think PJ is here for?'

PJ was here mostly to get payback for Brigid and Tomás and partly to see how much of Hamilton's cash he could pocket, that was a no-brainer.

'PJ won't let you hand me over, he can't. He is here to nut me. And you have to go too.'

He said it with such a calm matter-of-fact delivery that it *should* be true.

'No, Paddy, he's here because of what *you* did to Brigid, yeah, and Tomás also, but mostly Brigid. So you can expect to suck up a little pain but you'll survive if you co-operate, if you aren't too stubborn.'

'Ballicks! He fucking knows I had nothing to do with that! Ask him! He knows! He knows that couldn't happen, the lying bastard!'

Now he faked anger, indignant that I dare pin Brigid on him.

'Go on, Maknazpy! Why not? Why couldn't I have anything to do with it?'

He was goading me now, taking over, jockeying me into doubt.

'Because we had a fucking relationship, you stupid bastard! PJ knows I couldn't have hurt a hair on her head! I was set up, and so was she!'

'The last time I saw the two of you together Brigid was beating shit out of you.'

'Well, it wasn't always like that. Twenty five years ago it wasn't like that, before PJ and his fucking snoops broke it up it wasn't like that.'

There was something in Hamilton's eyes, not emotion, not regret, but there was something, like PJ's eyes on the bridge – maybe it was history.

'We had a thing going, not something I can explain, really, not a normal relationship. It was a war, she was the enemy, I don't know how to fuck it happened, it just did. It did, until PJ found out and set us up. I was supposed to get whacked by the IRA, she was supposed to be arrested for it. Well, I wasn't hit but she was lifted. She got twelve years, got released early because of the Peace Process.'

'So? What? You're telling me PJ was the Brit mole in the IRA?'

'He still is! He's on the payroll. I told you that before as well, maybe you weren't listening. You need to fucking listen now!'

I was listening, but everything Hamilton said had to pass through a mighty bullshit filter.

'And what about your man "*Jimmy*"? Who's he supposed to be? Some old comrade's son that has just turned up to help? Is he fuck! He's a Brit! Supposed to be living in Munich, isn't he? See that licence plate, why is it not a Munich "M" plate then? How come it is "BI", as in Bielefeld? You know what's in Bielefeld, don't you? That's right, British Army HQ in Germany. And your man just sails down here with a bag of Rugers? Fuck's sake, Maknazpy! Wake up! PJ has been sent to get those recordings and the cash, all you and I will get is one in the back of the head!'

This was too much. I shoved the towel back into Hamilton's mouth and made for the bathroom to wash some new blood off my neck. PJ and Jimmy were standing behind the kitchen door, I couldn't say if they had heard much.

'He changed his mind,' I said. 'He picked the easy way. We are going over to his apartment to pick up his bank ID - me, Hamilton, Beikle and Michael.'

PJ did his eye-screwing, head-tilting routine.

'And what are we supposed to do? Wait here scratching our balls until you decide to come back?'

'I'll be back, no problem, because I have some old business of my own to take care of. You stay here and compare notes with Artie about that ambush on Ferdia McErlane's uncles, you know, back in the old days? I'll be back to see you about it, believe me, I'll be back.'

CHAPTER THIRTY-SIX

Hamilton keyed the entry code. The security muscle was behind his desk, swivelled away from us to peer at the CCTV monitor as if he hadn't just killed the system. I rapped the desktop, he used his pen to swipe the sachet of Pyotr's white powder across the polished surface, still not seeing us, because we were never there.

The apartment was A-List extravagant but sterile and cold. Hamilton needed a shower and clean clothes. I put Michael in the bathroom with him and told him not to lock the door.

'Smack him if he tries anything,' I said, 'but you don't need that gun, I'll hold it, less chance of any accidents.'

I scanned the high ceiling in the lounge first. Everything in here looked solid, no signs of any patching or double skins, but then there wouldn't be – Hamilton was the *man*. Beikle hovered at my back, careful not to touch anything and shifting about as if he would be stained by our air if he stood still. A screwdriver rattled on its own in the bottom drawer in the kitchen. I've seen you at work, Paddy, this means there's *something* in here to be unscrewed. Back to the hallway, Michael standing outside the bathroom door.

'He's doing a shit! He's stinking!'

I booted the bathroom door open and went in gun first. Hamilton squatted and strained, his burnt face even redder. I pulled Michael in and looked around, all marble and chrome, no exposed screw heads that I could see. And Hamilton *was* stinking, I closed the door behind me.

A tall cupboard beside the bathroom held the heating system. Down on my knees, I stretched to feel around the pipes at the back, the only place in the whole apartment with clutter. I dragged the rolled up carpet out, saw the wooden strip, neatly fixed with six shiny screwheads – knew this screwdriver would fit.

'Can you open these?' Beikle didn't touch the disks. His nose twitched and his right knee shivered. 'Perhaps they will provide all the bank details we need.'

'It'll be encrypted but Hamilton knows he's not the only wizard in town with the magic key.'

I knew Hamilton, a pimply kid trashing his genius after he was gone would be the unkindest kick in the balls of all. His ego would do my trick, and a couple of lines of nose candy.

I told Michael to pull him out of the shower. Hamilton swaggered into the lounge with the towel over his head, all exhibition waxed butt, legs apart, bollock naked. Beikle shifted sideways and looked down at his shoes.

'You found them, Maknazpy, well done! Does that make you feel like a big boy now?' Hamilton said.

I let that go, I knew I had him.

'Go get dressed, Paddy, I'd rather talk without that wrinkly worm shaking around in my face.' I tossed the coke down on the coffee table. 'Get dressed and we'll have a going away party for you, just as soon as you hand over the entry card for the bank and the key to the deposit box.'

Beikle could see his comfort zone drifting further away over the sin horizon. 'This is not acceptable behaviour. I will not permit this.'

Beikle started to get up, I eased him back down into his seat. I hadn't liked him from the moment Artie had told me his name and I was liking him less every minute, but I would need him to decipher Hamilton's banking babble, he was staying put.

Hamilton looked like a nearly new man, oiled and groomed, cream linen suit, crisp white shirt, lavender and lime tie, a hint of his vodka musk. He crouched over the table with the fifty forint note at the ready. I tapped his knee with the Ruger, he pulled the plastic card from an inside pocket and flipped it in the air, the gold colored key jingled across the table.

'For all the good it will do you, you dickhead! That bank uses fingerprint recognition technology. The card gets you in the door, then a fucking big ugly security man is going to watch you press your finger on a sensor and he's going to expect my beautiful mug to appear like a vision on his screen! The only one who can get in there is me, understand?'

'That's my problem then, isn't it?' I said. I dipped the bank card and key into my pocket and stowed the pistol in my belt. 'You'll be on your way to a new life in the land of the free by this time tomorrow, so forget about it!'

Hamilton snorted like a pig, almost sneezed, clamped his nose with finger and thumb until the bitter surge settled, slumped back into the deep zebra-patterned leather armchair and curled up like a baby.

'Michael, son, do me a favor? There's a bottle of Stoli in the freezer, crack it out, will you? Take one yourself.'

Michael looked to me, I nodded.

That was it, Beikle was out the door, into the kitchen.

'That priest is a thief,' Hamilton said. 'I didn't do anything wrong except catch him at it. Fucking Italians hadn't the balls to finish the job, fucking Pope probably pulled rank!'

Michael set two glasses on the table, tipped the bottle, I gave him the eye to top Hamilton's to the neck.

'Getting me smashed won't get you into that bank, you know, but keep it coming, I don't care!'

'The bank won't be a problem,' I said. 'Certain Italian customers of theirs have made arrangements. Beikle will fail the fingerprint test, the guard will ignore that and open the door.'

Hamilton nodded, laughed, it didn't matter.

'Aye, well, I don't give a fuck what you do! My race is run!'

He nosed another line, knocked back the vodka, shivered, slapped the back of his neck, sunk into the chair. I wanted him high, high and talkative and stripped of his hate armor. I didn't want him on a downer, or unconscious.

'Is it true about PJ?' I said.

His eyes crossed as he tried to focus on my face.

'Absolutely! The bastard is here to put you and me in the grave! 100%! No bullshit!'

'Well, he isn't here now, is he? He won't get past security downstairs, we're safe, and my job is to keep you safe until I hand you over tomorrow night. After that, you are home and dry, make your deal with the CIA and forget all this shit.'

Hamilton threw back another vodka but missed his mouth, most of it ran down his chin.

'You don't know the slippy tit! He'll get us, one way or another. He'll fucking blow up the boat if he has to, CIA and all.'

He squatted to snort another line, lost his balance and fell forward on one knee.

'Is this the recording from that house?' Nice and easy, not pushing.

'Yeah, that's it! Fucking disaster! Wish I had just stuck with the Vienna money! Would be sitting here now with five mill clear and nobody on my back!'

I laughed with him, clinked my glass against his, knocked it back, reached for the bottle.

'It's all connected, you know, *they* are all fucking connected!'

He was talking to himself now, talking without listening, needed to spin himself back to the top, needed to absolve himself if he was going to move on.

Beikle poked his nose in, I shook my head, he backed out.

'You know I'll be handing this over to the CIA tomorrow, Paddy, anything on it I should know about? Anything about me?'

'*You*, Maknazpy? Why the fuck would there be anything about *you*?'

'It's encrypted, right? Run it for me, Paddy. Those bastards will be down on my neck about it, one way or another, and I don't understand anything about it.'

'That's your problem right there, Maknazpy! You aren't suited for this world. You like to think of yourself as some sort of High Noon cowboy, don't you? The heroic Knight Errant, a man of virtú, that's you, isn't it? But you swallow all the shit they feed you and keep coming back for more when really they're all laughing their balls off at you.'

Another line snorted, how much is an overdose when you are Paddy the Brit Hamilton?

'Michael, son!' Hamilton shouted, 'bring that laptop in here from the bedroom, will you?'

Hamilton was on automatic pilot, tapping and scrolling, until the screen squiggles stalled, then fell into place. He tapped the screen, a video played.

It was that house, that room. Seven men, middle-aged or older, tailor-made well dressed, cigars and brandy, silent eye contact across the round table like a séance.

'Is there sound? Did you record what they're saying?'

'Fuck's sake! They aren't saying anything, not yet. Anyway, it's not what they *say*, it's *who* they are!'

He was nearly gone but I couldn't lean too hard.

'That gentleman there, him there, that fat baldy dickhead, his boss sits on the Joint Intelligence Committee at Westminster. He's a wanker and so's his boss!'

'Were they there that night?'

'Aye, most of them, a couple were away back to their hotel. They were all over in Belfast for that investment conference, supposedly. *A Pledge for Peace,* they called it, supposed to raise £50 million to keep the Peace Process moving. Raised fuck all, as far as I know, but it was a nice cover for these boys to get together.'

'So who are they?'

'They're boys who are known to make the odd donation or two, that's who. See that one there beside the baldy Brit? He's a Yank, his da has a known personal wealth of $4 billion. The one beside him is the son-in-law mouthpiece for a slightly impoverished utilities and media baron, another Yank, he only has $2 billion behind him. Let's call those two Chuck and Hank. The others are Brit and European big business, bankers, what have you.'

Hamilton scrambled to his feet, clutched his gut, fell over, I called Michael and he helped him to the bathroom. Talk on the video now but too low, increased the volume but just white noise, needed Hamilton to work on the sound file.

Hamilton bumped into the table, his zipper undone. 'They shift billions of dollars easier than I've just shifted my bowels but the poor lads aren't happy, Maknazpy, not happy at all! They can never have enough and they're afraid the likes of us are coming to steal the pennies they have already scraped together.'

Dark splashes of piss down his linen pants, his deep gut stink masked by designer cologne.

'Power and fear - that's a dangerous combination right there, manifest around that table by entitlement and paranoia.'

He snorted the last line of coke, I figured he might last 20 minutes, tops.

'You'll have to keep it simple for me, Paddy,' I said, 'I don't have your IQ firepower, remember?'

'No, I know you don't! But, listen, the biggest fear for these prick princes is that they miss out on a big money deal. Like Iraq, say, they creamed it when trillions of dollars were invested in the Bushworld Wars, right? But then they were left outside the dealing door when the Chinese moved in and mopped up the oil industry and everything else that goes with rebuilding a country, right?

'Well, the writing has been on the wall for a couple of years now about Iran being brought back into the profit pool. That's half a million barrels a day when back in full flow, and a major infrastructure re-fit. These guys have denied themselves any share in that for a generation but they won't miss the bus this time.

'Only problem is, they have been out of the loop for so long that the Chinese and Russians are *already* fucking in there, and have been for years. No, if they want to play they'll have to speak nicely to an Oligarch or two. Now, see the big blond guy? Aye, him, he's a big wheel Latvian banker – I'm sure Yana briefed you on him, right?

'So, you are Hank or Chuck and you want to get tight to a Russian oil king? Latvian Blondie is *the* man. Okay, his bank is small town but his *connections* are big time. And with hundreds, thousands, of shell companies between them to play with in the US and Russia, he can matchmake like heaven.

'But it's always a two-way street, as a friend of ours would say, and the Russians need payback. So, that Russian money Yana told you about, the $200 million? Too big to be absorbed easily through the usual routes but that's where the matchmaker hits gold for his clients. With that sort of money Chuck and Hank could do serious damage in the United States – property, hedge funds, whatever.'

'These two?' I said. 'They are laundering Russian cash in the US?'

'With kickbacks, yeah, and preferred status as far as Iran goes, and a slice of Iraq and Syria, too, when things settle down and an honest robber-baron can get down to making some dirty money again, why not?'

'What made you think you could take a slice?' I said.

'Yakov got in my ear, said if I could pull it off in Vienna I could do likewise in Riga! The bastard didn't tell me Blondie was Russian Intelligence!'

I tipped the Stoli into his glass, guided his hand to his lips.

'But Hank and Chuck aren't as fireproof as their ass-licking flunkies let them believe! Maybe not yet, but the CIA will be sitting on that tape until the time is right, like a threatened budget cut, or a big mouth new President needs his balls squeezed.'

Hamilton's chin fell on his chest. I poked him, shook him back to life, asked him what he meant.

'Hank and Chuck's mom and pop empires invest in all sorts of things. Like, a Presidential candidate lucky enough to hook them can expect a campaign boost of something like $10–20 million from each of them! Money can't buy you love, Maknazpy, but it'll buy an election, and a prime seat on the inaugural platform to cheer their baby trashing the oath of office. And the CIA can wait. They'll have the donor golden boys on tape in a murder pedophile rape orgy and colluding with Moscow and the Mafia to screw the US taxpayer. CIA have a name for that, Maknazpy, they call it Blackmail Gold Dust! That's the olive in their martini!'

'Of course, I know the bank routines, I know where that money filtered, I know which righteous God-fearing American moguls are on the Moscow ticket, and I know who they have in their deep pockets. Aye, I can make life a lot easier for CIA – but it won't come cheap.'

He replayed the tape and repeated his ramble, snorting and sniggering as his world spun around his head. Mostly he sniggered at me, how gullible I was, what a victim, what an easy mark.

'Our American Dream would be a nightmare without the sheeple lumpenproletariat like you, Maknazpy, if you even know what that means,' he cackled.

When he crashed I had Michael haul him to the bathroom.

'Look after him, Michael. I need Paddy the Brit to be alive tomorrow.'

CHAPTER THIRTY-SEVEN

Artie answered in German, he was rattled.

'It's me,' I said, 'I'm using your pal's phone, we're on our way, everything is fine.'

'Everything is not fine! We said two o'clock, it's nearly three! I have been standing here like a lemon for the last hour!'

Hamilton had been out cold all night but woke screaming and raving this morning just as me and Beikle were leaving to meet Artie at the bank.

'We'll be there in five, Artie, keep your cool, don't attract attention.'

I found a parking space on the other side of the Parliament Building. Beikle left me to it and was striding across the street before I had finished the maneuver. I followed at a distance. The pairs and triples of police were at the usual spots, checking out the nice cars and girls passing by. Artie and Beikle mimed their formal greeting on the steps of the bank. The red light sensor blinked above our heads. Two priests in black uniform, heavy woollen overcoats to their ankles, here on holy business with briefcase and laptop. A security man that looked more like a 5 star concierge pulled the double doors and clicked his heels in some sort of parade ground salute.

Beikle approached the first desk, his voice was too loud when he spoke German but the lady smiled and inclined her head, nodded when he showed the key and card, and directed him to a door at the back of the reception area.

'No chance Hamilton is going to drop us in shit?' Artie whispered.

'No chance,' I said. 'Strung out, tied up and Michael on guard, he knows this life is over, already working on his new start in the US.'

Beikle swiped the card, the door opened, stone steps bowed in the middle led down to the basement. Another set of doors, but heavy steel this time. Beikle swiped, doors opened, a narrow corridor, red carpet, ornate brass wall lamps, a smoked glass booth ahead, a fat security man behind a grille in the wall. The booth was tight, no room for Artie, Beikle pressed his fingers to the glass screen, a camera flashed, we waited, then nothing, Beikle shuffled, we waited... 'Heh!' The fat head leaned out from the wall, mimicked the action of swiping a card. 'Ach! Armleuchter!' Beikle cursed himself, swiped the card, we were in.

The door floated closed behind us. An oval cave with an antique green baize covered table and chair, and rows and columns of brass boxes nested into the wall between knee and head height. Our key was number 187. The box slipped out silently on oiled rails.

Beikle claimed the only chair and started his systematic process of lifting one item at a time and placing it carefully on the green baize according to some ordered image in his head. I bent over him and tipped the contents across the table.

'In the name of God!' Artie said. 'It will take all day to sort through this pile of crap.'

It was a pile – data storage in all shapes and sizes, some with coded labels, others without, scuffed manila envelopes and plastic folders crammed with documents, bank papers and statements, mixed currency in a small silver box, five tattered notebooks, and a wad of pencil scrawled index cards strangled with a frayed elastic band.

'The life and crimes of Paddy the Brit!' Artie clapped an echo around the cave and rubbed his hands in delight.

I shoved the index cards into a pocket. Beikle processed the rest of the material, pulled a roll of sticky labels and printed a neat number on each item, then stowed it all into the two briefcases before slipping the box back into the wall. Artie used his elbow to press the buzzer, the door opened, the guard made a big deal of covering his eyes with his cap.

'Hey, Johannes,' I said, 'the poor guy is afraid you will have him whacked.' He ignored me, Artie smirked.

Beikle led the way back through the foyer and out to the street, took a right into Sas street and down to St István's Basilika. He stopped at a doorway, pushed a buzzer, then up a narrow staircase and into an office. One middle–aged man and six young guys waiting with blank computer screens, Beikle took their German greeting with a wave of the hand and started issuing instructions.

'You know what you're doing, Johannes, I'll leave you to it,' I said. 'Michael is back there baby-sitting Hamilton, I don't want to leave him on his own too long.' I winked at Artie and pulled him out to the stairway. 'Listen, Artie, Hamilton told me some scary stuff. He says PJ was and is a Brit spy. What do you make of that?'

Artie screwed up his nose. 'I wouldn't wipe my arse with Hamilton's lies! Divide and conquer, standard Brit tactic! He's trying to set you against PJ so he can exploit any aggro between you. Don't listen to him!'

I expected Artie's standard reply but something about Hamilton's eyes still niggled.

'He also said he was in a relationship with Brigid years ago. You ever hear anything about that? He says PJ found out and broke it up, set Brigid up for that gaol time.'

Artie rocked back on his heels. 'Are you seriously asking me that? Don't you think that poor girl suffered enough without you repeating the filthy lies of that scumbag?'

I patted his shoulder and started down the stairs.

CHAPTER THIRTY-EIGHT

The security man at Hamilton's apartment block had been replaced by two younger guys with shaven heads, forked lightning in their eyes and steel cables as neck tendons. One stepped from behind the desk, tapping his Rolex, 'Pyotr say 18.30.'

'Too early,' I said. 'I told him eight, like last night.'

He rocked his granite head, 'Now I tell you - 18.30!'

Michael was watching Hungarian TV in the lounge. Hamilton lay naked on the bed with the laptop perched on his fat gut, a white shirt and a black Knize suit draped over the chair.

'Michael! I told you to keep your eyes on him at all times!'

'Leave the lad alone,' Hamilton said, 'shut up and listen to this.'

He clicked the audio file, nodded for me to wait, the audio hissed, then a calm and determined voice.

"I want to take this opportunity to express the sincere gratitude of Her Majesty's Government for your courageous service. Your bravery is an inspiration to us all and continues to fortify our message to the IRA – all attempts to destroy our British democracy by terrorism will fail!"

I knew this voice. It was a weapon. It was the Iron Lady.

"Thank you, Ma'am. We are only soldiers doing our duty and it is our honor to serve Her Majesty and our country!"

He sounded weak and nervous in comparison to Thatcher.

"Indeed, Mr Nelson, I dearly wish I could acknowledge our gratitude to you in the most public way but I know you will understand our enemies within would seek to manufacture difficulties for us if we were to be seen in public together. These subversive civil liberties charlatans in the Labour Party and their acolytes in the BBC and press are really as much enemies of freedom and democracy as the IRA terrorists themselves! They are either too blind or too wicked to see that their road is the road to anarchy and tyranny!"

"I understand, Prime Minister, and perhaps if your enemies on the mainland were confronted with the terrorists they would change their minds."

A voice in the background makes a comment, Thatcher laughs.

"Yes, yes, Lieutenant-Colonel, there may well soon come a time when we will have no recourse but to root out the leftist extremists who threaten democracy here in Great Britain. When that time comes we will defend our British way of life against all enemies, from within or without, using all means necessary. In the meantime, you know you have our support for your sterling work in Northern Ireland, Mr Nelson, our fullest support. We are all agreed that the IRA terrorists have forfeited their own right to life and those who refuse to defend our British democracy are equally culpable. We must prevail! They will be eliminated!"

Hamilton clicked the button.

'That's Thatcher licking Brian Nelson's arse in 1989. He was chief intelligence officer for the Loyalists in Belfast. Nelson was our agent, we fed him the intell, we directed the hit squads through him.'

'Sure this isn't a fake?' I said.

'I was there! It was me brought Nelson over to meet her. This is Thatcher in her own words, and I have hours more of it – going back to their deceit regarding the Belgrano in the Falklands War, the hit squad in Gibraltar, and not only Thatcher, I have the New Labour cover up of the WMD fiasco!!'

If this *was* genuine then it was Artie's Holy conspiracy Grail, the endgame of his lifetime pursuit of a truth he needed.

'The Brits will kill to keep this buried, of course. That's what PJ and "*Jimmy*" have been tasked to do, they're here to get the evidence and then shut you and me up for good.'

'You'll be in the US this time tomorrow, Hamilton. My advice is play nice at the debrief and you really won't need to worry about the Brits or anyone else ever again.'

'Don't worry! Those MI5 bastards shafted me when my only crime was loyalty,' he said, 'so fuck the lot of them! And I have plenty more like that for the Yanks, if they have the money.'

He pulled the disk out and tossed it to me.

'See McCooey gets that,' he said, 'although it breaks my heart to give that two-faced prick more than the skin of my shite. And there is a copy in that envelope over there addressed to a human rights group in Londonderry. I'll get the concierge to post it after we are gone.'

'It'll be time to get moving soon,' I said. 'I could send Michael to get food. You hungry?'

'Hungry? I'm so hungry I could eat a donkey's arse through a five-bar gate!'

The motorcycle cop waved traffic away from the Danube. Michael dropped us at the bridge and we took the steps down to the embankment. Hamilton looked like a bank manager, dark suit, black cashmere overcoat – and the paisley pattern silk scarf pulled up to hide his burnt face. He carried a small overnight bag in his left hand, I clamped his right elbow to my ribs. Michael had searched him for disks or anything else he might want to hide. He said

Hamilton was clean but he hadn't checked up his ass. I told him not to bother.

Jaded workers squeezed through the ranks of shuffling tourists, cyclists wheeled through the logjam, Hamilton was in full risk assessment mode.

'We are too vulnerable here,' he said, 'this is where PJ will hit us.'

The space opened up before us, I marched him on. He twisted his neck to search for danger and bumped into a small woman. She stopped to complain but we kept moving without looking at her.

'Watch out for that wee runt Jimmy,' he said. 'He'll come from behind.'

'Just keep moving,' I said. 'You can forget about PJ and Jimmy, they won't be a problem.'

Hamilton scanned the wall separating the embankment from the road running parallel with the river. People ahead slowed down, tourists bunched around the iron shoe memorial.

'What are your plans now, Maknazpy? I hope you got yourself a decent deal.'

'I don't know yet.' I said. 'I'll just see what turns up.'

'Aye, right! Well, take my advice and never show your face in Ireland again. You were safe when you had CIA protection but you're on your own now. The Dark Side still have you fingered for old Swansea and now for McIntyre. If they can't go through normal channels they'll have you taken care of by other means.'

We were at the shoe memorial now, just another sight to snap and instantly forget for most people but one man had rigged up camera lights and narrowed the pathway with his tripod. I kept Hamilton close and pushed through. The Parliament Building was up above to the right, most tourists headed that way after the massacre memorial, the path ahead curving along with the Danube into the dark was empty. Hamilton scanned far ahead, then looked back over his shoulder. Two police uniforms were up above to our right, then two more dark shapes further along.

'Fuck! It's them!' Hamilton planted his feet and tried to pull away from me. 'That's fucking PJ and Jimmy up there! Where's that fucking boat?! It should be here! Where's the boat?!'

I stretched my arm around Hamilton's back to grip his left arm and pin him tight against my chest. The Ruger screwed in hard against his ribs.

'There isn't going to be a boat, Paddy, not for you, not this time.'

He froze, it settled slowly into the core of his being like a pebble dropped in snow, then rippled through his body and world like a shockwave. He stumbled, I held him up, he choked, his red eyes stabbed with panic, his tongue rolled out of his gaping mouth.

'You won't feel a thing, Paddy.'

He puffed his cheeks, blowing hard, blinking, steadying his weight against me. I willed him not to piss himself.

'Why? Fucking why? You have all the disks! This isn't right! You have the bank accounts!' The sense of injustice welled up in his throat, 'I gave you everything! Fucking why?!'

The two policemen drifted in the other direction, ushering stray pedestrians away from the embankment. I dragged Hamilton further into the dark. PJ and Jimmy kept pace with us up there in the light, squinting down at me and Hamilton in the shadows.

'You set up the ambush on Ferdia McErlane's uncles. He was my brother. This is what he would do if he was here.'

'What?! That's over twenty fucking years ago! That's bollocks!'

He tried to wrestle out of my grip, I gouged the barrel into his burnt skin and clipped the handgrip off his skull.

'It wouldn't matter to Ferdy if it was a hundred years ago, or a thousand. You did it, this is payback time. That's just the way it goes, nothing we can do about it, Paddy, I'm just the message.'

'It was a war! They were soldiers! We took them out but now that fucking war is over! Who's pulling your wire? McCooey? There's a big world out there that hasn't even heard of that shit! It was a dirty small-time cut-throat war for a two-bit piece of dirt!'

I might have said the entire world is made up of small-time people dying for two-bit pieces of dirt but I wasn't there to argue with him, I was there to kill him. A group of tourists came from the other direction, the cops hadn't blocked it off. I wedged Hamilton against the wall and forced his head down with the pistol drilled deep into the soft skin between his ear and jaw. He grunted like a rutting pig and clouds of steam poured out of his head. I could smell his smell, that sick vodka musk that could only be him. The tourists saw us but it wasn't their business to intervene, they kept moving, speeding up after they passed and not looking back.

'Don't fight me, Paddy, you'll only make it harder for yourself.'

Hamilton collapsed beneath me, all strength wasted, he knew it was over.

'Okay! Okay! But not here! Not in the dark like a fucking dog! Do it back there, back at that memorial for the other innocent people murdered by fascists!'

He wasn't in a position to dictate terms, and there was a limit to how much cover Pyotr had bought.

'Treat me like a human being and I'll make it easy for you, Maknazpy. Otherwise I'll fight like fuck!'

I could make out about a dozen camera-ready tourists around the shoes. PJ and Jimmy were waiting up above but we were out of their view. The two cops above and the others rerouting the traffic had only been told to keep people away and to go blind if something happened.

'People pray at that spot for the innocent souls massacred by evil,' he said, 'their prayers can be for me also.'

'Alright, Paddy, if it means so much to you, why not?'

He relaxed, pumped his lungs a couple of times then held his breath for ten seconds before releasing the tension with a long whistle. I released my grip but kept the barrel screwed into his neck. A few of the tourists moved off. I wiped the sweat off his brow with the paisley scarf and he took it to blow his nose.

'Fuck! I suppose you're laughing your balls off, aren't you, Maknazpy? Fucking big joke at Paddy the Brit's expense! You and McCooey and fucking PJ, all laughing your Fenian balls off!'

'Nobody's laughing, Paddy, that's not how it works, you know that.'

'I give you what you want, you let me go – that's how it works!'

Four or five figures hovered around the memorial, slowly moving away from us.

'Yeah, well, there's also the money to consider, Paddy, don't forget the money. See, I left Beikle with a squad of his bank guys earlier. He tells me he has identified $11 million of your money, so far, and another $25 million that they figure was Yakov's cut from the Latvian bank.'

'You don't have to do this, Maknazpy! Give me fifty grand and I'll disappear forever, you'll never see me again. You don't have to fucking murder me!'

'That money will do a lot of good when you're gone, Paddy, and that's the point – you *have* to be gone. All those bank accounts are set up with that dead man's lock you boasted to me about. You *have* to be gone.'

'What are you talking about? Just let me disappear and you take the fucking money! Beikle can transfer it wherever to fuck he likes!'

'No, not really, Paddy. Beikle says there are hundreds of accounts spread out all over the world, some legit banks and others not so much. Most of them, the big ones with the real money, all have that quarantine lock. Beikle can make the transfer but the cash is held somewhere in limbo until you activate another code after ten days. If you don't hit the activate button the funds bounce back to their original accounts and then they rebound here to Budapest and then finally are automatically filtered out to another set of banks we don't even know about yet. Beikle's guys say it is some weird banking algorithm they have never seen before, and these guys are all Swiss technicians that know their business.'

Steam plumed out of his silver head, I tasted his sick smell far back in my throat.

'Exactly! You murder me and that money disappears with me! Think about it, Maknazpy! Is that Ferdia McErlane revenge bullshit worth $36 fucking million?! And there is more they haven't found yet! Let me live and we'll work something out to suit everybody!'

The last of the tourists were far enough away, another group were coming this direction but stopped to fill up on photos of the light show at the castle across the river.

'It *is* worked out, that's *why* you have to be gone. I told Beikle about your boomerang trick so his team have changed your algorithm. He transfers the funds and they are still held in quarantine for ten days, okay, but you won't be there to hit the confirmation code and so *all* the cash will still bounce back here to GMC in Budapest, right? But that's where Beikle has screwed up your box of tricks, see? Instead of rebounding out of Budapest to a new set of unknown accounts, Beikle has fixed it so *all* the money rebounds to a special account he has set up in the Vatican Bank. You *have* to be gone, Paddy, that's how big banking works.'

I cracked his head off the stone path and trailed him up by his collar. He was dazed, didn't resist as I forced him back toward the massacre memorial. PJ and Jimmy were at the top of the steps.

'I knew the McErlane story was bullshit! You *are* murdering me in cold blood for the money, at least admit that much.'

'No, this was always inevitable, money or not, you should have known that.' And Hamilton *should* have known it that time he laughed at Ferdy being more maggot than corpse but it wouldn't have mattered – his ticket was stamped the moment I set foot in Ireland. 'You asked me before why I am here. This is the *why*, payback for Ferdy's people.'

'How much is my cold blooded murder worth to you?'

'I'm not a greedy man, Paddy. And I told Beikle to make arrangements for that Polish girl, Alina. She's doing serious gaol time because of you.'

'What about Michael? How much is he getting?'

We were at the memorial, Hamilton caught his foot on one of the iron shoes and staggered. I pulled him up straight. There were figures along the path coming closer. A massive working barge churned along the middle channel.

'Speak to your God now, Hamilton, if you have one.'

'It's true about me and Brigid, you know. Just ask McCooey if Michael is Brigid's own child, not her nephew. I guarantee he'll shit himself. Make sure the wee lad gets his fair share of my money, that's what Brigid would have w...'

I squeezed the end of Hamilton's history, Paddy the Brit dropped like a stone into the black Danube and tumbled like a doll in the strong current, baptized and buried in the same dark grave. And I did it cold this time, no magic trauma demon, no out-of-body immunity, no sham doppelganger. Cut loose from the Ríastrad shit, full circle and free from Ferdy's proxy revenge voodoo. I did it cold and the night around me was still and silent, nothing moving except the Danube. I watched until he disappeared, until PJ and Jimmy hauled me to the steps and flanked me as we jogged to the black SUV.

'Hamilton is done,' I said. 'Your observers will confirm it.'

Pyotr reached out from the back seat, I passed him the disk. There was a dark shape beside him.

'This is the CIA disk? The only copy?'

'The only copy,' I said. 'Beikle has recovered almost $5 million of Yakov's rip-off. It will all be paid back into your banks in fourteen days.'

Pyotr was young but not stupid, he was bringing the CIA's blackmail bonanza back to Moscow and what they did with it wasn't my problem so that bought me some plunder rights. The dark shape nudged his elbow.

'Follow us through the checkpoint,' Pyotr said, 'after that you are on your own. Good luck!'

The blacked out window closed, Pyotr disappeared.

PJ led me across the road, Jimmy trailed behind, watching our backs. Michael revved the engine, Artie kissing his prayer beads in the passenger seat. I dumped Hamilton's index cards into PJ's lap.

'That's all the politicians and journalists in his pocket, all the informers he ran in Ireland back in the day. You might recognize some names.'

Another SUV closed tight behind us, the blue strobe beacon ricocheting high on the Parliament Building.

'Well?' Artie said. 'What other filthy lies did Paddy the Brit tell you before he was called to account for his sins? Any last requests?'

'Yeah, Artie, he said a woman told him once that those who know history are condemned to repeat it. His dying wish was that you explain that to young Michael.'

Artie snorted, PJ and Jimmy sniggered.

Pyotr pulled a left into Markó Street, three SUV's with blue lights blocked our route. Eight men in SWAT gear stepped out of the darkness, one approached Pyotr's car, a quick look and bow before he jumped to attention and parted the road block with a wave of his hand. Pyotr's driver inched through the gap and accelerated off into the darkness. The SUV's rocked back to block the street.

He called us forward, I really hoped he would wave us through. I really hoped Pyotr wasn't laughing his Russian balls off.

DEIREADH

AUTHOR'S NOTE

The Irish proverb says "Ar scáth a chéile a mhaireann na daoine" – we live in the shadow of each other. This is an observation that we depend on each other, and should therefore be benevolent and supportive of other people.

It could also mean that none of us are the autonomous individualists as idealized by modern western culture – the free thinking independent, responsible only to our individual conscience which we have each created in isolation.

I was born in the north of Ireland in 1959, and was therefore 10 years old when the Troubles restarted in 1969. Like every other 10 year old, I learned to live a life we thought was normal, even if that normality was a heady fusion of the shadow cast by warrior-heroes, the baggage of competing cultural realities and our collective premonition that it would get worse before it would get better.

I only read Irish books when I was younger - James Stephens, Flann O'Brien, Michael McLaverty, John McGahern, John Banville, the Blasket books. Or else Irish politics, history and philosophy. I lightened up a bit later on, started reading about murder as entertainment. Hammett, Chandler, Cain, Himes, Parker, Ross Macdonald, Jim Thompson. Then Ellroy, Mosley, Burke, Ian Rankin, John Harvey, the Scandanavians, and, belatedly, discovered that William McIlvanney's 'Laidlaw' series was perhaps the best of all.

I started to write the Maknazpy books as standard thrillers, no big messages. Then realized I couldn't help it: all that stuff about being an underdog, free will limited by inherited cultural baggage and everyone's basic human right to be treated with dignity, it was all bound to come out.

Of course, it isn't only the Irish who receive cultural certainties, and I hope Maknazpy's travails, global and parochial, help to shed a little doubt on the self-confirming shibboleths that turn slogans into self-prophetic war cries.

Gerard Cappa @maknazpy February 2017

18362961R00180

Printed in Poland
by Amazon Fulfillment
Poland Sp. z o.o., Wrocław